DISOBEDIE
Sangee

First published 25th November 2022 by Fly on the Wall Press
Published in the UK by
Fly on the Wall Press
56 High Lea Rd
New Mills
Derbyshire
SK22 3DP

www.flyonthewallpress.co.uk
ISBN: 9781913211851
EBOOK: 9781915789006
Copyright Sangeeta Mulay © 2022

Dedicated to the Indian rationalists who lost their lives fighting
for rationality

"*Never have things of the spirit counted for so little. Never has hatred for everything great been so manifest — disdain for beauty, execration of literature. I have always tried to live in an ivory tower, but a tide of shit is beating at its walls, threatening to undermine it.*"

- Gustave Flaubert

Prologue
4th May 2016. Time: 15:00

Padded leg-holders protruded from a stainless-steel bed covered with a thin rexine mattress. A black wire sprawled from the bed onto the grey tiled floor. A poky toilet with the door ajar released a hint of dehydrated urine into the windowless room. In contrast, the doctor exuded efficiency through her crisp cotton sari. She sat behind a desk, facing Aparna. A medical assistant hovered.

"Name and date of birth?"

"Aparna Soman, 26th of April 1976."

"Do I have your consent to proceed with the examination?"

Aparna nodded.

"Sign here, please. Just a formality that you're giving me this consent voluntarily and without any coercion."

Aparna's hand shook as she signed.

The doctor scribbled. "So—full name Aparna Soman; you reside at the Prerna Bungalow on Senapati Bapat Road in Pune, and you came to this hospital with your husband, Mr Manish Joshi. Correct?"

"That's right," Aparna said.

"Two identification marks on your body?"

"A mole on the upper right side of my lip, and a scar in the middle of my right calf—childhood injury."

"When did you have your last period?"

"Two months ago."

"Any surgeries in the last five years?"

"No."

The doctor stood up, put on gloves and walked around the desk to Aparna. Aparna turned to face her but remained seated.

"Extend both hands so that I can check your fingernails." The doctor took a wooden swab stick and broke it in half. Using a separate swab stick for each hand, she poked underneath Aparna's fingernails and placed the scrapings into a sterile bottle. She then proceeded to cut Aparna's nails and placed the clippings in a separate sterile bottle. After examining Aparna's hair, she took twenty strands from her head. She placed the strands on a piece of paper and folded it. The assistant put the paper in a bag and sealed it.

"Open your mouth so that I can take a swab." She swiped a cotton bud under Aparna's tongue and handed her a glass of sterile water. "Rinse your mouth and spit in that container over there."

Aparna rinsed, trying to be as noiseless as possible. The container was labelled and sealed.

"Now go and stand over that newspaper behind the curtain. Hand over your clothes to me, one by one. Make sure you stand completely over the newspaper so that any evidence is collected. I will examine the clothes and write down my observations."

Aparna hobbled to the curtain. She took off her sari and handed it to the doctor.

"White sari with a red border. Signs of brown smudges. Measure these and record them in the report," the doctor said to her pale-faced assistant. Aparna handed over her other garments one by one, as instructed. The doctor kept up a steady stream of commentary which her assistant noted.

"Yellow and orange cotton *bandhani*-print blouse, and white cotton panties. A splodge of blood on the panties. Write down the measurements of the stain."

The assistant scribbled.

"I'm going to examine your whole body, starting with your hair. This may take some time," the doctor said.

Aparna could clearly see the printed paper with columns titled: *injuries, fractures, nail marks, bite marks, cuts, lesions, boils, discharges, and stains*.

Her slumped body found the energy to nod.

"Lie down on the bed here."

Aparna lay on the white sheets and her eyes went to the wall which had a faded picture of a red rose. She closed her eyes.

"Mild bruise on upper right arm. Seminal stains on the lips, stomach and vagina." The doctor proceeded to take swabs of the seminal fluid. "Area around the vagina raw and bruised. Stray pubic hairs and other foreign material observed." She collected the hairs and put them in a sample bottle. Then, she took a sample of Aparna's matted pubic hair. "I have to examine you internally." The doctor's expression did not change.

Aparna clenched herself. She wondered if, given another chance, she would do things differently. Shun controversial topics; suppress prohibited thoughts; only articulate palatable views.

"You need to relax. Don't worry, this won't take long." The doctor's voice yanked her thoughts into the present.

Aparna clenched again as the doctor lubricated a sterile speculum with warm, saline water and gently put it in. The probing commenced.

"No internal bleeding or injuries observed," the doctor said. Aparna relaxed. "Can you turn over?"

Aparna turned over and kept her eyes closed while the doctor prodded and probed.

"Seminal stains near anal opening. Slight swelling with mild bruising. No discharge observed." The doctor straightened. "There, that's done." She walked to the sink located in the toilet, and Aparna heard the plop of the discarded gloves and then the washing of hands. The doctor returned. "Have you brought the second set of clothing we asked you to get? These will remain with us." She indicated Aparna's clothes now lying in a sad heap in a sack. "You can get dressed while I sign and date the report."

Aparna dressed carefully behind the curtain. When she was ready, the doctor handed her a bottle.

7

"Give a urine sample in this. It will help establish pregnancy, if any."

Aparna lumbered to the bathroom and collected her sample.

"My assistant will collect your blood. This will give us an indication of possible disease."

"Take this," said the assistant as she handed a pill to Aparna.

"What's this?" Aparna asked in a quiet voice.

The doctor said grimly, "To prevent an HIV infection. And you will have to take a contraceptive pill immediately. It's available at the pharmacy within the hospital premises. I'll write you a prescription for a sedative which will be required in the initial days.".

Like an obedient Indian woman, Aparna did as she was told.

"Here's a preliminary copy of your report. Your samples will be handed over to the police and other reports will follow. We're done," the doctor said with a tight smile.

With that, the forensic medical examination, Aparna's second ordeal of the day, was over. Almost ten hours after the incident, she could finally take a shower.

BOOK ONE

Chapter One
17th January 2016. Time: 11:00

"What do you mean you won't register a complaint?" Aparna shouted at the thin policeman with a resplendent moustache, seated behind a cluttered desk. A badge pinned to his chest declared his name to be Inspector Ram Shinde. The police station was located in the tiny village of Karli in Maharashtra. With space to accommodate only three desks, it was cramped with files, posters and two rotund policemen who sat adjacent to Inspector Shinde, eating *wada paav* with tea. Table fans whirred to keep the smells, heat and mosquitos away. Darkness pervaded the few unoccupied spaces in the room while birds chirped madly in the sun outside.

"Why aren't you registering our complaint, Inspector Shinde?" Aparna asked in a calmer voice. Dressed immaculately in a cotton, hand-loom sari, with a large black *bindi* on her forehead, Aparna knew her handsome face wore a look of assurance; the kind that comes with experience of dealing with sluggish bureaucracy. Standing tall opposite the policeman's diminutive frame, her imposing body and greying temples hinted at her stubborn tenacity. As a young girl, she had been called Bhim behind her back. Bhim, the second of the Pandavas from the mythological epic *Mahabharata*, was believed to have shattered mountains on falling off his mother Kunti's lap as a child. The insult had been enough to set any sensitive young girl into a spiral of eating disorders, but Aparna had remained indifferent to the taunts.

This was her first visit to the Karli police station. Had things gone as planned, her complaint would have been registered in less than ten minutes, allowing her to head back home to Pune.

She wiped droplets of sweat from her brow with her sari *pallu* and stared at Inspector Shinde, openly impatient now. He found it difficult to meet her eyes, though his face remained amiable. Something was not quite right in this small, rural police station...

"*Bai*, wish I could help, but Godman Baba Omnath has supernatural powers. I don't want to upset him by registering a complaint against him," Inspector Shinde said. "Who knows what he'll do?" The other two policemen had turned around to listen. Inspector Shinde looked to them for support. They nodded their agreement.

Now Aparna finally understood their problem. It wasn't laziness but fear preventing the policemen from helping her. Nobody wished to tangle with a Godman experienced in black magic, not even the police.

"How can you refuse to lodge a complaint?" Aparna said. "Where will she go for justice?" Aparna pointed to a demure woman standing next to her, dressed in a raw henna-coloured cotton sari, red *bindi* on her forehead and a black *mangalsutra* around her neck. "Do you even understand the courage it takes to lodge a sexual harassment complaint? Especially against a powerful man?"

"Everyone fears the Godman, *bai*. That's the problem."

"*Arre*, you're the police! You can't refuse. It's against the law. Where will common people like us go?" Aparna said.

"You rich people will find a way." Inspector Shinde looked at his *wada paav* as if afraid it would disintegrate in the stifling heat.

"And what about the poor? Where will they go?" Aparna said. Sweat trickled in annoying rivulets down her back. She fanned herself with her sari *pallu* and, when that didn't work, she turned the table fan on Inspector Shinde's desk towards her and stood in its direct gaze. Inspector Shinde turned to look at his colleagues, with a brief roll of his eyes. The last thing they needed on this hot morning was to grapple with a determined, confident woman. Aparna bent down a little to get the fan's full benefit. For the next few minutes, she unabashedly enjoyed the cool air as the policemen looked on. She reverted the fan back to its original position.

"What can mere law do against the power of black magic, *bai*? I'm not willing to take such a risk." Inspector Shinde said after a few seconds. He shut the register that lay open in front of him with a force which flurried the tips of his moustache.

"I wish to speak to a senior officer." Aparna moved away from the fan and stood in front of Inspector Shinde, her hands crossed.

"You will have to make an appointment for that," Inspector Shinde said, wearily shaking his head.

"How do I make one?"

"Write down your name and number here." He pushed a notebook in front of her and gesticulated towards the other woman. "How did you get involved in all this?" He sounded like a concerned grandfather chiding a wayward granddaughter.

"I'm a volunteer for the Rationalist and Anti-Superstition Society of Pune," Aparna said. "We held an anti-superstition workshop in this village. That's when Kamla told me her story." The gaze of the woman in the henna-coloured sari did not shift focus.

"What did he do to her?" Inspector Shinde asked, shifting weight from his left bum to the right.

There was a pause.

"He promised to change the gender of her foetus using black magic," Aparna said in a tight voice. "In return for sexual favours." A slight frown rumpled her forehead, like a strict teacher about to reprimand her errant pupil.

The whirr of the fans and the chirping of birds seemed louder as a silence fell. Kamla's downward gaze did not shift.

"It's dangerous for her to complain."

"Why don't you let us worry about that? Your job," Aparna pointed her index finger at Inspector Shinde, "is to lodge our complaint."

"That, I won't do," Inspector Shinde shook his head at his closed register.

Aparna made a noise of disgust, but the Inspector refused to look up. She wrote her name, address and phone number in the notebook and then asked, "And why isn't there a lady police officer present here? It's the law!"

Inspector Shinde gave a helpless smile. "We will contact you," he said, focusing his gaze on his *wada paav*.

As Kamla looked up, Aparna nodded at her, and they left without another word.

"Sorry." Aparna lightly touched Kamla's shoulder as they stepped out of the gloom, "but don't lose hope. The city police will lodge our complaint."

"Don't worry about me, *bai*," Kamla said. "Want to come home for a cup of tea?"

"Thank you, Kamla, but I'd better get going."

"You have a comfortable journey back home then." She took both of Aparna's hands in her own. For a few seconds, the two women just stood there.

"Thank you," Aparna said, "I'll talk to you soon. With better news, I hope."

Aparna covered her head with her sari *pallu* and remembered Naseem's instructions to keep drinking water throughout the day as she set off. After a ten-minute walk under the cruel sun, she reached the bus station. She glugged warm water from the bottle she carried with her—a gift from Naseem. The state transport bus arrived and, after a two-hour journey, she returned home to Pune.

A month passed, but she received no communication from the Karli police station. In despair, Aparna phoned her uncle's brother-in-law, Amar, who worked in the city police force. The phone rang for a while, but just when Aparna was about to hang up a booming voice greeted her.

"A-ha, the do-gooder," Amar said before Aparna had a chance to speak. "How many men have you bashed today?"

Humour-coated sarcasm wasn't new to Aparna, nor were authoritative male acquaintances, who'd made it their mission to patronise her.

"Look, I need a favour," she said in a controlled voice.

"Where are your band of women, eh?" He laughed heartily, before adding, "Just joking."

"Ha, ha... look, the Karli police station refused to file my complaint against Godman Omnath because all the policemen there are terrified of his black magic. I've never heard anything quite so bizarre," Aparna said.

"You know how it is, Aparna. Common in villages," Amar replied.

"I'm not even sure whether to make a complaint against those policemen," said Aparna. "If they get suspended, it simply means more hungry families... but something needs to be done. They can't just refuse... I can't ignore this. Training should be arranged for the police force, especially in rural police stations... gender sensitisation... anti-superstition workshops."

"How many complaints will you lodge? Relax! Look, give me the details of the Baba Omnath case and I will do what's necessary," Amar said. "We will worry about training superstitious policemen some other time."

Aparna gave him the required details. "I will be making a lot of noise about this. Do you realise how serious this is? I will file a petition—"

"You can't do it all, Aparna. These things take time."

"I'm aware. But—"

"I will contact you soon," Amar said, and the jocular attitude returned. "Take a break from your mission to change the world and come home with Manish for lunch sometime. Pure home-cooked food."

"Appreciate it."

"Still waiting to be invited to your house," he chuckled.

"Soon. Thank you so much, Amar."

She hung up and mentally prepared herself for a long wait.

Chapter Two
18th April 2016. Time: 19:00

In their small bungalow, tucked in a cul-de-sac away from the steady rumble of Pune's chaotic traffic, Aparna's family finished the preparations for dinner. The tantalising aroma in the air of roasted garlic and green chilli paste tempted the staunchest of taste buds. A five-arm brass chandelier illuminated the Raja Ravi Varma paintings of subtly adorned, voluptuous Indian women draped in saris, telling glorious stories of times past. Even the routine fare of dill vegetable with mung dal, sliced cucumbers, chapatti, lemon pickle and rice, seemed exotic in the hue of intimate lights. It was almost seven. On their cushioned dining chairs, the family settled down to eat.

"One fraudster down, four thousand more to go," Aparna said, as she eased into her chair. "Complaint lodged. Summons issued. Godman arrested."

"Which Godman is it this time?" Naseem asked.

In the soft light of the dining room, Naseem resembled a muse of the celebrated painter whose works hung on their dining room walls. Despite being only eighteen, she had the aura of yesteryear actresses, those of the black-and-white movie era. As she reached out to take another chapatti from the tin, the elegant, cursive letters of her tattoo, 'MA'—short for Manish and Aparna—lurked like a malignant spider on the soft, dusky skin of her wrist.

"You must start reading the papers, Naseem. He is all over them," Aparna said.

A kitchen tap dripped at regular intervals.

"Baba Omnath. A self-styled, fraudulent Godman who used religion for profit. Hordes of devotees, blind in their adulation," Manish explained. Middle-age was playing her usual tricks on him, rounding off his angularity and eroding his hairline. Despite this, his eyes, framed in dark-rimmed glasses, reflected a friendly acceptance of people's shortcomings, and with his quiet strength, he cut an appealing figure.

"This *dal* could do with some salt," Aparna said. Manish pinched a few grains from the salt jar and sprinkled some on her *dal* as she continued, "Baba Omnath's modus operandi was to make promises to exorcise ghosts, change genders of foetuses and solve problems of impotency by using black magic. All this in return for sexual favours. He even claimed to be the husband of a woman in her previous life so he could have sex with her."

"Ew! Why did the women agree?" Naseem said. She was the only one who used cutlery to eat. Her parents ate with their hands.

"He is seen as a religious figure." Aparna said, her voice tight. "One woman saw through the abuse and agreed to register a police complaint. That's all it took. Several women filed complaints after that."

"Is he in jail?" Naseem asked.

"Yes, his bail was rejected. But he is powerful. His stooges will do everything they can to make the women revoke their complaints. Can someone please get up and turn off that annoying tap?"

"I've called the plumber. Until then, we have to put up with the drip," Manish said. He left his lunch and washed his hands. After rummaging in a cavernous kitchen drawer, he found a thick tea towel. He tied the cloth tight around the tap, stopping the drip. Satisfied, he returned to the table and continued his dinner.

"The identities of the complainants won't be revealed. Right?" Naseem asked.

"Hopefully not. He is powerful, so he may very well bribe the police. But then again, not everyone is corrupt, so he has a tough fight ahead," Aparna said, her face grim.

"Hope the women are aware of the dangers." Naseem dabbed the edge of her lips with a tissue.

"Of course, they are. It's really brave of them to do this," Aparna said. "The aura around him was a problem. But finally, we nailed him."

A silence followed. Manish reached out for the remote and switched on the TV.

A mother-in-law with thick make-up was berating a traumatised-looking woman in a crumpled sari, presumably the daughter-in-law, on the TV screen.

Aparna groaned, "The daily dose of regression. Opium of Indian women. Had Marx lived in India, I'm fairly certain he would have included Indian soap-dramas in his profound sentence on religion."

"You can't expect everyone to have similar tastes, Ma," Naseem said. "These TV serials may be their only escape." Naseem felt duty-bound to discourage others, especially her mother, from judging people too harshly. That's not to say Naseem did not enjoy Aparna's often outrageous comments, because she did, but she assuaged her guilt by reining her mother in when needed.

"I'm entitled to my opinion. Thank you very much." Aparna scoffed. "Try and find a nice Bollywood movie, instead."

"You find the TV serials regressive, but not the Bollywood movies," Naseem said, an eyebrow raised. "Strange!"

"Well... Bollywood was our only entertainment when young." Aparna's mouth was full of food, but she continued, "Going to the cinemas to watch a movie was such a treat for all. Difficult to get Bollywood out of our systems now. The damage has been done."

"I blame Nehru. Bollywood tempts us with undiluted escapism and glamour because we grew up in a socialist India." Manish laughed loudly at his own joke.

"Do all those folks who invite you to speak at important events know, Ma? About your love for the regressive world of Bollywood? They'd be shocked," said Naseem. She looked at Manish but got no encouragement from him. He had turned back to the TV. If there was one thing Naseem loved to do, it was to collude with one parent to tease the other.

"Well, we all have our foibles, don't we?" Aparna said, neatly side-stepping Naseem's teasing.

Manish said over his shoulder, "I, for one would be unwilling to let go of the camaraderie Bollywood induces. Put a group of Indians together and watch them bond over Bollywood songs, dialogues, and dances. If they aren't too snooty!" Changing the channel, he asked, "What do you want to watch?"

From the TV, Faiz's poem 'Bol' boomed into their dining room, causing a dramatic halt to the conversation. But where Manish and Naseem continued to eat, Aparna, feeling the full brunt of Faiz's brilliance, remained riveted. "Powerful! And so beautiful! How can you even think of eating when the poetry of the revolution is unfolding before you?"

"We *are* at the dinner table, aren't we?" said Naseem, putting a piece of chapatti in her mouth and refusing to look up.

"Hope this is a full-fledged programme on Faiz," Aparna said.

Instead, an advertisement for sanitary pads, displaying sparkling blue menstrual blood came on next. The chirpy jingle muffled the sounds of the family chewing.

"Why don't they show menstrual blood in all its sticky, scarlet glory?" Aparna moved her plate aside. "And if women bleed sparkling blue blood, then why stop them from entering temples on their period?" She sat erect; her food forgotten.

"Ugh, Ma. The things you come up with!" Naseem squealed, wrinkling her nose. "I'm trying to eat here!"

"I fail to understand why women have to be pleasing and palatable. Show us with our boils, piles, warts and farts," Aparna said, "and real menstrual blood."

Naseem guffawed. Manish continued to eat, his face calm.

"Ma has gone into one of her moods. Ignore her, Baba," Naseem said, laughing.

The doorbell chimed.

"Who could it be at this hour?" Aparna said. Three worried faces looked at each other. Manish got up to check. Aparna followed him. A group of young men stood at the door.

"Donations for Lord Ganesha festival. We're planning a huge pandal this time so please donate generously for your favourite god," said a scrawny young man with a budding moustache.

Aparna pushed herself forward. "We're not believers," she said.

"Meaning?" the man said. He put a finger in his ear and gave it a good jiggle.

The others looked puzzled.

"We're atheists," Aparna said, in a loud voice.

"Meaning?" the man repeated. His face adjusted itself into a question.

"We don't believe in God."

The man stared. No one spoke. Then he said, "But everyone in the neighbourhood contributes! No one refuses Lord Ganesha."

"Why should I contribute? For what? All that loud music to raunchy Bollywood songs at odd hours... traffic chaos and hassles. I'd rather donate to a charity for the environment or something," Aparna scowled. A stray dog out for a walk stood still watching them, wondering what the fuss was about.

"The Muslim loudspeakers for *azaan* don't seem to trouble you. It's only the Hindu gods that are a problem, is it?" the scrawny one said. "Are you Muslims?"

"I just told you. We're atheists," Aparna said.

"Yes, but Hindu or Muslim?" the man persisted.

21

"Or Christian?" A young boy poked his head out and asked with a grin.

Manish stepped forward. "Look, why don't you come back tomorrow? We will pay a token amount."

"Uncle, if people like you pay token amounts, then how will we collect enough? You must make a substantial donation. Look at the size of your bungalow." The young man let his gaze wander over the house.

"We don't want to contribute, and you cannot force us." Aparna appeared unruffled.

"You can't refuse Lord Ganesha," the man said smoothly. "Even Muslims contribute. They have to! Look, there are ways... best that you donate without a fuss."

There was a silence.

Naseem debated whether to pull her mother away from the door. Manish thought of ways to shut the door without a confrontation.

"Look here..." Aparna shouted, hands on her hips.

Manish placed himself between Aparna and the men. "Hold on. Hold on. What's the minimum amount you expect?" The man told him. "We will pay and look on this as a social event instead of a religious one," Manish said. Aparna glared at him. "Let me get my wallet. I'll close the door until then, if you don't mind." He nodded to the men. Before they could answer, he reached out, shut the door and scrambled for his wallet.

"Let them wait. No need to pay those bullies." Aparna ensured that her voice carried not only across the door but through the adjacent four bungalows as well.

"We don't have the time to get into a tangle with them. Let's just pay and we can complain at the next neighbourhood society meeting," Manish said in a low voice.

"Ma, come here. Please!" Naseem shouted from the dining room.

"I won't give in to this bullying." Aparna said to Manish. She stood up straight, crossing her arms.

"You're not giving in. I am." Manish took some notes from his wallet and opened the door. He handed over the cash to the men.

"No one refuses. Muslims, Christians... they all pay willingly," the man said with a look of disgust as he pocketed the cash.

The men walked away. "Sickular liberals," the scrawny one said to his friends within Manish's earshot. "It's become fashionable for Hindus to scorn our gods, but they'll be all over the Muslims respecting their religious sentiments."

"They have to, *dost*. Otherwise..." His friend imitated an explosion and pointed to the heavens. "They don't have those kind of guts." They laughed.

Manish locked the door. He went back to the dining room with Aparna.

"Every year, it's the same," said Naseem, her brows creased.

"I do wish you'd stop playing the peacemaker every single time," Aparna said, looking at Manish, her eyes serious.

"Leave it now. Let's enjoy our dinner," Manish said.

Aparna did not comment. They turned their attention back to the TV. As if on cue, a Hindu and a Muslim started sparring vocally on a debate, intent on proving the supremacy of their respective religions. Aparna frowned. Naseem turned her eyes to meet her father's. A wordless code was exchanged between them. In sharp contrast to Aparna, Manish's demeanour generally exuded warmth. If Aparna was like a cryptic crossword puzzle, Manish was as easy to read as a child's picture book.

"We're suffocating," Aparna said, pointing to the pickle bottle.

Manish dug out a piece of lemon and served it to her. The TV continued to flash images, but no one paid any attention.

As a young journalist, Aparna had worked for a major news media organisation but, fed up with the constant curbs on her anti-establishment voice, she had left active journalism. Five years ago, she had started a periodical to promote rationality and atheism. Manish was the owner of a printing press, and this allowed easy distribution of her periodical in a physical format. With a decent membership of six lakhs, her periodical had even been nominated for an award, but then the central government changed, and the selectors did not wish to put themselves in the spotlight by awarding a publication which promoted atheism. They mentioned their regret to Aparna in private and her periodical did not win. Against all popular advice, Aparna refused to publish advertisements or promotions in her periodical. Her voice had been silenced once and she refused to be silenced again.

"Whatever your beliefs, Ma," said Naseem, "don't go and tweet anything outrageous about religion. It's not worth it."

"I agree," said Manish, nodding at Naseem. "Aparna, please be careful with your tweets."

"And since we're on the topic, please can you stop with the constant criticism of the ruling party?" Naseem said. "It's dangerous."

"My Maths teacher, Karkhanis sir, was jailed during the Emergency," Aparna said. "It didn't stop others from criticising Indira Gandhi. And now we have to watch what we tweet?" She swallowed and continued, "The way these wily politicians fool the gullible masses by dangling religion in front of them for votes! If we don't speak out, then who will?"

"Gullible, regressive masses. And who are we?" Naseem frowned. "All we do is sit in our posh dining rooms and give everyone lessons on liberalism and atheism."

"Are we not allowed even an opinion?" Manish smiled at his daughter. "At least let us criticise the politicians in the safety of our dining room."

"I think it's really pompous of us to turn up our noses at believers just because we're atheist humanists. Everyone's journey takes time," said Naseem, her voice rising. "Is it so hard to understand why a mother who struggles to feed her children turns to God?"

Aparna and Manish looked at each other, conveying silent congratulatory pats on the back to each other for having raised a wise, idealistic daughter.

"Democracy is failing us," said Aparna, only partly serious. "Everyone wants only religious supremacy these days, and they vote for politicians accordingly." She waved her hands as she spoke, and a grain of rice landed on the table.

"Breathe, Ma, and count to twenty," Naseem said, raising and lowering her hand in front of her mother's face to calm her. "Just because the party you support is not in power doesn't mean democracy is failing."

"Maybe it's time to ring the death knell on democracy, which isn't as absurd as it sounds. When one system fails, make way for another," said Manish. He licked his fingers and both women gave him a look of disgust.

"What else is left? If not democracy, then what?" Aparna turned her dal-laden fingers of her right palm outwards as she asked her question.

"Only time will tell. I don't have the answers," said Manish, helping himself to a liberal dose of the roasted chilli–garlic paste; he scooped some of it with the chapatti, put it in his mouth, and sat back, content. "Aah! Willing to trade democracy for a life-long supply of this chilli–garlic paste. It is divine! Can I use that word with atheists sitting around the table, or will it cause offence?" His eyes smiled at Naseem and Aparna.

"Don't worry. We atheists aren't easy to offend. It's the other lot that are a problem," Aparna said, suspiciously polite.

The silence that followed was broken only by minor sounds of cutlery being moved. The TV had been muted while their conversation was in progress.

"Free thought... free expression... as Tagore said, where the mind is without fear and the head is held high," Aparna said softly to the ceiling. "Someone needs to write the truth. The message needs to be repeated consistently until it becomes normalised."

Naseem sighed. "You really need to conform, Ma. It's about time."

"Since when did you start using words like 'conform'?" Aparna asked.

"She's *your* daughter, Aparna," Manish smiled.

"I conformed enough when I was young. Now's the time to rebel," Aparna replied, lost in the soothing thought of rebellion.

"I'm serious, Aparna," said Manish. "You have the ability to reach lakhs of people. Use your voice responsibly."

"Thank you for patronising me," Aparna said, bringing her palms together but not quite touching them, in a *namaskar* gesture, and bowing.

The silence that followed threatened to go on forever.

Then Aparna flashed them a quick grin, revealing the dimple in her left cheek. "I hereby promise, I will make outrageous statements about religion only within the four walls of our dining room. Is that okay, Mama Bear?" She reached out and pulled Naseem's cheek with her clean hand.

"I'm not Mama Bear, but you're definitely Goldilocks. Finicky about everything. Neither too hot nor too cold. You want things just right," Naseem said. "Correct, Baba?"

Manish smiled but refrained from replying.

"But Baby Bear's porridge was always right for Goldilocks! Goldilocks and Baby Bear were a team, weren't they?" Aparna said.

"Argh! You make me cringe, Ma. Baba seems lost in all this talk about Mama Bear and Baby Bear," Naseem giggled.

"He's never heard of Goldilocks."

"No, I haven't, and neither do I want to. I went to a simple SSC school and they didn't read out these stories to us," said Manish, switching the TV channel.

"Fairy tales, Baba."

"What?"

"Never mind." Naseem exchanged a chuckle with her mother.

The rest of dinner passed in silence. They retired, each to their own bedroom, after clearing up the kitchen.

The rooms reflected their owners' idiosyncrasies. Aparna's was filled with books and paintings: Mario Mirandas picked up during a brief visit to Goa; Raja Ravi Varmas bought during visits to Kerala; Gond and Warli tribal art purchased from various exhibitions. She had her laptop placed in the centre of her long writing desk. As she was not overly fussy about household cleanliness, it was normal to find streaks of dust and an unmade bed in her bedroom. Naseem's, on the other hand, was scrupulously clean, full of books, paintings, and smaller knick-knacks collected over eighteen years. Manish's was the messiest with clothes strewn in all corners. He hoarded receipts, old newspapers, bills, magazines, and all kinds of disposable junk. Aparna and Naseem had given up on his room a long time ago. Sometimes, they visited simply to marvel at his collection of useless things. Naseem had once even spotted a broken tooth, which Manish had forgotten to discard, in his stack of receipts. They half-expected to find dead rats, cockroaches, and lizards in the clutter and considered themselves lucky when they never did. Unlike other Indian middle-class families, they refused to hire cleaners. The responsibility was their own.

Aparna pulled out her laptop and typed out an article for her periodical. Outside, the wind pulled strings to make the trees dance; they obliged without a fight.

27

Breaking News — Times of Hindustan
19th April 2016

Case registered against *Imran's Dhaba* for insulting Hindu gods

PUNE: A case has been registered against the owner of the famous restaurant *Imran's Dhaba* following a complaint accusing him of insulting and demeaning Hindu gods in a newspaper advertisement for his restaurant. The Pune police station registered the case under Indian Penal Code section 295A (deliberate and malicious acts, intended to outrage religious feelings of any class by insulting its religion or religious beliefs). The advertisement which carried the caption "Gods too relish our Biryani" was found to be offensive because, according to the complainant, "Hindu gods do not eat Biryani". A letter of apology posted on the restaurant's social media handle read, "if our advertisement campaign has inadvertently hurt the sentiments of a religious community then we would like to apologise to the public at large". Complaints in four different states have been lodged over the same issue. All of them have accused the restaurant owner of hurting their religious sentiments.

Chapter Three
20ᵗʰ April 2016. Time: 09:00

Aparna rang the doorbell of the Rationalist and Anti-Superstition Society office. Fifty-year-old rationalist and anti-superstition activist Kumudini Pathak had established the society fifteen years ago using her own funds. Since Kumudini lived alone, her flat was used as the society office. Meetings were conducted every week. Aparna was greeted at the door by Rama—one of the permanent members of the society.

"Congratulations on the Baba Omnath case," Rama said as Aparna walked in. "I got these for you." She unwrapped a small newspaper parcel to reveal a sprinkling of Prajakta flowers. Aparna beamed and bent her head to savour the delicious fragrance of the coy, white and orange flowers.

"How lovely, thank you."

"From my neighbour's garden. I plucked them early in the morning and hoped to make a garland but didn't have enough time."

"Not to worry. They're lovely as they are." Aparna took another whiff. She wrapped the flowers in a tissue paper and placed them in her bulky bag. "To breathe in their fragrance from time to time," she said, pointing to her bag.

Years ago, Rama had arrived on Aparna's doorstep, a broom in her hand, begging for work.

"*Bai*, I will leave your house sparkling. Hire me as a cleaner. I'm desperate for work."

Aparna had noticed the pallor of anaemia on her face. Her thin, young body had looked like a stick draped in a sari, and yet, despite her troubles, she'd tried to look presentable with whatever little she had. A painted black *bindi* graced her forehead. A shabby red ribbon bundled her oiled, dark hair into a strict bun. Her eyes, lined with kohl, highlighted the oxymoronic mix of hope and weariness.

"We mop and clean the house ourselves. Making someone else clean my house is against my principles," Aparna had said gently.

"*Bai*, I admire your principles, but if everyone starts to think like you, then how will I feed my children?" Rama pleaded.

"I can't. I'm sorry." Aparna looked away, but then the woman grovelled.

"I've got hungry mouths to feed at home. You look kind. Can't you ignore your principles for a few years until my children become older? Please?" she begged.

Aparna's shoulders slumped.

"Can you come and meet me tomorrow? I will find some work for you."

"*Bai*, I can only clean. I don't know anything else. Please will you ask your friends if they require a cleaner?"

"Did you attend school?"

"I did. Up to the eighth standard on the Government's free girls' education scheme. When the scheme was dropped, my education stopped," she said, wiping her brow with her sari.

"What's your name?"

"Rama."

"I'll see what I can do. Meet me tomorrow. We require someone with your skills at the office."

"To clean?" Rama asked, widening her kohl-rimmed eyes.

"Office work," Aparna said.

"*Bai*, how can I work in an office? People will laugh... I can clean the office if you want, but anything else..." she said.

"No one will laugh. Times have changed," said Aparna.

"All right, *bai*," Rama said aloud, but privately wondered what the *bai* was up to.

She met Aparna the next day.

"Your job will be to sort files, pass messages, prepare tea, get provisions from the stores... will you manage that?" Aparna asked.

Rama nodded.

"If you work well, we will train you further."

Aparna had mentioned the incident to Manish that evening. He was sitting on the living room sofa, a newspaper spread out in front of his face.

"You've hired a cleaner to sort files in your office? It will never work," he said, a spectacled eye peering out from behind the newspaper.

"Why not?" Aparna asked. "She has studied up to the eighth standard."

"C'mon Aparna. I doubt she's ever stepped inside an office before." The thin newspaper made a delicate sound as it moved in his hands. "Helping someone is fine, but you take it to the limit sometimes. Try and get out of this saviour complex of yours."

Aparna hadn't replied.

Over the years, Rama flourished. The pallor on her face disappeared. Her saris were now of brighter shades. Stick-on *bindis* replaced the painted ones. Her bangles changed colours daily based on the colour of her saris. The liberal progressives on the committee did not allude to her previous profession and, though progress was slow at the beginning, Rama's intelligence had ensured an active participation. She was taken on a trial basis but managed to impress everyone with her agility. Three years later, she had been recruited as a permanent member of the team. Rama regularly travelled with volunteers to villages to help spread the anti-superstition message. She managed to establish an immediate rapport with the rural women and they found it easy to confide in her.

As Rama and Aparna walked towards the main office, Kumudini joined them, a tray with glasses of *Kokam Sarbat* in her hands. Taller than the average Indian woman, Kumudini's greying hair and simple cotton sari encouraged trust. Aparna took a glass from the tray and sipped. The sweet and sour beverage offered respite from the oppressive heat.

The setting of the main office was informal. Mattresses covered with traditional Indian fabrics worked as a seating arrangement. Sunil, the Vice President of the Society, previously the CEO of a software firm, was seated with the nine other permanent members. Sunil displayed a certain lightness prevalent in those who had managed to escape the corporate world. The treasurer, Milind, not being a fan of the *Kokam Sarbat*, was preparing coffee in the kitchen.

Everyone clapped as Aparna walked in.

"Welcome, official Godman-buster!" Sunil said.

Aparna gave an exaggerated bow. Due to space constraints, she was the only volunteer present. The seated members shifted to make place for the three of them. Aparna and Rama squeezed into their respective spaces. Kumudini offered the glasses of *sarbat* around. Milind joined them with his cup of coffee. The meeting commenced.

"Let me officially congratulate you on the Baba Omnath case," Kumudini said. "Well done. And I believe you've now got another Godman on your radar."

"Yes," Aparna said, "another one, but not as dangerous as the Omnath fellow."

"These Godmen spring up as easily as wheat," Sunil laughed. The room sighed and murmured.

"Overall, our progress hasn't been good. I have the numbers right here," Kumudini said. She put on her Gandhi framed glasses and peered into the papers in her hand, "In the past three years, we were aware of two thousand fraudulent Godmen and Godwomen in Maharashtra alone using religion to cheat people. We've received formal complaints against two hundred." She kept the first paper behind the rest and started with the next one. "Seventy per cent of the complainants are women. Only ten cases from the two hundred have been brought to trial—eight convictions and two acquittals—both the acquittals were cases of sexual exploitation by the Godmen."

The room erupted with sounds of exasperation.

"We're simply not agile enough! And we're always short of funds," Sunil said, throwing up his hands in the air.

"Our voice is not being heard," Rama added.

"We need the Government and the media on our side. Even now, there are a bunch of petitions gathering dust in a government office somewhere. We need to telecast anti-superstition messages constantly over the TV, the radio, and the newspapers. We need to get into schools. But where are the funds and the resources? Where is the support?" Kumudini said. Despite the disappointing figures, her back remained straight; her eyes displayed an unwavering confidence.

"And how does one do that when the Government itself is a bottomless well of superstition and religious dogma?" Aparna frowned.

"It's difficult," Milind said.

"The problem is, we only hear of these cases after the damage is done," Sunil gesticulated as he spoke. "These Godmen target remote villages teeming with superstition where the villagers are often ignorant and uneducated."

"Don't blame the villages. City people are fond of them too." Aparna raised an eyebrow. "The Godmen which appeal to city people spout mumbo jumbo in English. That's the only difference."

"They're like slime slipping through fingers. Look at the number of ways they think of to cheat people. One Godman asks his disciples to eat a *dosa* each time they face a problem. One Godwoman gives hugs as blessings. Another dresses up as a bride in red saris and jewellery and says she is an avatar of Goddess Durga! The English-speaking one talks of electro-magnetic waves affecting one's karma and all the deluded educated fools follow him. I mean, how on earth do they come up with such nonsense!"

"The ones with the largest followers are excellent orators. Charming too, with a knack of peddling mumbo jumbo with a straight face," Aparna said. "They know all the tricks to win over followers."

"The demand for their services is excruciatingly high," added Sunil.

"What can one do when the police themselves are terrified of black magic?" Aparna said, gazing at the floor.

"The cult of the Godmen and the religious lobby is too powerful," Sunil said.

"Well, let's look at our victories. Over the past three years, the society has shut down fifteen *ashrams* of the Godmen and Godwomen. Miracles have been busted by demonstrating the science behind them. Numerous workshops have been held in the villages to educate, inform, and raise awareness. Most importantly, after countless years, thanks to the efforts of activists and volunteers, we have managed to get the anti-superstition law passed in Maharashtra. That's certainly something. Think of all the lives saved," Kumudini said. There was a shift in the atmosphere of the room. The mention of the anti-superstition law always cheered the activists.

"Which brings me to my report," Aparna said. "As some of you may be aware, the society was informed of a Godman who claims to cure medical ailments by whispering religious chants into the ears of believers. Each whisper costs five hundred rupees, and apparently, it takes a minimum of five whispers for a cure." Aparna cleared her throat. "Villagers flock to him, desperate for a divine solution; pouring their hard-earned money into his lap."

"Where did this take place?" Sunil asked.

"Partas in Maharashtra—a small village of around twenty-five houses. The main occupation is agriculture, and most villagers have sugarcane farms." Aparna gulped down a sip of her *sarbat*. "I went there to assess the situation with Rahul and Neha. A fifteen-minute walk from the bus station led us to where the Godman operated. Clad in a white dhoti, wearing just a white *janeu* across his chest, his long beard made him look like a typical religious *baba*."

Sunil smirked.

"It was like a king holding his *durbar*. Villagers gathered in front of him while he sat on a raised platform under a banyan tree. His devotees told him of their troubles, and he talked. He spoke of the universe, the gods, nature... and anything else to make his charade believable. Two men stood beside the platform, handing him water when required."

"How does he ask for money?" Milind enquired.

"We asked around. The whispering sessions always take place in private. Money never exchanges hands in public."

"What's your gut feeling?" Kumudini asked.

"His operations are restricted to this village. I don't think this one will give us too much trouble. A warning will suffice." Aparna cleared her throat. "We advised the Godman to try and find other ways to earn money. If he doesn't stop, we warned, a police case would be registered against him."

"His reaction?" Sunil asked.

"Nothing. He said nothing. Neither did his men. I think they were surprised. I don't think he wants the hassle of a police complaint," Aparna said.

"Frankly, neither do we," Kumudini said.

Aparna nodded. "We informed him that it was in his best interests to stop fooling the villagers.

"Did you have time to pass around the leaflets?" Sunil asked.

"Did you take the latest ones?" Kumudini asked.

"We did have time, and yes, I took the pictorial ones to overcome the problem of illiteracy. We managed to cover almost all families, I think," Aparna said. "We split up and went to every house. We talked to villagers; advised them to take their health complaints to a doctor instead of the Godman. The main problem is that the hospital is a couple of kilometres away." She took another sip.

"Good job. Well done," Sunil said.

"You've planned a follow up?" Kumudini asked.

"Yes. We'll return next week to assess the situation; go from house to house to deliver the anti-superstition message and urge them to stay away from frauds. We may also challenge the Godman to prove his claim of curing medical ailments."

Aparna took her last sip, but her throat was dry and itchy from her speech. She went into the kitchen to get herself some more *sarbat* and returned to the room with the full glass in her hand.

"Good progress so far," Milind said to no one in particular.

Kumudini shook her head. "We must do more. Something radical."

Aparna sat in her assigned place. "The belief in superstition is too strong."

"One village at a time. Change will happen," said Sunil.

"If only the Government allowed us to conduct workshops in schools. Catch them when they are young," Aparna said.

"Now that the Government at the centre has changed, it seems unlikely," said Milind.

The next hour was spent discussing the workshops the society was planning to arrange in several small villages. After the meeting, Aparna covered her head with her sari *pallu* and headed home under the scalding afternoon sun.

She reached home in fifteen minutes. The first thing she did was to take the wilted Prajakta flowers from the tissue and gently place them in a bowl of water on the dinner table. The flowers would perk up. She looked forward to being greeted by the heady fragrance of Prajakta over breakfast.

Breaking News — Times of Hindustan
21st April 2016

Case registered against Bollywood actor for hurting religious sentiments

Bengaluru: A case has been registered in a local court against Bollywood actor Shaan Kumar for allegedly denigrating a Hindu god and hurting the religious sentiments of the Hindus. A case under section 295 (injuring or defiling place of worship with intent to insult the religion of any class) of the Indian Penal Code has been registered on a complaint filed by social activist Namdev Kamat.

In his complaint, the activist alleged that by posing for an advertisement in a women's magazine as Lord Vishnu, and holding a sanitary pad in his hand, the actor had denigrated the Hindu god and hurt religious feelings of the Hindus.

Chapter Four
22nd April 2016. Time: 16:00

"Shirish wants to shield his wife from me—from my feminist extremism," Aparna scoffed, making a fist and raising it into the air. Manish merely raised his eyebrows. It was almost four. The dolorous voice of Begum Akhtar saturated the room from a speaker. A verdant *jamun* tree outside the window allowed patterned sunshine into the room. They were sipping richly brewed 'Society' tea in clay teacups. A tin of *chaklis* lay open in the centre of their dining table. Manish's childhood friend, Shirish Kabra, had invited the family to the Grand Royal Club that evening.

"I've played cricket with Shirish, shared lunches, slept over at his place and know every embarrassing detail about his childhood. There's no friend like a childhood friend, I always say. You liked him too when you first met," Manish said.

"Those were good times, I agree," Aparna said, "when the three of us ambled out for a coffee or *dosa* somewhere whenever the mood took us. You with your printing press and he the founder of a software company... somehow that did not matter." She paused. "But then he got married and he changed."

"I don't see any change in his behaviour whatsoever," said Manish with a crunch of *chakli*, "no change at all."

"Observe today. He won't miss a single opportunity to belittle me," Aparna said, her tea growing cold. "What I find fascinating is how coy Mala acts around him. I mean, grow up," she gestured with her hands. "Evolve, for goodness' sake! They've been married for twenty-odd years now. She doesn't need to pander to his ego every single time!"

"Well, if it works for them..." Manish sipped his tea.

"It may work for them but it doesn't work for me." Aparna looked at him. "When will I ever get the pleasure of

38

gossiping with you? You see the good in them all. Forever trying to maintain peace!" Manish shrugged with a smile. Putting a wayward hair in its rightful place, Aparna continued, "A few days after his marriage, he told me I'd given his homemaker wife a complex because of my numerous achievements. From that day, he's downplayed me every time, in front of her."

Naseem came in just then and heard Aparna. A look passed between Naseem and her father. Aparna caught it.

"Naseem, it was Mala who talked about my achievements, not me. No need to snigger with your dad."

Naseem burst out laughing. "We love you, Ma, despite your lack of modesty." She took a piece of *chakli* from the tin.

"Most men do not like opiniated women and Shirish makes that clear. If I disagree with him or correct him, he starts to patronise."

Manish placed his palm over her cup. "Your tea is cold, Aparna."

Aparna ignored him, "Mala was never an insecure person. She has a healthy self-esteem and is fully content in being a homemaker." She turned to Naseem. "Plus, I haven't got the appetite to engage in this tug-of-war between the homemaker and the working woman. Mala probably said those words to Shirish as a joke, and there's nothing more to them. Shirish took them seriously and now tries to elevate his wife at every given opportunity." Aparna raised her eyebrows. "Mala doesn't need validation." She took a sip of the cold tea and pulled a face.

"C'mon Ma. I'm not saying this is your fault, but you intimidate people," Naseem said.

"I think you're reading too much into all this," Manish said.

"If Shirish believes Mala gets intimidated by you, ignore him. That's all I'm saying," Naseem said, switching off the ghazal.

Aparna frowned. "Mala is not intimidated by me, and Shirish does not get that."

39

"How would you know?" Naseem asked.

"I can sense it."

Naseem shook her head.

"I don't want to go," Aparna said making a face. "Shirish has evolved into a sexist pig who has made patronising women his profession. Mala coos at every word of his."

"We have to go for Baba," Naseem said, looking at Manish.

"I wonder at his choice of friends sometimes," Aparna said, "Shirish even wears the *janeu* for God's sake!"

"He is my childhood friend, Aparna," Manish said. "You don't really choose your childhood friends, do you? They just happen to you."

"Why couldn't you meet him alone somewhere," Aparna asked, "without the family tagging along?"

"He thought it will be fun for all of us to dine at his club," Manish said. "He thought you'd enjoy it."

Aparna shook her head. "I don't like posh places. Rather, I don't like the way people behave in posh places. Pretentious nonsense!"

Naseem sighed and Aparna turned to her.

"You will see first-hand today, Naseem, how the world treats an opiniated, feminist like me. No man likes a woman who disagrees with his world view."

"I'm sure it's not going to be all that bad, Ma."

"We'll see."

Chapter Five
22nd April 2016. Time: 17:30

"I'm looking forward to meeting Manish. But Aparna… Aah! A unique specimen all together." Shirish Kabra was getting his head massaged by his regular barber. Despite being forty-five, he had retained all his hair. With his pumped-up muscles, six-feet height, and dusky complexion, Shirish was an attractive man. Appearances were important to him, and he managed to polish his through regular workouts and massages.

Appearances extended to the décor of Shirish and Mala's living room. Colossal Thanjavur paintings, foiled with authentic twenty-four-karat gold and embedded with semi-precious stones, greeted visitors before they entered the living room where he now sat with his barber. A spectacular gold pendant chandelier shimmered above the living room windows stained in extravagant colours and beige sofas with gold linings, giving the room a palatial look.

The barber had placed a towel around Shirish's shoulders to catch the wayward streams of oil.

"She requires careful handling, I agree," said Mala, smiling. She sat at the dining table, a couple of feet away from her husband, cracking betel nuts with a help of a nutcracker. Mala was a wide-boned woman with a pleasant face. Like Shirish, she believed in taking care of her appearance. In her freshly washed and ironed white cotton salvar kameez, she appeared composed and elegant as if she was about to step outside.

"She is… shall we say… difficult?" Shirish closed his eyes as his barber vigorously massaged his head. "She nearly bit my nose off last time I shared a joke with her. You know that one about a bimbo wife? It had gone viral on WhatsApp. She told me I'm normalising misogyny and sexism. What! Just a bloody joke! She is… you know… that type," he mimed double quotes, "so we better be on our best behaviours." He wagged his index finger at Mala.

Mala made soothing noises.

"She is one of those women who has a problem with everything. Usually ends up missing the woods for the trees." Shirish laughed. "I wonder what made her opt for marriage and family. Women like her don't do domestics. Hardcore principles are all that matter to them."

"Fully agree," Mala said, busy with the nutcracker.

Shirish wiped off a thin stream of oil lurking near his eye. "I don't know if I told you this. She was invited to host a youth programme once. A typical millennial event. Aparna thought it would be a good opportunity to spread her message amongst the young. Manish and I tagged along, and by God, she left us cringing in our seats. She started to preach. Chill, woman! I urged her to be quiet, hoping my thoughts would be telepathically conveyed to her. But our madam went charging at them like an atheist rhino," he chuckled. "I will never forget. The remarkable thing was Manish did not say a single word to her. We all pretended as if the hosting had been an enormous success."

"She relentlessly pursues her goal… I've noticed. Why plan an evening with them, after so long?"

"I miss my friend. He's not a bad sort, and we were close."

There was a pause.

"Well, I'm afraid her habit of bringing religion into every conversation puts me off," Mala said. "She's relentless. Certainly wouldn't be my first choice to spend an evening with."

Shirish nodded in agreement, closing his eyes like a martyr forced to tolerate a world full of atheists.

"Do it for me," Shirish said, his eyes still closed, "and for Manish. Do it for our friendship?"

"Of course." Mala smiled her acceptance. "I'm not saying I won't come. Just that I'm not looking forward to it, that's all."

With the massage over, the barber left unnoticed, and the couple started preparing for the evening ahead.

Chapter Six
22nd April 2016. Time: 19:00

"Damn! Bloody difficult to get a parking space these days," said Manish. They were at the Grand Royal Club to meet Shirish and Mala. "Aah! there they are." He waved at Shirish and Mala and squeezing his battered Maruti between two posh cars, the models of which he did not recognise. His small car stuck out like the lost mother from rural India, come to encourage her son at a posh school event.

Shirish and Mala were waiting at the entrance.

"You look wonderful, Aparna," said Mala. "How tall you've become," she said to Naseem, holding her hand.

Shirish, resplendent in a suit, and Mala, in a ravishing turquoise silk sari, seeped luxury. As was his usual style, Manish had put on a *khadi kurta* pyjama and Aparna wore a simple, white sari with a red border. Her face was without make-up. Naseem, wearing a ripe mango-coloured salwar kameez, looked down at her feet, aware of how out of place they looked.

"Glad to see you again, my friend." Manish gave Shirish a hug.

"Of course, of course. How long has it been? Four years? To think that we live in the same city…"

"We must meet more often. I agree," smiled Manish.

"Where's Harshal?" Aparna asked, referring to Shirish and Mala's nineteen-year-old son, "I haven't seen him in such a long time."

"He's busy with his studies. You know how it is… they don't like to accompany their parents after a certain age," said Mala, smiling at Naseem. "I guess it's different with girls."

Everyone waited for Aparna to make a comment on gender stereotypes, but no complaint followed.

"Let's go in." Shirish indicated to the entrance to the club, and they followed him inside. The British-era club spewed understated grandeur. A relic of the colonial period, it continued to follow the old British traditions, taking its prestige and exclusivity extremely seriously. At the reception, Shirish signed them in as guests.

The man seated at reception hesitated. "I'm sorry sir," he said to Manish, "but as your attire does not conform to our dress code, you'll be allowed into the club but won't be allowed to visit the restaurant."

"In what way doesn't my attire conform?" Manish asked amused, observing the receptionist's stiff white shirt.

"You're wearing *Kolhapuri* chappals, sir. Shoes need to be worn in our restaurant."

"Aah, I see. The attire of the West. I understand." He paused. "A little too hot for shoes, don't you think?"

"Shoes or chappals—what difference does it make to your club?" Aparna said loudly. "It's ridiculous to assess an individual by their privilege. Even Buckingham Palace entertained Gandhi and *he* turned up bare-chested in his loin-cloth and chappals. Would your club turn away the great Mahatma too?"

The receptionist looked startled. People turned, their noses in the air, glad not to be a part of this troublesome brigade. Manish's glee was genuine, but Naseem was mortified, and Mala's eyes revealed discomfort. Shirish shifted from one foot to another.

"No madam," mumbled the receptionist.

"Ma, please. Gandhi?! Really?" Naseem whispered in Aparna's ear.

"Can we sit in the bar?" Shirish asked.

"Yes sir. That won't be a problem."

"Will you please serve us food in the bar, then?"

"Sure, sir," said the receptionist, smiling.

"The British left India, but they left one of their spies behind," joked Manish, winking at the stiff shirt.

"Ugh Baba. Stop fooling around," whispered Naseem.

"Sorry *dost*. Should've told you earlier. I was unaware of this rule until this moment. I don't wear chappals, you see," said Shirish.

"*Arre*, I understand. Only suit and boot for you." Manish grinned widely. Naseem met Aparna's eyes, their expressions guarded.

The five of them, finally, were seated in the bar.

"They opened up their membership briefly for three months and I pounced on the opportunity to secure mine. Exceedingly difficult to get membership." Shirish showed his teeth.

"Good, good," said Manish. "So, how've you been, *dost*?"

"Doing well, by the grace of God, as you can see," said Shirish, spreading his hands to indicate the surroundings.

"Which engineering college does Harshal attend? I forget. Is it the Government College?" Naseem asked.

"Bah! We decided to enrol him in Bharti. At least it is private, so it gets a select crowd," said Shirish.

"Is that what untouchability has evolved to nowadays?" Aparna said loudly.

Manish gave her a worried look. Mala pulled at her earlobe.

"How're you doing, Aparna *Bhabhi*? How is your periodical going? I've not had the time to read it, I'm afraid," Shirish said, leaning towards her.

"Periodical is going well. You should read it one of these days." Aparna relaxed back in her chair.

"Good. Good. It's good to keep busy. It gets boring sitting at home all the time," said Shirish.

"I don't do it to keep busy," Aparna said, her face expressionless.

"Of course, of course. The other day, I had a conversation with my sister who is also a social media warrior like you.

Sitting in her armchair, sipping fresh coconut water (she has it delivered to her house by the coconut *wallah* every morning, by the way), she furiously types out all these anti-right-wing posts. Believes she will change voting patterns. Yet, we have a right-wing government in power. Where are the mindsets being changed?" Shirish's laugh at his own joke reverberated into the sedate room.

Aparna leaned forward, eyes widening. "Oh, but mindsets are being changed. Slowly, but surely. It may not be evident on social media, because that's just a miniscule number of the population. But we activists managed to get the Maharashtra Government to pass the anti-superstition bill. Isn't that a great achievement? Would that have been possible without the written word, and of course, the sweat of our activist volunteers?"

"Why do you need a law against superstition? What is superstition anyway?" He placed a hand on his wife's shoulder and squeezed. "Mala here fasts every Monday for Lord Shiva. Is that superstition? I visit a temple every Wednesday. Is that superstition? Should the law get involved in every one of my personal, religious decisions?"

"You misunderstand, Shirish *bhai*. There are pockets in our country which are extremely superstitious. Even cases of human sacrifice are not uncommon." Mala made a clucking sound in the back of her throat, but Aparna spoke over her. "Are you aware that before the anti-superstition law came into effect, cases of human sacrifice were treated as murder? But you see, neither the Godman nor the believers *knew* that a murder was being committed. The Godman performs a religious ceremony before the sacrifice, and that's enough to convince everyone that they're dabbling in religion, not murder. Now, we have the anti-superstition law, which lists the act of human sacrifice specifically as an offence. So, both the Godman as well as the believers *know* that the act is a criminal offence. It serves as a deterrent."

"I love this drink," Naseem said, pointing to her glass. "Never had it before."

Everyone ignored her.

"Wasn't the bill passed during the tenure of the previous government? Try and make the current government pass such a bill, and then I will be convinced," Shirish said.

"Law and order are a state subject, Shirish *bhai*, not a central subject. Anyway, the efforts are always on but, as you know, the road ahead is not easy." She took a breath, "And Naseem, that's just a lemonade. Don't know why you're saying you haven't tasted it before."

"Well, as long as it gives you satisfaction, that's the main thing," Shirish said, leaning towards Aparna. She moved back to put some space between them.

"But you fail to understand my point. This is not about me finding a hobby or satisfaction."

"Yes, yes. I agree, but I don't like the attitude with which these liberal activists go about things. My sister is the same. She's the only one who is right and all the others who do not agree with her are the uneducated, bigoted masses." Shirish cleared his throat and Mala passed him his glass. "Now, taking on our great religion... is that advisable? There are several other regressive religions that you can take on. Why exclusively target our own? Also, is it really necessary to write so... aggressively?"

"Ah! Shirish *bhai*. I thought you don't read my periodical," Aparna smiled.

"I'm aware of your overall style," said Shirish. "But why not take up the issues of the burkas and hijabs?"

"We do take those on too, Shirish bhai," said Aparna. "Look, it is not for me or any man to tell a woman how to dress." She wrinkled her nose, a glint in her eyes. "I *do* raise awareness of the sly ways of patriarchy though."

"A-ha. Taking the easy way out," Shirish wagged his finger at Aparna.

"Our country is not used to radical thoughts, Shirish *bhai*, whether it is atheism or feminism. I wish to normalise them." Aparna stressed every word with a tap of her fist on the table. Naseem reached out to steady a wobbly glass.

"What's the need? Let believers believe," said Shirish, holding on to his glass.

Aparna tipped her head to one side, considering this. "Okay, how about this? Let believers believe—as long as their believing does not trample on the rights of others. Also, if theists can promote their religion, then why can't I promote atheism?"

Manish looked at her, his eyes softening.

Shirish's jaw tightened. "Extremism of any kind is not good. There are extremists in religion and then there are these militant atheists like yourself. Good women who lead their lives on an equal footing with men, and then there are the radical feminists who are out to insult all men." Then, abruptly changing tracks, he said, "There's no greater happiness in life than to have a wife at home who cooks and cares for you. I keep telling Mala that I must have done some remarkable deeds in my previous birth to get a wife like her."

Naseem placed her hand on Aparna's lap.

"Well, who doesn't like to be served a plate of delicious, hot, home-made food. I know I do," said Aparna, and sensed the relieved sighs of her family. But she had not finished yet. "Your views are terrifying, Shirish *bhai*. It helps all of us to think beyond stereotypes, and just for the record, I believe in atheist humanism, not militant atheism. There's a difference."

The dinner threatened discomfort. Mala looked around, a smile still pasted on her face, angry with herself for not avoiding the dinner as her instincts had suggested. Manish searched furtively for a topic to break the conversation. Naseem kept her hand firm on Aparna's lap like an owner used to the rage of his pet dog.

"Let's just say, this is how I do things. Right or wrong, I don't know. I'm especially unable to keep quiet when asked to," Aparna said. She took a sip of water, her smile wide but firm.

"Which is a good trait. I wish I could do half of what you do," came a surprising rejoinder from Mala.

Naseem turned to Mala and gave a small smile.

A silence descended. When Shirish said, "You must hear this latest joke," everyone looked uncomfortable.

"How do you know when a woman is about to say something smart?" Shirish grinned as he looked at each face. "When she starts a sentence with 'A man once told me...'" He laughed raucously—the only one to do so. "And there's one more... You'll agree that this one is the best. How many men does it take to open a beer?" He looked around again, urging them, by gesticulating, to give his question a go. "None. It should be opened when she brings it." More laughter, again his own.

Aparna's hands tightened into fists.

Naseem whispered to her, beyond caring whether anyone else heard, "Ma, let it go. It's just a silly joke."

Manish looked worried.

"This joke is misogynistic, and you very well know it. And Naseem, I will always publicly object to misogyny wherever I see it."

People on other tables turned around to look. *It's those same troublesome people again.*

"Hey folks, I don't know about you, but I'm hungry. Let's order," said Manish, forcing joviality into his voice. Aparna gave him a piercing look as everyone except her moved plates, forks, and knives around desperately.

"Misogynist jokes do not have a place in the current times, Shirish," Manish said gently.

Shirish gave him a look full of pity which Manish ignored.

"*Bhabhi*, will you like to have some wine?" Shirish asked, "You prefer red, right? Manish, what about you? Whiskey?
50

Mala, red for you too?"

As the wine flowed, it muted strong emotions. Ideologies aside, they conversed simply as friends. And then, when no one was looking, Shirish whispered in Manish's ears, "Ply them with wine to keep them quiet. Always works," he winked.

For a moment, Manish was tempted to smile but instead his eyes flicked to Aparna. With a serious look, he simply shook his head.

Chapter Seven
23rd April 2016. Time: 21:00

"What's this thing I've produced, was my thought when I first saw you. There you were—tiny, miserable and wriggling."

Snug under a mosquito net, Aparna was lost in the past. She lay on her back, gazing up at the net, one arm under Naseem's head. Naseem lay facing her, with one leg on Aparna's knee. A single night-lamp glowed yellow. Outside the net, mosquitos set up a merry buzz.

"Why, thank you, Ma," said Naseem, "you make me sound cute."

"It's the truth. Your birth absolutely overwhelmed me. It's not true, you know, what they show in films. I felt no love towards you in the first two months—just an overwhelming sense of responsibility."

"That's so good to know."

"Aji had warned me, just like I'm warning you. But despite all that, it was still difficult."

"But why? It must be nice to have a baby to play with. Your own doll."

Aparna rose up on her elbows and looked at her daughter for a moment.

"It's not that simple," she said. "I wasn't willing to put myself at your disposal for twenty-four hours a day. This tiny, tiny baby who loved to bawl her lungs out. I wanted to be free! But I toiled on." She turned her gaze back to the net. "Then the nursing… All this politics around breast-feeding… this pressure that new mothers are subjected to. I started tentatively and didn't know what to expect. I'd heard horror stories of pinched, bitten and bleeding nipples."

"Ew, Ma."

"I didn't want the hassle of sterilising bottles in the middle of the night, so I stuck with it, but I was pleasantly surprised to be given an easy ride by you. Good-natured and sweet, you were easy to love once you grew out of the bawling infant phase. Day by day, we started to fall in love, and by age five you declared to the world that your Ma was the one great love of your life."

Naseem's smile went unnoticed.

"My parents didn't believe in physical affection, you know, but you've always grown up with cuddles and kisses."

"Aw! Were you never hugged as a child?"

"It wasn't as common as it is now." Aparna turned to lay on her back.

"But didn't Aji hug you, like ever? I'd die if that were to happen to me."

"We had other things to worry about," Aparna said. "Your *ajoba* lived in his own mind with alcohol to keep him company. He probably suffered from depression but there was a lot of ignorance about this back then."

Naseem nodded slowly. "I didn't know that, Ma. Seeing him like that must have been hard for you."

"Yes... Money was also a problem. Your Aji and I took tuitions. When a home does not have an earning male, the predators circle around. The world did not take us seriously because we did not have enough. It was difficult."

They fell into a comfortable silence, Naseem playing with the ends of her hair.

"What was your house like?"

"Oh, it was a gloomy one. Three rooms, so I guess still privileged in a way. We did our best to cheer it up using as little money as possible. Plants used for the décor. Curtains crafted from old saris. Aji and I painted pictures in vibrant yellows and oranges to bring in some colour."

"How was Aji back then? Was she nice?"

"She was an intelligent woman. She educated me—not in the traditional sense though there was that too, of course—on borrowed books and by hunting down books sold by weight—these are cheaper. She read. She learned, and she shared her love of reading with me. I did not own any picture books but the way she regaled me with fairy tales was remarkable."

"I love that," Naseem grinned, and Aparna returned her smile.

"Yes, my world was full of beautiful princesses and handsome princes in mesmerising, three-spired castles. So expertly did she weave her stories, I remained lost in their magic for years. But as I grew older, she took on the task of exposing the realities of the riveting tales that she had narrated. Isn't it strange how all stepmothers in fairy tales are wicked? Why does the prince have to rescue the princess *every single time*? Why are girls always in distress? Why aren't they resourceful enough to get out of tricky situations? These exposés of the fairy tales left me spellbound. That was my first lesson, I guess."

"Did she believe in God?"

"Initially, she followed all religious traditions. Bathing the gods daily; lighting *diyas;* offering flowers; chanting prayers—maintaining fasts. Until one day she decided to give it all up. She could no longer ignore the futility of it all. All of it, so time-consuming and unnecessary! And as with everything else, it falls to the woman of the house to do it all." Naseem snorted in agreement. "The gods remained in the house but were no longer worshipped."

"Your journey was made simpler by her."

"My other journeys too. She allowed me my thoughts. Didn't restrict my freedom in any way."

"So, that's how you got into the habit of speaking without thinking of the consequence," Naseem laughed.

Aparna stroked Naseem's head. Naseem snuggled closer.

"Ma, what if I choose to marry someone who is not liberal enough to understand feminism or atheism?" Naseem asked.

"A feminist Indian man is very difficult to find, anyway," Aparna said.

"C'mon, Ma," Naseem said impatiently.

"No feminist men in high-paying jobs. In a creative field like yours, perhaps there's still a chance. But in the corporate world—never. You'll have to lurk around in journalism or social work circles to find one. They usually hang out there. Atheists, on the other hand, are almost impossible to find. As rare as finding a rational right-winger."

"I'm serious, Ma! So, will you please stop goofing around?"

Aparna turned on her side to face Naseem.

"Don't make the mistake of choosing to marry someone with my approval in mind. Marriage is a huge compromise as it is. Marry someone you love. It becomes a little easier then." Aparna sighed. "As it is, feminist men have this nasty habit of springing patriarchal surprises on you now and then, so don't get your hopes up even if you do manage to find one."

"Baba is not like that. Sometimes, you're too negative."

"I didn't have it easy, and neither will you. Despite your privilege."

"Why? What's so difficult?"

"The pressure to conform. Whether you choose to cross the line at all costs or allow yourself to be subdued by societal rules depends on your resilience. Become financially independent, and then it's easier. No need to bow down before anyone else. Earn your money, spend it the way you want and lay your own ground rules."

There was a silence and then Aparna sighed. She touched Naseem's nose again. "You're an adult now. I'm done with all the mothering and the nurturing. You can bloody well look after yourself without relying on me."

Naseem looked at her mother, mock horror all over her face.

"What a luxurious thought!" Aparna said, "No more responsibilities."

"Oh no, Ma. I'm not going to let go of you that easily."

"Don't you have all those glass ceilings to smash?"

"I'm in no hurry," Naseem chuckled.

"Well, goodnight. Time for me to go."

"Be careful. Don't let the mosquitos in."

"That's my next challenge," Aparna said as she squeezed out of the tightly bound mosquito net. The glow soothed for a few minutes until Naseem switched the lamp off.

Chapter Eight
24th April 2016. Time: 08:00

Like a gourmet chef selecting the finest ingredients for an elegant lunch, Naseem took care to choose her outfit. Delicate enough to feel Ronit's touch through the fabric. Flexible enough to shed, should things head that way. A push-up bra gave her breasts a false, exaggerated effect. *Cater to the male gaze. The most potent of desires. Why pretend?* The thin muslin of the pastel-pink *chikankari*-embroidered kurta gave her the desired level of transparency and delicacy. Her *dupatta* was the palest of greens, like summer caterpillars; her *salvar*, the colour of burnished mud from the Konkan region. After painting her nails the colour of a spicy pickle, she added bangles to complete the look.

She had first spotted Ronit in the university café where she studied Interior Designing. Subtle, wordless messages had been exchanged. They started visiting the café in the hope of spotting each other. Finally, Ronit had asked a mutual friend for introductions.

"I didn't know you're a Muslim," he said to her, a few minutes after the introductions.

"What makes you think I'm a Muslim?" Naseem said.

"Well, your name... Isn't it obvious?"

"My mother decided to name me Naseem. It's a name of Persian origin, synonymous with the breeze."

"That's... unusual. Hindus don't give Muslim names to their children."

"Oh, Ma is weird that way. Baba was reluctant to give me a Muslim name. Didn't want me to experience the bigotry that Muslims face here, but Ma was firm. She refused to let the bigotry of others control her choices. So, Naseem it was!"

"Interesting," Ronit said. Naseem would have liked to probe his comment further, but she left it for another time. They met daily in the same café, flirting and teasing until it was useless to pretend any further.

On the fourth day of their meeting, they ventured into a park and found a lonely spot—almost an impossibility in Indian cities. They kissed, and Naseem discovered the potency of lust. During her lessons, she dreamed of Ronit's hands on her breasts. She thought of his touch during dinner. Her lust for him fully controlled her, which disturbed her a little. Yet, she revelled in the experience, yearning for more.

The first time she had understood what sex involved was at age twelve in a sex education lesson at school. She was astounded. *One of the first lessons we're taught as girls is to sit like ladies. Don't spread your legs when you're sitting. Sit properly. And then they hoist this on us!*

Now that she had a boyfriend, she found herself thinking of sex all the time. *Will I enjoy it? Will his desire for me see me through the potentially painful experience?*

She had giggled through the few erotic videos she had watched with her girlfriends. She'd giggled but the videos terrified her. *Is this what sex is? Pounded through frontal and posterior orifices, swallowing body fluids, and moaning loudly until the neighbours can hear? Is this the natural, ultimate basic instinct that indicates love between two humans? Why does it all feel so alien? Perhaps it wouldn't feel quite so extreme if we could see our aunts, neighbours, friends, teachers, librarians and other normal people having sex. But this is supposed to be a private act to be performed when the lights are out, and the doors closed. Has civilised society got it all wrong? Perhaps nature intended sex as a public performance. Out in the open for all to see and learn. Just like the animals. Do animals become anxious about sex too?*

She turned to fiction, but it painted an ideal. *All women must conform to this perfect way of making love. Do women write about their experience of sex with honesty? Is it all really so glorious? Or are we all bogged down by male fantasy?* After reading, questions faced her more than answers.

Despite her misgiving, she read some more. *Boys and men get anxious about their performance too? Baapre! One would think that a natural act would be... well, natural and easy to perform. How on earth did nature get this all so drastically wrong?*

Desire, doubts, confusions and worries jumbled together with a breathless, fevered anticipation. Ronit did not push for more. Neither did she. Both luxuriated in new sensations and pleasures.

The summer that year was a rampage of colour. Scarlet blooms of the Gulmohar competed for attention with the shocking oranges, pinks, and whites of the Bougainvillea. Jamun trees, lush with fruit, thrived in the gardens. Treasured mangoes, like pampered sons, showed off on green branches. The days started off well, but then the heat grew steadily oppressive. The sun was treated like an ex-lover: to be avoided. Still, it continued its pursuit, relentless, the air heavy with desperation for rain prolonging the suspense. Finally, the ruthless sun disappeared into the clouds. The rains gave a hint of their impending arrival, turning the air aromatic. Mynas refused to stop singing. Unseen peacocks gossiped. Families gathered to have potato fritters with cups of hot tea to welcome the showers. And when the rain finally arrived, the petrichor was lovely enough to be bottled as perfume and sold by savvy entrepreneurs. The poor, who sleep out in the open outside their houses sighed with a mixture of relief and trepidation for the monsoons. Children rushed out to dance, and parents, for once, did not stop them. One of the most anticipated free events every year, the first rains of summer were greeted with celebration.

With the weather set for romance, Naseem was greeted by Ronit at the university gates. Ronit could have easily found his feet in the Indian modelling world. Standing at six feet, he had chocolate boy looks and a compelling physique. His quick glance of appraisal turned into appreciation after spotting her, which made Naseem ridiculously happy. She admired the sleek line of his shoulders beneath his casual, cotton shirt and felt the familiar twinge of lust.

"How late you are! I was waiting ages," he said, his eyes smiling.

"Just getting a few things ready for Ma's birthday day after tomorrow. I mentioned that, I think."

"Of course. I was just impatient to see you."

They wanted to touch each other physically but they could not. Even in the twenty-first century, Indian society did not allow a couple to kiss or show much affection in public.

"Hey, let's bunk the lectures and go to Ash's flat to hang out. I have the key right here," said Ronit.

Naseem bit her lip. "We hardly attend lectures. Don't want to get into trouble for my attendance."

"Oh, c'mon. We have all the time in the world to attend lectures. Come, let's go." They headed towards the parking lot where Ronit had his bike parked. He jumped on and put the bike in gear. Naseem climbed up behind him, holding him tight, eager to experience the times ahead. *How little I know him,* Naseem thought to herself. *An attraction based on physical characteristics, lust rather than love!* The thought troubled her. *Am I as frivolous as that?* But she was unable to do anything about it.

Ronit parked. They climbed the stairs to the first floor where Ash's flat was located. After fiddling in his pocket for a few seconds, Ronit produced the key, unlocked the door and they went in.

It was a one-room kitchen flat with a large, looming unmade double bed. Below the bed was a half-eaten plate of Biryani and a banana peel. Plates encrusted with dried up curry and empty beer bottles filled the kitchen.

Naseem took in a breath, trying to assess the quality of air. Looking around the filthy room, she sat on the edge of the bed and asked, "What do you think of feminism?"

Ronit mimicked a jump.

"Oh, all serious and all, huh?"

But Naseem did not smile.

He sat next to her and placed his arm around her shoulder. "Feminists are feared in my family," he said with a laugh.

"And you're okay with that?" she asked, her face sombre.

"It's got nothing to do with me. The women in my family have no interest in going out to burn bras."

"Is that what you think feminism is? Burning bras?"

"Who cares?" He said, lunging towards her.

She paused, the disappointment of his response unsettling. But, as his hands moved all over her, she thought: *here's to the power of lust! It eclipses ideologies. And filthy rooms. You simply bow your head and do as lust instructs.* She welcomed his arms and gave in.

Chapter Nine
24th April 2016. Time: 17:30

The flowery aroma of the room freshener, diffused with the odour of the cooking meat, swept through the dusted and mopped living room. The artefacts were chosen with care, not merely for aesthetics, but to display wealth and status. Malaysian flower vases bragged on the coffee table. Porcelain plates purchased from Singapore gleamed. As the cook chopped the tomatoes, coriander leaves glistened, ready to garnish.

Ronit's mother, Vaishali Mehendale, reviewed the proceedings with a critical eye. Vaishali was a petite woman with a clear complexion barring a medium-sized mole on her chin which, in her opinion, made her look evil. She hated the mole. It did not help that one of the famous, yesteryear villains of Hindi cinema had sported a prominent mole on her chin, and since then, moles had been blatantly used to portray immoral female characters in the movies. Vaishali planned to get rid of it but something else always came up.

Despite attending the neighbourhood laughter club at dawn, Vaishali was stressed. Kitty parties were demanding work! The sheer amount of effort required was enough to bring tears to the eyes of the strongest of women.

"Why join kitty parties when you don't enjoy them?" Ronit asked, putting on his shoes.

Vaishali wrung her hands. "Oh, but I do enjoy them! It's only when I have to host one that the stress gives me hot flushes."

"What's there to stress about? They're your friends, aren't they?"

"Yes... but you see, everything must be perfect. It must have that wow factor. Pointless doing it otherwise." Vaishali wiped her face with a tea towel.

"That's just silly," said Ronit, putting on a cap and getting his sunglasses from a nearby drawer.

"Now, Gayatri the other day had prepared a full Thai meal for us, complete with starters. Her gift for us that evening was an adorable knick-knack she'd purchased from Thailand. I *must* outdo that."

"What gift have you selected?" Ronit asked, curious.

"That's what I'm most worried about. I spent an hour yesterday hunting for one. Then, I saw these beautiful silk scarves in Bombay Stores, and I thought that they would do the trick."

"Good, then. Problem solved. They look expensive."

"They are," Vaishali said in a small voice. She whispered the price to him. "We're allowed to purchase gifts within an agreed budget only. This one far exceeds the budget… but what can I do? I had to get something with the wow factor. I'll end up being a total laughing stock otherwise. So, I'm going to lie and say that the gift is within the agreed budget."

"Amma, that's crazy," said Ronit.

"I know, *beta*. Don't tell your papa…"

"Hmm, okay… Anyway, I'm off. I'll see you later. Tata!" said Ronit as he left the house, closing the door behind him.

Vaishali's husband was out of the city on a business trip, so the evening was all hers. She spent the next hour adorning herself. A black silk sari with magenta bangles, a subtle diamond necklace, Dior foundation, and lipstick to match. *I look gorgeous, except for that evil mole.* She spent a few minutes deciding which music to play in the background for the evening. She wanted something classy, so Bollywood music was ruled out. *A ghazal will work. It will also go with the theme of the evening.* She selected a Jagjit Singh ghazal and as the tender tune filled the living room, it put her in a better mood.

At the appointed hour, one by one, the ladies sashayed in.

"Sit down. Sit down ladies," said Vaishali, waddling around like a worried hen. To the sound of 'Aahs' and 'Oohs', she sprinkled rose water on them. Something to distinguish her evening from theirs. The ladies shot comments as they looked around the room.

"Ooh! What an adorable vase this is."

"You look gorgeous, Vaishali. The colour suits."

"I love this Pankaj Udhas ghazal."

"Er…it's Jagjit Singh."

"Dear me. They sound the same, don't they?"

"Such a difference from trashy Bollywood! I love ghazals."

"I can smell… umm… mutton kebabs, are they? What an aroma! That boy Hussain refuses to purchase mutton for us. He says people will mistake the red meat for beef and lynch him, now that the Government has banned beef consumption. Now, what to do? I can't go to the mutton shop on my own. Yuck! We had to stop eating red meat because of these Muslims."

The ladies tutted sympathetically.

"Well, serves them right. To think that India had been selling sacred cow meat for so many years. For what? India is a Hindu country. Don't kill our sacred cows," said Mrs Yadav, exuding righteousness.

"I agree. I'm so glad our dear Prime Minister has banned beef. It's been our one desire for years. I finally feel as if I belong here," said Mrs Kulkarni, though her ancestors had been living in the country for centuries.

"But these liberals! They aren't happy. The usual suspects are making loud noises, saying food choices should not be policed. Absurd," Mrs Shah added.

"I've *almost* given up meat. It gives me gas," Mrs Joshi said.

"The other day, I read an article by that Aparna Soman. She says Dalits and Muslims prefer beef over other meat and there should be no food bans. *Arre*, how much more can we do for the Dalits? Our children don't get admissions to medical colleges because they take away all our seats… Now, they want to eat beef too?" Mrs Kulkarni tittered.

"*Waise*, your son seems to be a big fan of Aparna Soman. Or a fan of her daughter, most definitely," said Mrs Shah, looking at Vaishali.

"My son?" Vaishali was puzzled.

"You don't know? He has been spotted with Aparna Soman's daughter several times. They are probably girlfriend–boyfriend." Mrs Shah's face throbbed with satisfaction.

The cook came in to place the kebabs on the coffee table. She went around handing empty plates to everyone and the ladies started to help themselves.

"Who is this Aparna Soman? I haven't heard of her," said Vaishali.

"*Arre*, that radical feminist. She writes all these angry articles which no one reads," said Mrs Kulkarni, gnashing the kebab with a fork held in manicured fingers.

"Feminist?" Vaishali looked aghast. The possibility of getting a feminist daughter-in-law made her armpits moist.

"Nip it in the bud while you still have the chance," said Mrs Shah, waving her arms and her perfume towards Vaishali.

"You can imagine the kind of upbringing the poor girl must have had. She's either been royally ignored because of her mother's whims, or she must be a staunch feminist herself. I don't know which is worse," Mrs Kulkarni chewed the kebab like a sparrow.

"I agree. These feminists are the limit. I hear, they don't even give blowjobs to their husbands," said Mrs Joshi, giggling.

"Hay, Mrs Joshi. Where did you hear that?" Mrs Kulkarni snickering. "If that's the case, then I wish I was a feminist too, but in this respect only, *haan*."

"Why Mrs Kulkarni? You don't like giving blowjobs to your husband?" Vaishali asked. The women burst into raucous laughter.

"Do you?" Mrs Kulkarni asked, with all seriousness.

"We all have to do whatever is needed to maintain peace at home," said Vaishali. The women nodded.

"We're all in this together," said Mrs Kulkarni, droplets of perspiration emerging from her face like a sieve.

"She doesn't believe in religion either," Mrs Joshi added, mid-chew.

"Who?"

"That Aparna Soman."

"Is she a celebrity of some sort? You all seem to know a lot about her," Vaishali said.

"A certain section of people cannot stop raving about her. She's well known in the social work circles. You know the type, finding a problem with anything and everything."

"It's just a fad to attract attention. Saying outrageous things to make people talk about you. She lashes out and mesmerises the idiots," Mrs Kulkarni soothed.

"Like I said, Vaishali, stop it before it gets serious. You want your Ronit to get regular blowjobs, don't you? Find a nice, domesticated daughter-in-law who will keep you all happy," Mrs Joshi said.

"I'll speak to him today."

An hour or so later, a volley of burps went around the living room. With the ladies satiated, it was time to bring out the gifts.

"Hope you like them. It's not much," Vaishali mumbled as she handed out the silk scarves to the ladies.

"*Arre* Vaishali, I saw these in Bombay Stores yesterday and they were bloody expensive. These aren't within the stipulated budget," said Mrs Joshi.

"Take them anyway. I spent so much time searching for the right gift," said Vaishali, miserable at being found out.

"We cannot. Rules are rules. They cannot be broken," said Mrs Joshi, moving from side to side to make some room for the gas in her stomach.

"Just take them. Next time, I'll get a cheaper gift to even things out," Vaishali pleaded, nearly in tears now.

"Vaishali, I'm not going to take these, and neither will the other ladies. We will have ladies gifting gold, silver, and diamond trinkets next. Give them back. I'm sure they're returnable," said Mrs Shah. The ladies handed back the scarves. Vaishali wanted to cry. Despite all her efforts, the evening had not been a success.

"Bye then. Wish you could have taken the gifts," she mumbled.

"Don't worry so much Vaishali," Mrs Kulkarni said.

Easy for you to say. You with your imported knick-knacks. Vaishali thought to herself. The women left after their muah-muahs, leaving her alone.

That night, Vaishali waited for Ronit. She did not believe in unnecessary wastage of energy, so she sat in the dark. Eventually, she heard his key turn in the lock. As soon as he came in, she said, "Who is this girl that you are dating?"

"Good God, ma! You made me jump. What are you doing in the dark?" He switched on the light.

"First, tell me about the girl," Vaishali demanded. She sat on the expensive sofas with her arms crossed and her face determined.

"Girl? What girl?" Ronit feigned ignorance, knowing fully well which girl his mother was referring to.

"Aparna Soman's daughter. Are you serious about her?"

"What if I am?"

"Is she a Brahmin? Soman is a Brahmin name but these days you can never tell. Does she speak Marathi with an accent? That's the easiest way to guess... She is good-looking, isn't she? Must be a Brahmin then."

"Good God, ma. Give me a break."

"Look, I'm telling you for your own good. You will attend high-class parties after marriage. Do you really want your wife to speak accented Marathi at such events? That will reflect poorly

67

on you. How does she look? And I hear that she is a feminist," Vaishali continued without letting Ronit get a word in. "Don't ever marry a feminist, *beta,* your life will be utterly miserable. I'm telling you from experience."

"What experience do you have of feminism?"

"You know Harshal uncle, don't you? His wife is a feminist. Doesn't let him get a word in! Throws her views around everywhere. Works at odd hours and makes poor Harshal look after the children. He even has to cook, for heaven's sake! How greedily both his sons eat when they come to our house. As if they haven't seen decent food for decades. God save us from these feminists."

"Ma, I've just met this girl. I don't know whether she is a Brahmin feminist… nor do I care."

"Are you telling me you aren't serious about her?"

"I've just met her, ma. I'm not in that space yet. Can I get something to eat now?"

"Of course, *beta,*" said Vaishali, and while Ronit plonked himself in front of the TV, she went to the kitchen, heated the kebabs, garnished them, and got them out on the platter for her son to eat. She watched him devour the food, biting her lip. She was determined to foil her son's attempt to bring a feminist daughter-in-law into the house.

Breaking News – Times of Hindustan
25th April 2016

Controversy over Bollywood movie *Rock n Roll* for hurting religious sentiments

Mumbai: #BoycottRocknRoll has been trending on Twitter for a week, after claims that superstar Rashid Khan's upcoming movie hurts religious sentiments of Hindus. Netizens are upset because a scene in the song 'Aaja', which shows sadhus clad in saffron, dancing with guitars in their hands, is aimed at maligning and insulting Hindu sentiment and culture, and hence demanded boycott of the film.

Aparna Soman's Blog
25ᵗʰ April 2016. Time: 21:00

Have you counted the number of activists, comedians, cartoonists, writers and rationalists jailed for blasphemy in recent times?

Scrap section 295A. Normalise blasphemy. Free the jailed.

Any action or word that insults religion or God is considered an act of blasphemy which is a criminal offence in this country.

When social activist Periyar smashed the idol of Lord Ganesha in 1953, he was taken to court. The magistrate ruled that a mud figurine resembling Lord Ganesha cannot be considered sacred and he dismissed the petition. The case was then taken to the High Court which ruled that an idol not installed in a temple is as good as a toy and cannot be considered sacred. The appeal was dismissed.

What is remarkable about the Court's ruling is the level of tolerance displayed for offences against God. Such a courageous, rational judgement would be impossible in the current times, where even trivial incidents and opinions cause huge moral uproar, attract charges of blasphemy and give a free rein to radicals and fanatics, allowing them to riot, plunder, and murder. Instead of counteracting this dangerous trend, the media, religious organisations, and the state remain mute. These excesses must be curtailed before they disrupt any more lives. The nation does not have the resources to spend on every blasphemy. Does a modern, democratic nation need an archaic blasphemy law?

To believers, I say, why does it matter if a mad Hindu somewhere criticises the Prophet or a loony Muslim insults Ram? Your faith is strong. Your belief is not fragile. They can withstand insults.

Scrap 295A. Normalise blasphemy. Free the jailed.

Chapter Ten
26th April 2016. Time: 09:00

On the morning of her birthday, the ringtone of Aparna's mobile sang an unfamiliar tune. *Damn! Naseem must have changed the ringtone without informing me.* The name of her staunchest friend and ally, Benazir, flashed on the screen. Aparna had few friends, but one friendship she valued was Benazir's. Both women did not have time to nurture their friendship, and this worked well for them. Months passed before they contacted each other, but they could always catch up from where they left off. Birthdays were forgotten, anniversaries missed, but none of that mattered.

They'd met during their journalism days. In a society that was inhibited and conformist, their outspoken natures had drawn them together; their refusal to bow down to authority made them good friends. Benazir now lived and worked in the US, so Aparna was surprised to receive her call on her birthday.

"Loved your tweet promoting the normalisation of blasphemy. You nailed it!" Benazir said.

Aparna smiled. "I haven't checked the feedback, but you know, it's been brewing inside me for quite some time. Bound to come out eventually."

"You'll be given grief over it. Mark my words."

"So, what's new? I'm never given the bouquets, always the brickbats. Never the praise, always the trolling."

"Wait patiently for the what-aboutery. What about Islam? Why don't you say something about Islam? Why is it always about Hindus? And so on…"

"Well…"

"No, really. I want to ask you too. Why don't you write about Islam? If you're writing about blasphemy, then an article which does not include Islam does not have much merit."

"It's not for a Hindu or an atheist to reform Islam. The change has to come from within."

"That's labelled as Muslim appeasement. When Hindus see you consistently give negative examples from their religion with no reference to Islam even once, you've lost their vote."

"Well, I'm glad I'm not standing for an election then. On a serious note, I'm not sure, I agree with you."

"Everything okay at home?"

"Yup. Daily routine. How about you? Things alright?"

"Chugging along. Look, I've got to go. Will give you a call again. Meanwhile, keep churning out those articles. Make them even bolder."

"What would I do without you?"

Only after the call ended did Aparna realise no birthday greetings had been given or expected.

She did not look forward to celebratory events like birthdays or anniversaries. The unnecessary fuss over them put her off. *All this, just for the unremarkable feat of being married or born!*

Manish and Naseem entered the room and wished her a happy birthday. Naseem placed a neatly wrapped parcel in front of her. She took time to admire the golden wrapping paper topped off with a flamboyant red ribbon. Naseem excelled in gift-wrapping, a feat which Aparna had not mastered. *This wrapped gift looks perfect. It smells of luxury.* She unwrapped it slowly, taking care to preserve the beautiful wrapping paper. *You can never let go of your middle-class roots. My ma always salvaged and recycled precious wrapping paper from the few birthday gifts I received from my friends. I've inherited her trait.*

The paper unravelled to show an intricate Madhubani painting. The tiny, geometric patterns worked together to create a dazzling picture of a peacock in bold colours.

"It's beautiful, Naseem. Did you buy this?"

"I painted it. My secret project for more than four months," Naseem said.

"Where should we hang it? Let's put it in the living room," Aparna suggested.

"Our living room has become an art museum of sorts," Naseem remarked.

"And your contribution to this?" Aparna said, looking at Manish.

"To help you hang it in the living room at the exact angle you want," said Manish. He was a reluctant gift giver. When they were courting, he would donate to a charity and hand over the receipt for the donation to Aparna on her birthday. "I've donated to a charity, in your name, on your birthday." Aparna had been alarmed when he'd done this for three consecutive years, but then she'd resigned herself to receiving a receipt every year on her birthday. Eventually, even the charity receipt stopped, and Manish simply went through his normal routine on her birthday, bearing no gifts and feeling no shame.

"No paper receipt for a charity donation this time?" Aparna asked, smiling. Manish smiled back. Aparna looked forward to spending the rest of the day in fuss-free peace, but Naseem wasn't done yet. An organic green kiwi fruit cake was placed in front of her.

"Such myriad flavours! I hadn't even heard of kiwi fruit back then, and now we have kiwi fruit cakes!"

"The pleasurable effects of economic liberalisation," mumbled Manish.

She cut a slice, and Naseem sang for her. The celebrations ended. Manish and Naseem left Aparna free to carry on with the rest of the day without further expectations.

Rehana was expected but hadn't turned up. The household did not believe in hiring domestic staff but if there was one task which they'd failed to accomplish, it was preparing chapattis. None of them had been able to master the craft and so Rehana came in daily to make the chapattis. She'd been working with them for more than two decades. If Aparna was known to intimidate people, then Rehana was doubly intimidating. Tall and thin, she had tattoos, in keeping with the ancient practice, on her forehead, hands and feet. Children avoided her. She was known to chase the neighbourhood boys with her broom if they annoyed her in any way, often shouting if they made a racket. Rehana's attitude was always surly, and her words soaked in sarcasm.

That day, she failed to arrive at the Soman bungalow at her usual time. Aparna waited, watching the window. After an hour, she decided to go to Rehana's house to investigate. It was a scorching day and by the time she arrived she was sweating profusely. She was astonished to see Rehana dancing outside her house, waving the Indian flag.

"What in the world is going on, Rehana?" Aparna said.

"Oh, Aparna Madam. India has won the match against Pakistan, you see. We are celebrating. I will come to your house in a jiffy."

Back home, as Rehana kneaded the *chapattis,* Aparna said, "I didn't know you were such a cricket fan."

"Aparna Madam, I don't even watch that silly game," Rehana said.

"It didn't look like it. The sheer joy with which you were celebrating."

"Well, what can I say. That was just drama. Our slum is a potent one. The Hindutwa people have us Muslims in their sights, especially on volatile occasions, like cricket matches between India and Pakistan. The fools still believe that all Muslims support Pakistan. Now I don't want to start a religious riot here, do I? So, I make it fully obvious to all that I support the Indian team. Let there be no doubt in anyone's mind. After every India–Pakistan match, you will find me dancing like a monkey outside my house. That's the easiest way to prevent any misunderstanding. Otherwise, who has the time to clean up the mess after a religious riot?"

"Very imaginative," Aparna said with a morose look.

"True, Aparna Madam, and more so now that the Government has changed. Earlier, I didn't bother, but now I'm always alert. I'm worried. We're suddenly viewed as enemies by the Hindus. And to make matters worse, this stupid son of mine has fallen in love with a Hindu girl! 'Couldn't you find a Muslim?' I asked him, but the fool refuses to listen. You tell me, Aparna Madam. How will such a girl be accepted in our community?"

"*Arre,* Rehana. Let your son marry whoever he wants to. Hindu, Muslim, who cares?"

"It's easy for you to say this, Aparna Madam. Difficult for us people living in the slums," said Rehana.

"It's fine. This isn't the first time a Muslim boy married a Hindu girl."

"Aparna Madam, it was different previously. Now that the Government has changed..."

"Try not to worry. Tell your son not to worry about a thing, and you shouldn't either."

"Hrmph" Rehana made an exasperated noise. "You will never understand," she said under her breath. Aparna ignored her.

"It's your birthday today?" Rehana asked, "Do go to your temple. I don't like this constant, 'there is no God, there is no God' attitude. Go to the temple, at least on your birthday. It can do you no harm, only good."

"But Rehana, I don't believe. You know that."

"Even so, will going to a temple cause you any harm? Just go," said Rehana. "Anyway, I have done my duty by telling you. Rest is up to you. Have you at least prepared something sweet to eat in the house? Do you want me to make something?"

"*Arre*, no. Naseem insisted on buying a cake and we all had a piece each. Take some home with you. I'll pack it for you. Too much sugar today. It causes nothing but harm. Just like religion does," Aparna said, winking at Rehana.

Rehana kneaded the dough with exaggerated motions, making her displeasure apparent. Aparna left her to it, making mental notes for the day ahead. After a while, Rehana surreptitiously started the preparations for *kheer*. *A birthday is an auspicious occasion, and auspicious occasions demand traditional sweet dishes, something other than the silly cake. As long as I'm a part of this house, I will ensure that the family celebrates with a traditional sweet dish.*

Breaking News — Times of Hindustan
26th April 2016. Time: 11:00

Anonymous social media account threatens to cut off rationalist's nose

PUNE: A social media account going by the name of 'Hindu Warriors', yesterday threatened to cut off the nose of feminist, rationalist and atheism campaigner, Aparna Soman, for her call to normalise blasphemy.

"Indian men treat women as goddesses but if the need arises we will not hesitate to cut off their noses just as Lakshman did to Shurpanakha," a masked man said in a video which he uploaded on his social media account.

"Indian culture teaches us to respect all religions and we strongly condemn this irresponsible call to blaspheme. Women who lose their way need to be taught a lesson to prevent chaos in the set order. We would like to offer a reward of fifteen *lakh* rupees to anyone who would chop off Aparna Soman's nose."

Chapter Eleven
27th April 2016. Time: 06:00

A series of loud, hoarse caws outside his window woke Manish up. He turned his head to look at his clock. It was only six. Cursing the disgruntled bird outside, he reached for his phone. The next moment, he sat up, put on his dressing gown and strode into Aparna's room.

"Your blasphemy article and tweets seem to have gone viral, Aparna," Manish said. "It's spiralling out of control."

Aparna opened a sleepy eye. "Umm, what?"

"Your article! It's gone out of control."

Aparna sprang up and sat on her bed. In the haste to get her phone from her bedside table, she knocked off a book from a pile left there haphazardly.

Without averting his gaze from his phone, Manish picked the book up. "An organisation called Hindu Warriors has threatened to cut off your nose."

"What?" Aparna said, furiously scrolling. "That's hilarious!" She was silent for a few seconds as she read. "It says here that a case has been filed against the Hindu Warriors account for threatening a woman with bodily harm. That's taken care of, then." She chuckled. "The nutters with fragile egos are having a field day at my expense."

Manish sat next to her, and they both read the latest tweets on Aparna's phone as she scrolled:

Smart_alec: When the privileged liberals get bored, they come out with crap like this

Upright_Rightwinger: You have offended my faith, you anti-national, sickular, anti-Hindu

Proud_Hindu: Now wait for the liberal vultures and hyenas to defend this woman

Champagne_Liberal: How is your religion offended by a view? Why is it offended?

Proud_Hindu: Here they come!

I_luv_beef: Why is your faith so fragile?

True_Hindu: @I_luv_beef Why don't you draw cartoons of Prophet Mohammad and then ask them the same question?

I_love_Vedas: That woman has the gall to insult our religion!

Organic_liberal: She hasn't insulted your faith, merely offered an opinion

Ancient_India: Go to Pakistan and offer your opinions

True_Hindu: Cut off Aparna Soman's nose.

Champagne_liberal: @True_Hindu Reporting your profile for threats of violence

India_my_pride: Stupid woman. Our society is not ready for such radical ideas.

Nationalist: Go and take care of babies. Don't meddle in our religion.

Shy_snowflake: You've hurt my religious sentiments.

Strong_Man: How dare you?

Ban_Beef: This woman is not anti-religion. She is anti-Hindu. Why doesn't she criticise Islam? Does she have the guts?

I_love_my_PM: Who is this woman? Why does she have this staunch anti-religion sentiment?

True_Hindu: This is a conspiracy by Pakistan

I_luv_beef: Aparna is not a woman. She is a Muslim man in disguise

Aparna chuckled again as she turned to look at Manish's worried face. "The loonies are digging up my older tweets and retweeting them," she said. "You know, my thoughts on religion made over several years now dredged up from the depths of the virtual world for all to view and mock."

"This is no laughing matter, Aparna."

"Me volunteering for the Anti-Superstition Society has been taken as proof of my offensive against religion. Can you believe it?"

Mafia_Don: This woman cannot be Hindu. Is she in fact a Muslim?

Proud_Indian: This is an elaborate plot of the Muslims to disparage the Hindu religion.

Aparna guffawed. "My religion has become a question mark! I've stated everywhere that I'm an atheist humanist but that's conveniently ignored. They now think I'm a closet Muslim!"

Manish opened an article on his phone. "Hold on, Aparna, it says here that a public interest litigation has been filed against you for hurting religious sentiments." He turned to her, his eyes concerned. "This is getting serious."

"Relax! Nothing that I cannot handle," said Aparna grinning. "Just the believers from all over the country coming together to deride the vile woman who dared question their religion."

"They are calling for your arrest," Manish said. "Hope this doesn't escalate."

"You worry too much," Aparna said. "Nothing will happen. Wait and watch."

"I don't know if you have read all the news articles... the political parties have now gotten involved. The official spokespeople of the ruling party have vocalised their disgust at your article. They're stressing the importance of preserving

Hindu religion and the need to protect it from evil dark forces intent on destroying it."

Aparna's laugh rang out in the room. "Yes, I have seen those. Their PR teams have been busy. I've seen at least a hundred memes showing me as the destructor of Hindu religion. We have no appetite for rationality is the new *mantra* of our times," Aparna said.

"The media are interviewing common people." Manish looked up. "They're expressing anger and distress."

"You know how it works. Politically unsavvy and religious Hindus will now automatically gravitate to the political party which offers to protect their religion. What's the opposition party saying?"

"They've expressed disgust at the article," Manish said slowly.

"They don't want to lose Hindu votes at the cost of their secular credentials."

There was silence, and then Aparna exclaimed, "But see this, the rational voices have come out to fight armed with barbs, arguments, and logic."

Atheist_Pride: Aparna Soman has merely offered a comment on the times that we live in. She has the right to do so.

Organic_Liberal: Nowhere has Aparna encouraged anyone to break idols, neither has she been disrespectful to religion.

Sensible_man: Aparna is not anti-Hindu. She is not even anti-religion, but yes, she does propagate atheist humanism.

Cow_not_my_mum: Just like believers are free to propagate their religion, atheists and humanists are free to propagate their beliefs.

Secular_girl: The Constitution gives the right to freedom of speech.

Liberal_women: We protest the outrageous call of the Hindu_Warrior.

Manish placed a hand on her shoulder. "Lie low for a while, Aparna, until this dies down."

"Don't worry about me, Manish. I can look after myself."

"But there's a death threat. Rape, facial disfigurement! They're even threatening your mother and Naseem."

"These are empty threats, Manish, and this is not the first time I've received them. You know that. Ask any woman who speaks against the norm, and she'll tell you the same."

Manish was silent for a while. He got up and paced around the bedroom.

"Loonies hiding behind anonymous social media accounts, that's all they are," Aparna said. "Do calm down."

"Aparna, it's different this time. Religion…a right-wing Hindu government in power…"

She sighed, placing her hands on her hips. "Look, I'll report all these threatening tweets. That should take care of them."

Manish nodded. He left the room to go into the bathroom.

The silence was sudden, and Aparna thought, *They all come clamouring in greed to twist my tweet to their benefit. Like the promise of a ministerial seat in Parliament, my tweet has given them a launch pad—a potential pathway to fame, power and riches. But enough of that. Nothing will happen.*

She threw her mobile phone on her bed and started her preparations for the rest of the day.

She whispered to herself, "Nothing will happen."

Chapter Twelve
4th May 2016. Time: 05:00

"Manish! You done?" Aparna was ready for her morning walk, dressed in a sari for ease. Tracksuits felt restrictive. Manish had indicated his willingness to accompany her this morning.

"I'll take time. Why don't you go ahead?" Manish bellowed from his room. Aparna was pleased. She enjoyed her own rhythm and power-walking with a partner did not work for her. Naseem was still in bed.

The beautiful morning was tinged with a pinkish-yellow glow. The frenetic pace that characterised most Indian cities was missing at dawn. Even the smell of the morning air was different. *Pity only a few people are up to enjoy it.* A couple of joggers sprinted past, but none that she knew personally.

At home, Manish read his newspaper in peace. After two hours, he got a call on his mobile: an unknown number.

"Hello," he said, preparing to hang up even while he spoke.

"Saheb, I'm calling from Nagnath Stores. You're a regular at my shop. You buy Glucose biscuits from me, remember?"

"Maybe. What's this about?"

"Saheb, I came in to open my store and saw Madam had fainted near the door. I recognised her immediately. She comes in every two weeks to place the grocery orders. That's how I have your phone number."

"What!" His newspaper glided noiselessly to the floor like blood flowing from an open wound as Manish shot up from his chair. "I'm coming. Is this the same Nagnath Stores which is at the main junction?"

"Yes, but Saheb, I was worried... er... there was blood on her sari... uh... so I called the ambulance. They've taken Madam to Sai General Hospital."

Manish hung up. His hand went to his thudding chest. His pores moist with sudden sweat surprised him. Trying to calm his heart, he took a quick inhale and a longer exhale—information he'd read on the Internet to stop a panic attack. He made a silent entreaty to his heart to behave and then spun into action.

Car keys, house keys, money, inform Naseem, his brain urged. He couldn't remember where the car keys were kept. Rummaging through the drawers, he finally saw them hanging on the hook by the main door—their usual place, along with the house keys. Taking the keys, he rushed out, and then realised he had left his wallet behind. He ran back to retrieve it. He decided not to wake Naseem up. No need to leave her alone in a state of worry. Finally, he got in the car and drove, his left hand touching his chest now and then.

The traffic signals decided to punish him, but he broke the last two and got a judgemental look from a lady in a Mercedes. Ashamed, he decided to drive safely. Aparna would never approve of this rash driving and the risk wasn't worth it. After driving for fifteen minutes, the white building of the Sai General Hospital came into view. The hospital parking lot was full. Parking illegally in front of a corner shop outside the parking lot, he got out.

People were milling around outside the hospital. Two elderly gentlemen sat on a brick wall under a mango tree, loose sheets in their hands, discussing what looked like medical reports of a loved one. Three empty ambulances stood parked within the campus. The hospital was upmarket, so the usual crowds were missing. He strode to the main building. A lady behind a desk outside the main door looked up enquiringly.

"I'm here to meet a patient," he said, his voice trembling.

"Ask at the main reception," she said with a nod. "They will guide you."

He opened the main door. The sweet, cool air of the air-conditioner provided immediate relief. Ahead, he saw the main reception. Taking long strides, he wiped the sweat from his forehead. There were just two people ahead of him in the queue. His chest continued to thud painfully. The sweat had dried off.

It was his turn.

"I'm here to meet Aparna Soman—my wife. Please can you give me her room number?" The tremor had still not left his voice.

The receptionist looked up and then consulted a companion who was sitting alongside her at a separate desk. Her companion gave him a sharp look which confused him. The first receptionist shuffled some papers and asked, "Aparna Soman?"

"Yes," he mumbled.

"Room 28. Third floor. The lift is straight ahead." She indicated the direction with her hand.

Ignoring the worried looks of other visitors who had gathered behind him, he rushed to the lift and waited for its arrival. His hand went to his chest again. After a few seconds, the lift doors opened, and he stepped in. He gave a nod to the lift operator and then stared at the picture of a laughing baby stuck to the lift walls. The lift opened into a long, empty corridor. Breaking into a jog, he found the room and went in.

Breaking News — Times of Hindustan
4th May 2016

INDIA: India has been ranked 142 out of 180 countries on the World Press Freedom Index, making it one of the countries considered dangerous for free speech. At least thirteen Indian journalists have been murdered in connection with their work since the start of 2015.

Indian journalists are often the targets of violent online harassment and death threats over views expressed on social media when their views do not align with the followers of Hindutva, the ideology behind Hindu extremism.

BOOK TWO

Chapter Thirteen
20th September 1976. Time: 13:30

Painted Hindu gods cavorted on a whitewashed Tulsi *vrindawan* in the central courtyard of a small three-room house, located in a crowded residential area of Pune. An intricate, hand-drawn *rangoli* soothed the eyes of the painted deities. Cleaned with a mixture of cow dung and water, the courtyard released a strangely pleasing aroma of digested grass. In the living room of the house hung a Hindu calendar which displayed the traditional Hindu units of time, useful in keeping track of Hindu festivals, the phases of the moon and days allocated to Hindu gods. A lit *diya* in front of a picture of the Goddess Saraswati lent its light to a portrait of freedom-fighter Tilak.

In this living room which also doubled as an office, Vijay Sabnis sat with his client, a young man with a soft, unlined face who wanted to know a favourable colour for his first car.

"Blue colour will guarantee success," Vijay said, peering into his notes. At forty, his haphazardly cut hair had receded to a dull grey. Dressed in a white cotton dhoti, he hadn't bothered to put on a shirt in the fierce heat of the day. The *janeu,* which he wore diagonally across his chest, sparkled against his dark skin. An astrologer by profession, Vijay left it to his clients to pay him the appropriate fee. As prosperity increased in the nation, so did the anxiety, and Vijay was never short of regular clients, ensuring a regular income flow.

"I wanted yellow," the young man had an earnest face. "Please can you double-check?"

"There's no double-checking. Yellow will not be suitable. Prone to accidents."

"Oh, that's a shame," the young man looked morose. "You see, I'm getting married next month and yellow is the colour chosen by my fiancée for our first car."

"You can either choose to listen to your fiancée or listen to the wise advice of sages dispensed centuries ago. The choice is yours." Vijay closed his notebook.

"I will choose blue, of course," the young man said. "Prevention is better than a cure."

He smiled and stood up. After digging into his trouser pocket, he produced a wallet from which he extracted some notes, paid Vijay, and left.

Vijay got up and placed some herbs in the earthen water pot to add flavour. Hearing footsteps outside, he opened the door. Six-year-old Hari skipped in and hung his schoolbag on the hook near the door. On his way to the kitchen, he remembered something and stood still. He turned back, ran to Vijay and gave his father's leg a tentative hug.

Amused by the unexpected affection, Vijay asked, "Is everything all right, *beta*?" He ran his fingers through Hari's curly hair.

"Today is Father's Day, Baba. Your day. Teacher told us to buy gifts for fathers. Hug them. Love them. I want to say thank you." Still hugging Vijay's leg, Hari looked up expectantly.

Vijay bent down to look at his son, hesitant and awkward.

"Gratitude for parents cannot be displayed on a single day," Vijay said grimly.

Hari sensed his father's disappointment but did not understand the reason.

A few days passed.

One night, when Hari was getting the blankets out from the iron trunk kept under the bed, his father said to him, "No need to attend that English-speaking school. I've enrolled you in a new Marathi school. You'll attend this new school from tomorrow."

"Why, Baba?" Hari looked at his father, the soft, yellow blanket sown from his mother's old cotton sari, still in his hands.

"Listen carefully, *beta*," Vijay said. "There will be times when you will be tempted to follow the herd and engage in this... blind adulation of the West, prevalent everywhere in our country. Celebrating Father's Day and the other useless days that the West has imposed on us for nothing but commercial reasons. In our culture, we look after our aged parents. We don't leave them out to die in old-age homes like they do in the West. Our culture teaches us respect. Respect the elderly on all days, not simply on one day. No need to go to a school that's so Westernised. This new school is grounded and more in line with our culture. You're too young to understand these things, but you will one day."

"But... I like my school," Hari said in a small voice.

"The decision has been made," Vijay said. "You'll thank me later."

"Is it because I hugged you?" Hari asked an empty room. His father had returned to the kitchen.

Hari pushed the iron trunk back under the bed. Without a word, he snuggled under the soft blanket, worrying about the next day. Sleep was difficult that night.

Hari's mother had died due to the dreaded breathing sickness when Hari was just a few months old. Vijay didn't want any distractions from bringing up his son and wished to lead what he called a pure life and so had taken the oath of *brahmacharya*.

When Hari was four, his father taught him a Sanskrit *shloka* to be chanted while having a bath. "Chanting this shloka will activate every cell of your body. You will feel closer to god and perform your activities better." Mornings were meant for the Surya Namaskar, a yoga involving salutation to the sun. Young Hari, a quick learner, loved rattling off the *shlokas* and performing Surya Namaskars. Vijay watched him with pride.

"One day, you will perform more Surya Namaskars than me, but until then, it will be difficult for you to beat me," Vijay chuckled. He could easily manage fifty Surya Namaskars daily while Hari barely performed five. Father and son got up at six, did their namaskars, chanted their shlokas and, once spiritually fortified, were ready to tackle the day ahead.

Vijay taught himself to cook after his wife's death. The food they ate was simple and vegetarian, cooked without spices. Breakfast consisted of the left-over *bhakri* with milk, sugar, and cow ghee. Lunch and dinner were *bhakri* with some green vegetable, dal and rice.

"Lead a simple life, *beta*. Eat simple food. Exercise, and chant your shlokas daily. This will keep all psychological disorders at bay. Don't eat the meat of animals, and never eat food touched by an impure person," instructed Vijay.

Fresh urine from the holy cow was a monthly breakfast beverage. The owners of a neighbourhood cowshed allowed Vijay some free urine due to his piety. He set off at dawn carrying a clean utensil and didn't have to wait long for a cow to urinate. Rushing behind the urinating cow, he would hold the utensil under her flow.

"This is a life-saving drink, Hari. The urine of the holy cow, our mother, has medicinal properties. It can even cure cancer. We're lucky to be able to drink it."

Every Tuesday, Vijay prepared extra food for the beggars who waited outside the Hanuman temple which father and son visited. "We have more than we need. Sharing food leads to peace and happiness," he told his son.

When Hari became older, he was taught the Gayatri *mantra*. "This will purify your mind. Learn it and teach it to others."

Hari nodded, "Yes Baba."

At age eight, Hari had his *munja*, a traditional ceremony signifying the start of his journey towards education. He wore the sacred thread *janeu*, with three threads for the holy trinity. It was understood, the *janeu* would be worn for the rest of his life.

"Be proud of our ancestors, our culture, and our ability to assimilate knowledge and education. Wear your *janeu* with pride. Your *janeu* will signal your ancestry to the world, and you will be respected wherever you go. There was a time when we *janeu* wearers enjoyed utmost respect, but now the vermin cheat us of our birth right," said Vijay.

"Who are the vermin, Baba?" Hari asked.

"All these English-speaking elite. They think it's wise to reject our centuries-old traditions and ape the West instead. Fools! What do they know?" Vijay hissed. Had he been outside, he would have spat.

The clothes that Vijay purchased for Hari were of simple colours. "Only wear clothes that can accept and transmit positive waves into the atmosphere. They will protect you from the negative energies," he told his son.

"How can I recognise such clothes, Baba?"

"It's quite simple. Avoid black and bright colours. Plain, light clothes emit the right type of waves and don't attract negative energy. Never ever wear clothes with pictures of animals or ghosts. Only perverts wear them."

Once, when Hari was cutting his nails on a Saturday, Vijay stopped him. "Each day of the week has a certain significance. Cutting nails on a Saturday can lead to mental instability. If you cut your nails on a Wednesday, there is a possibility of acquiring wealth because Wednesday belongs to the planet Mercury, the planet of intelligence. Choose a day wisely."

Young Hari looked at his father in awe.

"How do you know, Baba?"

"The wise men of our country have documented it all in our books to make it easier for us. These lessons were conveyed from one mouth to another. There are guides for everything so you will never get confused. If you do, then just open one of our books or find a priest, and things will become clear," Vijay explained.

Hari loved to follow the rituals as explained by his father. The only thing Hari rebelled against was keeping a *shendi*—

shaving off his hair to keep only a tuft, as kept by traditional Brahmins.

"No, Baba. I don't want to do that. Everyone will laugh," said Hari.

"*Beta*, the tuft of hair acts like the antenna of the TV. It attracts good energy and will activate intelligence in your brain. It will only help you."

"No, Baba. I won't," Hari said firmly. Vijay decided not to force him. The boy was diligent, and normally gave him no cause for worry.

"If that's what you wish to do, then I won't force you. I've performed the *choul* when you were in your mother's tummy. It has already negated the sins of the ovum and the foetus, so you don't need to worry."

When Hari was ten years old, his father enrolled him in a spiritual organisation set up to extol and propagate the virtues of Hindu religion. Every evening, Hari hopped along to chant and repeat stanzas from the religious scriptures. His teacher narrated stories from India's two great epics, the *Ramayana* and *Mahabharata*. Given the scale of the epics, there was a lot to learn from the range of enthralling stories.

"Why doesn't Ram accept Sita after her rescue, Baba?"

"Her purity became questionable, Hari. Impure women have no place in our society," said Vijay.

When Hari became a little older, Vijay told him the story of India's independence and the aftermath.

"We were jubilant when India acquired independence from the British. Finally, we could look forward to living in our very own Hindu nation where Hindus would be given priority. But alas, the new Prime Minister disappointed us. He opted for a secular republic. What this meant was an erosion of all the privileges that Brahmins had enjoyed. We Hindus bloody lost! For this, I will never forgive Nehru and his entire clan."

"What happened then, Baba?" Hari asked, curious.

"Then partition happened, and yet some Muslims chose to live in India rather than go to Pakistan where they actually belonged. Bloody bastards! What is secularism other than pandering to these rogue Muslims? I bloody hate that word." Vijay fired saliva. "Muslims don't belong here. The Mughals invaded our country and demolished all the temples. Even our Taj Mahal was previously a temple. It even has a Shiva *linga* in a hidden room. Nehru should have shown those Muslims their place, but instead he played secular-secular with them!"

"Why are Muslims bad, Baba?"

"Their strict religion teaches them to hate. Our religion does not teach hate—only peace and love. We don't follow a strict code, but these Muslims do! And they breed. A lot!" Vijay paused to breathe. "There will come a time when Muslims overtake Hindus in this country. Be ever fearful of that, *beta*. Be vigilant. We must work to ensure this does not happen.

"I will never let that happen, Baba," young Hari said solemnly.

"Remember, if the Hindus get together to defeat the Muslims, then our nation can regain its past glory."

"I will make it happen," Hari said. His eyes took on a look of determination uncommon in children.

Chapter Fourteen
23rd May 1986. Time: 10:00

With a cotton satchel flung across his shoulders, Hari waited under a leafy mango tree opposite the main college building. It was his first day at junior college. An hour before the first lecture, all the first-year students loitered in the open area outside the main building.

Hari's eyes kept getting pulled towards a group of noisy girls standing some yards away, wearing attires that alarmed him—their tops and skirts covering the bare minimum. He devoured them with his eyes: their style; the dainty, pastel dresses they chose to wear; their confidence in owning the space with their voice and presence; their beauty which they enhanced with tantalising perfume, alluring eye make-up and jewellery that glinted when it caught the sun. They made his eyes water.

School had been full of boys just like him—proud of wearing the *janeu*, chanting shlokas and generally abiding by the rules of ancient Hindu culture. Junior college had students from all parts of Pune—the traditional, the modern and the ultra-modern. Brahmin boys were easy to spot, but these ultra-modern Brahmins did not seem to be taking their caste credentials too seriously. He failed to spot the prominent line of the *janeu* under their thin cotton t-shirts and their general air of joviality dismayed him. They wore the latest brands, eyed the girls, laughed and bantered. No signs of worry wrinkled their foreheads. As scraps of conversation fell on his ears, he understood that most of these ultra-modern, first-year students had no intention of attending any lectures on the first day. Their plan was to hang out in a café located just outside the campus.

Hari had cash with him; cash that could have been put to better use elsewhere, but he decided to tag along with these strange students because he was curious. He had never visited a cool, trendy café before and was unaware of the behavioural norms in such places, especially under the scrutiny of teenage eyes.

The group of girls left first, followed by the boys who bantered continuously. Hari followed them. They left the college campus and crossed a busy road which brought them to a small, whitewashed café. The outdoor seating area at the entrance seemed full. They walked in.

"Let's not sit here," the girl in a pastel-pink dress said. "Let's go to the garden section."

They walked across the interior of the café and came to an open-air garden buzzing with students. All the tables were occupied.

"No free seats in India, we'll have to sit in Pakistan," said a pretty girl with ironed hair, sporting a tattoo of a snake.

"Er... India and Pakistan?" Hari asked a quiet boy who was standing next to him.

"Oh, this café has a smoking section and a non-smoking section. We call the smoking section Pakistan," the boy grinned. Somehow everyone seemed to know this, except Hari.

After a short wait, they got a table in India. Hari avoided the girls and rushed to sit next to the boy who had answered his question. It took time for everyone to settle in. Handbags were propped on the tables, chairs moved with rebellious squeaks to make way for long legs, lips brightened with lipstick, deodorants sprayed, until finally, the flurry of activity around the table abated. A friendly young waiter arrived. Hari opened the menu card and decided to order an *idli-sambar*. One by one, they placed their orders by telling the waiter their choices. All the boys and girls opted for burgers or pizzas. When it came to Hari's turn, he felt ashamed to order the humble *idli*, so he opted for a pizza—his first one.

There was a lull until the girl with the snake tattoo threw a question at them. "What is the one thing that you really, really want?" she asked them. "Like if someone grants you a wish, right now."

Hari was surprised at the general lack of shyness as, one by one, the young people rattled off the answers.

"To date Deepa!" said a boy who looked like Bollywood star Rajesh Khanna.

"Cracking the IIT entrance exam," said another boy who wore a branded t-shirt. Hari recognised it from a billboard with a Bollywood star endorsing it.

"Owning a dress designed by Rituparna," said a girl with earrings circling her ear.

"Meeting Bollywood star Kumar Raj!"

"Mastering the Vedas and learning the positive and negative energy flows," stammered Hari.

A silence. For a moment, everyone stopped eating, and then a girl guffawed.

"Why on earth do you wish to do something as archaic as that?" she tittered.

Hari gave a tiny smile and shrugged. The pizza arrived, deflecting attention. He bent his head and ate his pizza silently. His skin burned with the girl's mocking laugh while the rich, creamy pizza provoked his tastebuds.

The quiet boy sitting next to Hari asked him to pass the menu card. As Hari reached out, a tall lad sitting on his other side, screwed up his nose.

"Man, don't you ever put on the deo? You smell."

Hari waited for the pending guffaws, and as expected, they came. Everyone laughed. *Do I smell? How dare that bastard pass such a personal comment? Am I expected to hide my sweat under chemicals to smell artificial?*

Quietly, Hari finished his pizza while the rest of the table continued to chat and banter. When it was time to leave, the same flurry of activity commenced. Bags were gathered, chairs pushed, dust brushed off clothes.

The group went to hang out, once again, under the mango tree on campus, but Hari decided to attend the lecture instead. Wearily, he trudged to the lecture hall hearing mocking giggles and subdued laughs behind him. Entering the cool, dark lecture room offered some respite from judgemental eyes. *I'm here to study after all. Who needs approval from others? Let them laugh and mock!*

The medium of communication in college was English. After passing out from a Marathi school, Hari knew this would be a struggle and carried an English to Marathi dictionary with him for this purpose. While he waited for the teacher to arrive, he quickly looked up the meaning of the word 'archaic'. *Am I old-fashioned?*

A boy with crumpled clothes and an unkempt beard, who did not look as scary as the ultra-moderns Hari had left under the mango tree, now came and sat next to him. When he saw Hari dipping into a dictionary, he asked, "Vernac, are you?"

"Er... vernac?"

"Vernac for vernacular," the boy guffawed. "You haven't done your schooling in English, have you?"

"No. I haven't," Hari said, surprised.

"You're a vernac," the boy said with a satisfied smile.

Is everyone expected to speak only in English here? If you don't speak posh English in a refined accent, you are mocked. If you speak in an Indian accent, you are ridiculed. If you come from rural areas, you are ignored. Is this really my own country, or am I in the land of the English Queen?

A subdued looking professor arrived. After just a few minutes into the lecture, Hari realised he had to put in extra effort to understand the points that the professor was making. To translate a sentence, sometimes he had to translate each word, as he hadn't encountered most of them previously. The professor shouted at him once, for reaching out to his dictionary too often. It took him double the amount of time to keep up

99

with the students who had completed their schooling in the English language. *I probably look slow and stupid to them, which is so unfair. Being unable to speak English fluently is a handicap in this country. You may be the most talented, successful, or the richest person around, but if you cannot speak English fluently then the ultra-modern elite will never accept you in their circles.*

Hari's first day at junior college ended at around two in the afternoon. Not wishing to go home, he decided to catch a Bollywood movie—alone. All he wanted to do was kill time. He left the campus and hailed an auto-rickshaw. After five minutes, the auto-rickshaw dropped him outside the cinema hall. The name of the movie wasn't familiar to him. Judging by the lack of crowds outside, it did not seem to be making good business. He purchased one ticket and went inside.

The cool, dark cinema hall welcomed him and in no time at all he got engrossed, for about thirty minutes until the movie too managed to annoy him. *Who are all these rich heroes living in mansions in England and cavorting in posh European locales? And the women! Their clothes get progressively tinier in every scene until they take them all off and dance only in bra and panty. Are these women Indian? In our country, we treat women as deities. Where are the movies about Ram and Sita? Where are the movies about patriotism? Where are the movies about our soldiers? Instead, they show us this filth.* He spat in the cinema hall and left.

Deciding against hiring an auto-rickshaw, he plodded home, weary from his first day. Mulling over the non-academic lessons he learned that day, he decided to stop interacting with the other students from thereon. *The hassle is not worth it.*

Two years passed in this manner. After he turned eighteen, he failed to secure admission in the Government Engineering College because he fell short by a few marks.

"See how they cheat us! The untouchables get the premium seats by doing no work whatsoever because of this reservation nonsense. The rich get their children into private colleges by paying stupendous fees. We Brahmins of meagre means have no way of giving our children a secure future. Who do we turn to? Where do we go?" Vijay lamented.

"Don't worry, Baba. I will make you proud. You wait and watch. I've got plans." In his eyes shone the familiar gleam of a mad determination.

Chapter Fifteen
5th November 1997. Time: 14:30

Frequently feeling restless and unable to concentrate, Hari found himself in the red-light area of Pune's Budhwar Peth, one afternoon. Girls of all ages loitered in a narrow alley with decrepit single-storey houses, posing in myriad ways, fiddling with their phones. Some stood in groups, others alone, some standing, others sitting on parked two-wheelers, chatting, hands on hips, waiting to be approached. Amidst a row of grocery shops, young girls looked out from shadowy upper-storey windows, while the traffic murmured below. Clothes hung to dry from open windows offered a glimpse of normality. As he walked, the aroma of jasmine incense tickled his nostrils outside one house.

The girls were everywhere. *How could father have remained celibate for so long? This is too strong. I will not win this fight.* Hands in his pockets, his pace quickened.

Around the girls, men worked in their shops, trying to earn money to feed their families. Hari avoided their gaze. He wasn't in the mood to check whether their eyes carried any judgement. Tyre and clothes shops; miniscule general stores with racks of eggs displayed prominently; tiny hotels that let out rooms by the hour; medical shops showing off glittering rolls of condoms and headache pills; restaurants selling tea; hawkers on handcarts selling peanuts, toys, and vegetables; betel leaf shops—all went about their daily business as if owning a shop in a red-light area was the most natural thing in the world. He spotted a group of boys chatting with the girls, the scene nondescript enough to be mistaken for a college campus.

He avoided the girls wearing long, boring, cotton gowns colloquially called nighties, glanced at those wearing jeans and the traditional salwar kameez, but looked lustily at those in thin, pastel-coloured chiffon saris. For some reason, they reminded him of the posh, snobbish girls of his junior college—the ones he could never hope to attain. Some girls turned around as he passed so that he could look at their posterior. None of them exposed body parts other than those normally exposed in a sari. All were decently dressed. *Even the whores are conservatively dressed in my country.* He was proud of that. *I expected to find dirt and filth here. But how beautiful and fair some of them are!*

Four girls came to Hari, aggressively cajoling and promising him an enjoyable time. They held his hand, pointed to his body parts, and almost dragged him away. Their aggression turned him off. Having heard stories of the girls stealing cash, he was thankful to have carried a limited amount with him. "Get lost," he shouted at the girls and waved his hands to get rid of them. Keeping up a steady stream of abuse, they followed him, but after a few minutes when they realised that he was not going to give them business, they lost interest and left him alone to wander.

As he continued to walk, he looked at the face, figure, and feet of every girl. The face to gauge signs of attractive features hidden beneath the thick layer of make-up. The feet to assess the colour of their skin under their make-up. *The face may lie but the feet won't.* Only then, did he look at their physique. These girls, unlike the aggressive ones earlier, waited to be approached. He decided to risk it.

He selected a woman, middle-aged but voluptuous who looked almost dignified in her pale-yellow chiffon sari. Sharp, kohl-rimmed eyes. Her feet confirmed her fair skin. He ambled to her and noticed her eyes change.

"How much?" he asked.

"Six hundred rupees," she said.

"Five hundred, okay?"

"Five hundred and fifty," she said. He nodded. She pointed to a nearby house, and he followed her in. The tiny room with blue walls looked dark despite the glare of the sun outside. Leading him to a double bed, she stood in front of him as he sat. He could hear a baby crying somewhere and this annoyed him. Struggling to relax, he wondered whether this tryst would work, but then the woman took off her blouse and he did not need further persuasion. The intent was there. His body screamed with yearning, but despite all the encouragement, the fifteen-minute relationship with the woman could not be consummated.

"It happens," she said, "don't worry. Just relax."

Hari was too wound up to relax. He paid her and left. The next day, he went back to the same woman, tried again and succeeded. At the point of climax, he shut his eyes and gave in to the fantasy of copulating with a classy snob who spoke refined English. His pent-up energy released, finally leaving him to enjoy his new freedom from frustration. *It's like a clean scrub of my interiors.* His visits became a regular feature. The woman was always the same.

"What is your name?" he asked her after a week. His satiation after the act had induced a heavy drowsiness. He continued to lie beside her instead of getting up immediately as normal.

"Naaznin," she replied.

"Muslim?" he asked.

"Yes," she whispered.

Hari got off the bed, put his clothes on, spat in her house and left. He selected a different girl on his next visit.

Chapter Sixteen
10th November 1998. Time: 10:00

"It's time you got married, Hari," said Vijay, conjuring up the tried and tested solution that Indian parents rely on to solve any problems that may come their unmarried child's way. "Marriage will calm you down, *beta*. I have a girl in mind who'll make a perfect match. I will speak to her parents today."

Vijay was unaware of Hari's extra-curricular activities but had sensed his growing restlessness. He had put off contacting a holy Godman for his son, hoping things would sort themselves out.

Hari was now a dark, stocky, six-feet-tall man. To enhance his macho looks, he sported a moustache. He thought of keeping a stubble but did not want to be mistaken for a Muslim, so dismissed the idea. In public dealings, he adopted a default tone of aggression. As predicted by his father, he could easily manage fifty *Surya Namaskars* now and regularly trained with weights to keep fit. In circles uninhabited by judgemental, trendy young people, he stood a chance and could pass as acceptable, but there was nothing remarkable to distinguish him from the billions of ordinary young Indian men other than his eyes. They carried a humourless look, as if he thought the nation owed him a favour for oppressing him. His *janeu* remained a regular accessory but now the pizza had replaced the *idli* as his comfort food. His father remained ignorant of this. Father and son continued to believe in the cancer-protecting benefits of cow urine and dosed on the beverage at least once a month.

"If you insist, Baba," said Hari, as he folded the clothes which he had just washed.

"She comes from a good *Chitpawan Koknastha* Brahmin family. They go by the name of Godbole. I'm not aware of the *gotra* they belong to, but I can find out soon enough. Her father is an Ayurvedic doctor. The girl herself is docile, good-looking and a wonderful cook. She will make an ideal wife," Vijay said.

"As you wish, Baba."

"We will go and meet her family tomorrow. Let me know what you think of her," said Vijay and hobbled to his room.

Father and son set off the next day for the Godbole residence. The Godboles lived in a small stone bungalow which had managed to survive the wave of reconstructions that had taken over the city of Pune where the older houses and bungalows were demolished to make way for modern, snazzy apartments.

"Please, do come in," said an elderly gentleman, presumably the father, who led them inside the house. Clad in a cotton, checked bush-shirt and dark trousers, his face was genial enough, but his eyes looked wary: a look, commonly found in the eyes of fathers seeking arranged marriages for their daughters. The stone bungalow provided an immediate respite from the afternoon heat as they stepped in. An embroidered cat in pastel pink hung on the wall. The room had a sofa and two chairs upholstered in grey; a colour favoured because it easily catches the dust. A small showcase was placed in a corner upon which sat assorted wooden animals. A wicker coffee table in the centre held a vase of artificial flowers. A photo frame of Veer Savarkar, hung in a corner of a wall, advertised the Hindutwa ideology subscribed to by the house owner. An Indian wooden swing hung opposite the sofa, on which the father proceeded to sit. Hari and Vijay sat on the grey sofa facing him. A timid, middle-aged woman wearing a yellow cotton sari, her hair neat in a bun, a red dot on her forehead and a necklace of black beads signifying her marital status, entered with two glasses of water placed on a flowery tray.

"This is the girl's mother," said Mr Godbole, smiling while introducing his wife. Mrs Godbole's smile was shy when she looked at them. Though brief, it managed to convey the humility necessary for the mother of a prospective bride upon meeting the prospective groom's parents for the first time. A girl's family putting on a surly attitude was not the norm in Indian society. The wrong kind of an attitude in a girl's family had the capacity to break potential marriage alliances. This norm was universally observed across caste, class, and wealth. The boy's family on the other hand were allowed unlimited airs, tantrums, and sulks.

Mrs Godbole offered the tray. After they each took a glass, she left the room. The three gentlemen made idle chat while they waited for the entry of the girl who they'd come to see.

After six minutes, a girl arrived bearing the same tray which now carried three bowls of steaming *pohe*. Dressed in a sari, with Madhumati flowers in her hair, she fixed her gaze demurely downwards.

Vijay noticed her flaws at once. *Her skin tone isn't that fair. This could've easily got me double the amount of dowry in the olden days. She's on the shorter side too, but her face looks pretty despite her complexion. Not much going on in the breast department either, but best to let Hari make the final decision.*

"Sit, my dear," said Vijay. The girl placed the *pohe* on the coffee table. Mr Godbole indicated that they eat. Everyone, except the girl, took a bowl. They kept it in their hands while staring intently at her. The girl still had her eyes to the floor.

"What is your name, dear?" Vijay asked.

"Lata," said the girl in a whisper.

"She is very shy," said Mr Godbole beaming. "Speak up a little, *beta*."

"Lata," she repeated, a little louder.

"Good, good. Did you make the *pohe* yourself , Lata?" asked Vijay. "They look delicious."

Lata nodded.

"Lata is an excellent cook. What's more, she loves to cook. Isn't that right, Lata?"

Lata nodded.

"How much have you studied, dear?" Vijay asked, rolling in the questions.

"I have completed my BSc in Zoology," she answered meekly.

"Any plans for working after marriage?" Vijay asked the crucial question, the answer to which would either make or break the alliance.

"After marriage, she will do as her husband and in-laws desire. Lata is very adaptable that way," said her father smiling, striving hard to please his guests.

"We aren't looking for a girl who wants to work after marriage. It's better to be clear about these things at the start in order to prevent problems further down the line."

"Of course. Of course. We appreciate your candour," said Mr Godbole, smiling.

"What are your hobbies, Lata?" Vijay enquired, now relaxed as he put a spoonful of *pohe* in his mouth. Hari carried on eating—one bite followed by another. Having sized up Lata in the first few minutes, he did not feel the need to look at her again.

"She loves cooking, of course, and she loves needle work. She is also an excellent singer," answered Lata's father on her behalf.

"Please can you sing two lines for us?" Vijay asked.

"Of course," said Mr Godbole, "Lata, sing two lines from the *bhajan*."

In a soft voice, Lata sang two lines from the religious song taught to her, not raising her eyes even once.

"Do you want to ask her any questions?" Vijay asked Hari. Hari shook his head.

"You can leave, dear," said Vijay to Lata. Lata escaped. Vijay whispered something to Hari and Hari whispered right back.

"Though her complexion is a little dusky, we liked the girl. It is a yes from us," said Vijay to Mr Godbole. "If it's all right with you, then we can go ahead and finalise the marriage."

"Yes, of course. Er... about the finances," said Mr Godbole.

"We expect you to bear the finances for the wedding. From our side, there will be fifty people," said Vijay.

Mr Godbole blinked twice. He looked worried. "Er... anything extra? It's best to be clear about these things to prevent misunderstanding later."

"If by extra, you mean dowry, then no. We are a modern family and don't believe in dowry. Just give us the girl—that's all," said Vijay.

"Oh, thank you. Thank you," gushed Mr Godbole. His face looked softer. "Shall we fix the date then? Who better than you to let us know an auspicious date? *Arre*, Lata's mother, please can you get the sweets out? The marriage is finalised." Mr Godbole smiled.

The atmosphere became celebratory. A wedding arranged! Lata's mother, now grinning widely, entered once again, this time with a plate of assorted sweets. She offered the sweets, and each person gallantly took one. It would have been rude to refuse the celebratory sweets, although as the family of the bridegroom they were free to be as obnoxious as they wished. Jubilation and smiles all around. Lata sat in the other room not knowing her future was now decided.

The marriage was thus arranged. A month later, Hari and Lata were married. Lata came to live with them in their three-room house. Vijay slept in the living room, and the newly married couple occupied the bedroom. The marriage was consummated on the first night itself. By now, Hari had become adept in deriving sexual gratification from a woman. The thought that the woman deserved some did not even cross his mind. Over the days, he came to believe that his demure wife was not the type to enjoy sex enthusiastically. After a few days, he continued his trysts with the sex-workers in Budhwar Peth. His wife had no such avenue to satisfy her urges, which her husband believed to be non-existent, and so her desires were squashed before they could even begin. In a society where women are often beaten, burned, and discarded in the first year of marriage, Lata considered herself supremely lucky.

A year after their marriage, Hari and Lata became parents to a baby girl. Vijay named her Kashi. Hari was indifferent to the birth of his daughter. *What is the point in investing any emotions in her when one day she will fly off to her husband's nest? My duty is to protect her until we hand her over to her husband.* He left parenting to his wife and involved himself in matters that evoked his passion.

Chapter Seventeen
5th October 2011. Time: 07:00

It was seven. Hari slumped over a gigantic Desktop which he had purchased from a scraps dealer, modifying it to suit his requirements. Kishore Kumar's melodious voice infused the gloomy room with meaning. Hari heard the heavy tread of footsteps as his father lumbered in. Vijay hung his *topi* on the rack and went in the bathroom to wash his hands and feet.

Wiping his hands with a towel as he came back into the room, he asked, "How was work today?"

"The same," Hari replied. "Nothing changes much from day to day." After completing his degree in Politics, Hari now worked from nine to five as a clerk in a government office.

"So, what is it you do day after day on this machine?" Vijay asked, peering into the monitor, his glasses on his nose.

"I interact with others," Hari said with a satisfied grin. "See, I will show you. Read what I've written." Social media had arrived like a Bollywood seductress claiming her victims as she swept through the nation establishing her hold. Over the years, Hari had felt an increasing need to express himself but found it difficult to do so with his peers. *Most of us are from the same caste, yet the differences between us are too vast. I have nothing in common with them.* So he turned to the easiest available option. He broadcast his ideas and beliefs in the virtual world for everyone to view and comment. He tweeted in his broken English, but mostly in Hindi and sometimes in Marathi. He swept his hands with a flourish towards the screen:

Devout_Hari: People may think that the tuft of hair which the traditional Brahmins maintain is old-fashioned. They may be surprised to know that there is a scientific reason behind this.

Devout_Hari: The tuft acts like the antenna of a TV and this attracts positive waves which help in promoting mental well-being.

Vijay slowly read the words Hari had written. He stood behind Hari as he read, the fingers of his right hand on his glasses and his left arm over his son's shoulder.

"Very well written, *beta*," he said.

"And see here, people are responding," Hari pointed.

Vijay peered to see the responses:

Sanskari_liberal: This has to be the funniest tweet of the day ROFL.

I_am_leftwing: Hail the new pseudoscience expert!

Hit_comedian: Whoa! Talk about regressive views!

Politics_expert: Casteist!

Feminist_nari: Backward oaf!

Champagne_liberal: India will never progress because of people like him.

Devout_Hari: Brahmins are the new Dalits. We are the most maligned.

Evolved_human: Look at this privileged fool. Forgive him, oh Hindu God, for he knows not what he utters.

"*Arre!* What in the world...?" Vijay jerked his head back in shock. "People are so rude!"

"This is a conversation, Baba, a debate. I write my views here."

"Be careful, *beta*. All this viciousness does not seem right," Vijay said, taking a step back.

"Don't worry, Baba. Why shouldn't we put our views across? Views that are important to us?"

"Yes, but...," Vijay said. "I don't understand this medium but if it gives you happiness..."

Hari wasn't listening.

Devout_Hari: How long will Bollywood continue to show us trash? We demand movies about our soldiers, our deities, our epics and our great leaders.

Vijay looked at him and realised that his son was lost to the machine.

It was almost ten when Hari switched off his Desktop. The to and fro interactions fortified him intellectually, something his nine-to-five-job failed to do. While he slept, his tweets continued to work. Like ants trickling towards a grain of sugar, they continued to attract attention and gain momentum.

Hari logged in again the next morning just before setting off to work. "Baba, come and take a look."

Vijay's eyes, which had brightened at Hari's invitation, grew dull again when Hari pointed to the Desktop. "What? That machine again?"

"Look!" Hari said.

Vijay bent and peered into the monitor.

"Look at the number of likes my tweets are getting. See the number here," Hari pointed excitedly, "and read the comments. The number of people who agree with me now outnumber those who ridicule. Positive comments outnumber the negative ones."

Vijay nodded his head in agreement, not really understanding. "Well, if it makes you happy..."

"This is not about happiness, Baba. Don't you see? Such an important lesson! The number of people who share my beliefs outnumber those who don't. I may not speak English as well as my peers, I may not be comfortable in a posh café, but I have my own following. There are people like me, and they outnumber the cheap imitators of the West. I am on the right path. You were right all along," Hari said.

Vijay had never seen him this animated. "And you know all this through this screen?"

"Yes," Hari said, laughing. "Trust me, Baba. We're on the right path and one day we will regain our past glory. See, every day I tackle a new issue. Today, it is about the holy cow."

The old man did a *namaskar* to show his respect to the holy cow.

"Look, this is what I've written today," Hari said, eagerly turning the monitor towards Vijay.

Devout_Hari: The cow is our mother. It is a sin not only to kill cows, but also to remain silent and watch as cows are being taken to the slaughterhouse. We request the Government to ban cow slaughter.

Non_resident_Indian: Bravo. You have my full support.

Ancient_Indian: Ban beef.

Champagne_liberal: These non-resident Indians have no problem with cow slaughter in their adopted countries but seek a ban in India!

Devout_one: We pamper the Muslims and their beliefs while our own beliefs are ignored. Why hasn't cow slaughter been banned yet?

Media_person: @ Devout_Hari can you give us a byte about your demand?

Beef_Lover: @Ancient_Indian I am a Hindu and I love beef! Who are you to tell me to stop eating beef?

Certified_Atheist: It is wrong to police people's eating choices.

Cat_Lover: Love all animals. Don't elevate the cow to such ridiculous heights.

Woke_Liberal: The cow may be your mummy. She certainly isn't mine.

All_that_Beef_Drama: You wish to worship the cow? Worship it. But please spare us.

Devout_Hari: This is a Hindu nation. The cow is sacred to us. Why should we allow her slaughter? In every country, the rules as decided by the majority must be followed.

Ivory_tower: I'm a practising Hindu. I don't eat beef but have no problem if others want to.

Hindu_king: What kind of a wishy-washy Hindu are you @Ivory_tower?

Organic_Liberal: India is a secular nation, not a Hindu nation. We have freedom of choice. I have the freedom to eat whatever I want, whenever I want. The Government cannot police me.

Devout_Hari: To massacre an animal that is sacred to billions of people is not freedom.

Iron_maiden: STFU you cow-piss drinker

Vijay read and was aghast. "It's more of the same! What in the world is this, *beta*? All these insults. This abuse! It all seems so... so unnecessary. I don't understand. Why waste so much time fighting with these useless people? Do they even have jobs?"

"Baba, I give it back to them good and solid. Did you see?"

Vijay's eyes revealed his incomprehension.

"I just wish you'd do your job. *Bas!* That's it. No need to fight with strangers like this. What will that achieve?"

"Baba, have you finished your yoga asanas? Won't you be late?" Hari stood up and gently ushered his father away from his Desktop.

Vijay took one last look at the machine, opened his mouth to say something, decided not to, and walked away, bewildered.

Hari started using social media like a concerned mother imparting life lessons to her children. His followers increased, his tweets shared, and his confidence flourished.

There are people who agree with me, but the power is held by those who do not. It is held by those who ridicule my culture. It is held by those who have sold their souls to the West. And when the people in power do not reflect your views, nothing can be done.

But he wasn't despondent because he wasn't done yet. He wanted more! He had plans. Grand, ambitious plans. It was his dream to establish his own organisation: a spiritual organisation to bring people of his faith together. Once he had the numbers, his ultimate aim was to convert his nation—from a secular nation to a Hindu nation and regain the lost glory.

Chapter Eighteen
30th October 2011. Time: 05:00

Vijay wasn't in the habit of using alarm clocks to wake up. The neighbourhood rooster crowed exactly at five every morning and his shrill cry worked as an excellent wake-up call. After performing the daily ablutions, he put a pan for boiling on the stove to prepare tea and that was when he normally woke Hari up. This routine had been followed diligently for several years. So, Vijay was surprised to see Hari awake before him, slouched in front of his Desktop. Vijay felt mildly irritated. His son seemed to be in front of that machine all the time!

Swallowing his irritation, he went up to Hari. "Everything all right, *beta*?"

Hari didn't look up, typing furiously. "Baba, I'm going to bring the glories of Hindu religion back."

"Don't you have to go to work, Hari?"

Hari turned to look at him. "Baba, I've taken the day off."

"A day off? What on earth for?"

"I'm writing a manifesto for setting up my own spiritual organisation. An organisation that will bring back the glories of Hindu religion and culture!"

"But... your job?"

"My job is not running away anywhere."

"And how will you find the time?"

"Baba, don't worry. Leave it all to me."

"But *beta*..."

"Don't worry, Baba. Ganesh will also help me. He can't wait to teach those bastards a lesson."

"Ganesh who? That loafer?"

"He works in his father's garage, Baba."

"And the bastards?"

"Muslims, Baba. Muslims. Never forget, as you rightly taught me."

Vijay opened his mouth to say something, but then kept quiet.

"I will show you my manifesto when it's ready. Remember what I said? I will make you proud one day," Hari said, talking to the screen.

Vijay did not show his alarm but decided to keep an eye on his son. Start his own spiritual organisation indeed! What next? The old man trudged to the kitchen to prepare another cup tea.

Father and son toiled separately but after about five hours, Hari rushed into Vijay's room, a sheaf of papers in his hands.

"Here it is," Hari said, his voice shaking with excitement.

Vijay peered through his glasses. "Here's what?"

"My five-hundred-page manifesto which gives the aims and ambitions of my organisation." Hari passed the papers to Vijay. "I have even named it. See. *Dharma Sanstha*. What do you think?"

Before Vijay could comment, Hari rushed on. "My plan is to start small—hold yoga sessions; narrate stories from our great epics; conduct classes for children to learn shlokas; arrange cultural events; celebrate Hindu festivals; volunteer; undertake charity work and so on."

"But—" Vijay interjected.

But Hari continued. "I want to reach not only every Indian state but every country, even the smallest of islands where Hindus reside. All I want is the numbers. Once I get those, WHAM, I will move towards my real goal—transforming India from a secular nation to a Hindu one."

"But... Hari, there is no need to do this."

"How can you say that, Baba? We cannot let the Hindu religion die out. Those bastards will overtake us otherwise. Look at the rate at which they reproduce. Do you want Mughal rule all over again?"

"No, no *beta*... but—"

"You leave it all to me." Hari put a reassuring arm around his father's shoulders. "Remember, I'm going to make you

118

proud."

"Hari, it's not easy…"

Hari led Vijay by the shoulders and sat him down on the bed. "Hush Baba, relax! Don't worry."

Vijay wasn't convinced, but he also knew that Hari's crazy plan would find no success whatsoever. It would remain within the sheaf of papers and, after the initial excitement died down, Hari would forget about it all. Vijay hoped he would.

That year, the monsoon was particularly terrifying, causing the Mula river to break her banks and flood Pune. By now, Hari had a considerable social media following. He got together several local volunteers by raising a call on social media to help those who had lost homes in the flood-ravaged areas. Under Hari's leadership, the volunteers collected funds; made temporary accommodation arrangements; arranged food, water, and other resources. A local newspaper noticed his efforts and wished to do a short feature on him about his flood relief work. Hari ensured that the name of *Dharma Sanstha* featured prominently in the article.

Vijay got the newspaper page featuring Hari laminated, and kept it on his desk. He took the newspaper copies with him when he visited clients or friends.

"My son," he would say to his clients when reading their horoscopes. "He cares about things that matter."

The old man boasted as his clients nodded and smiled their approval. Hari noticed his father's pride and smiled. *I always knew I would make him proud, but there's so much left to be done.* "This is just a step, Baba. There's more to come."

"What do you mean?"

"This is just to gain trust," Hari smiled. "Once we gain the trust, then WHAM!"

Vijay frowned. "Tchaa."

During the annual Ganesha festival, where it was the norm to set up colourful displays around the Ganesha idol, *Dharma Sanstha*'s pandal was the most appreciated. Unlike other displays which resorted to Bollywood gimmickry, Hari's display portrayed the cultural heritage of Pune. The local newspaper, impressed by the display, carried a picture which prominently featured the name of the *Dharma Sanstha*.

Devout_Hari: People of our ideology should get together to form a strong unit. We are a considerable force.

Devout_Hari: Let us get together and fight the secular forces of the country which are dragging our glorious culture backwards.

Hari tweeted, held meetings and shared resources. He gave talks and increased his network. Efforts to coordinate with overseas Indians were made to get them interested in the work of the *Sanstha*. The overseas Indians, always in search of God and desperate for a sense of belonging which they had failed to experience in their adopted nations, gladly contributed in the name of charity, culture, and religion. The donations continued to grow. Cultural festivals and charity work commenced in the *Sanstha*'s name. Over time, the *Sanstha* became famous in Pune, and so did Hari.

Vijay was happy with Hari's small successes, but then Hari came to him and said, "We're drawing up lists."

"Lists? What lists? And who is this 'we'?"

"Me and Ganesh are drawing up lists of Muslims and the non-believers."

"What on earth for? Concentrate on your job, *beta*, and continue to do your charity work."

"All non-Hindus must be shown their place. Lessons must be taught."

"What is the need? There is no need to do all this. You have already achieved so much. Brought people together. Made me proud. There's no need to do more."

"But Baba, there is a need to do more. Much, much more. The glory of ancient Hindu India needs to be brought back."

Vijay wondered if a *pischaaz* had got hold of his son. That mad glint that he sometimes saw in his son's eye probably required treatment. He wondered if he should talk to a holy Godman.

Breaking News — Times of Hindustan
1st November 2011. Time: 10:00

MAHARASHTRA: A five-year-old boy of Ramgadh village has been the victim of a sacrifice, according to the Pune police. His body was found in the early hours of the morning with a severed head. A thirty-six-year-old woman and a self-styled Godman have been arrested.

According to our reporters, the woman had visited the Godman to find a cure for her fifteen-year-old son who had been suffering from hallucinations for the past few months. The Godman informed her that the boy was possessed, and the only way to appease the demons that hounded him was to sacrifice a human child. The desperate mother kidnapped the neighbour's five-year old son and, in a ceremony organised by the Godman, killed and sacrificed the five-year-old to exorcise her son's demons. On being examined by medical professionals, the woman's son was found to have been suffering from psychosis.

Maharashtra has reported at least one case of human sacrifice every month for the past three years. Aparna Soman, volunteer and activist with the Rationalist and Anti-Superstition Society of Pune has reiterated the organisation's call for an anti-superstition law. "We need to prevent the exploitation that takes place under the garb of religion," she said.

Breaking News — Times of Hindustan
11th November 2011. Time: 10:00

UTTAR PRADESH: A huge procession was taken through the streets of the northern states to demand a ban on cow slaughter. The agitation for cow protection was launched by Hindu Warriors, a group of nationalist Hindus. Around 100,000 sadhus marched through the streets dressed up as Hindu gods, brandishing tridents and spears.

Chapter Nineteen
14th February 2012. Time: 06:00

"Today," Hari said, "is the most obscene of all days. An abhorrent day that corrupts young minds."

"True Hari *bhau*," Ganesh said, "the West corrupts our young." There was a pause. "But what are you talking about in particular?"

"Valentine's Day," Hari said grimly, "the 'let's celebrate obscenity' day. The 'let's teach the youngsters immoral things' day."

"Correct, Hari *bhau*," Ganesh moved his head in agreement.

"How dare these unmarried youngsters flaunt their love out in the open? Don't they have any shame? They will soon start having sex outdoors if not stopped now. The bloody West and their frivolities!" Hari shouted.

Ganesh had not opened his father's garage for the day. Two of Hari's trusted aides, Prahlad and Shakti, sat with Hari and Ganesh across a makeshift table in the garage. The four young men sat with ease, their legs sprawled. Outside, the air was bereft of voices. The coo of a restless *koel* could be heard periodically. A cool breeze sometimes made her way in through the open garage door providing relief from the heat. Hari took a quick look at his Twitter account:

Liberal_feminists: Valentine's Day is a celebration of commercialisation.

Liberal_feminists: Valentine's Day is a celebration of only one kind of love—the love between a man and a woman.

Liberal_feminists: For this reason, we deride the day.

"*Saala*! We and these so-called liberal feminists are on the same page today," he laughed.

The others did not understand and looked at him blankly.

"We must stop this corruption. Assemble into groups and visit all college campuses. Take *lathis*. Stop the young from celebrating this vile day," Hari ordered his goons. "Order flower shops to stop selling roses to the young. They must not encourage this obscenity."

"Rocking, Hari *bhau!*" Prahlad said.

Young men without jobs were eager to show off their prowess by bullying young lovers with the help of lathis. After giving them the instructions, the meeting concluded, and Hari left for work.

Dharma_Sanstha: Anyone who celebrates Valentine's Day will get a lathi on their bum.

Right_Wing_Hindu: Give a red rose and get a red bum in return.

Holy_man: Why celebrate love before marriage? Get married first.

Indian_parent: I applaud the Dharma Sanstha for showing youngsters the right path. Bravo!

Since most Indian parents were reluctant to let their young daughters engage in sex before marriage, a fate worse than death, *Dharma Sanstha*'s angst found favour with them.

At around nine, Hari's men grouped. Lathis in their hands, they toured the college campuses. Soon, they spotted a young man carrying a red rose. One of goons caught the young lad by the scruff of the neck.

"Drop it," he threatened "This is your age to study, not give roses to girls."

"What kind of dictatorship is this?" the young man exclaimed.

"Do you want a lathi on your bum? Drop the rose."

The rose was dropped with reluctance.

The group walked further. They saw a young girl with a red rose in her hand.

"Do you want us to send your photo to your parents?" the goons threatened the girl who had dared to accept a rose from an admirer. The girl dropped the rose with a shriek and ran away.

The group walked all over campus with lathis. Then they went to a flower shop which normally stocked extra roses on the day.

"No selling roses to youngsters today," the goons warned the owner, "else we will damage your shop."

"No, no… please don't do that," the owner pleaded. He waited until the goons left and then sold the roses anyway.

Hari's group found it difficult to be present everywhere at the same time, so it was easy for his offenders to break the imposed rules. The young people followed the same strategy and Valentine's Day was celebrated with gusto. No one was willing to let the goons stop them from exhibiting love. In fact, the day became even more significant because the celebrations carried on despite the threat from goons.

Liberal_feminists: Moral objections to the day are rooted in patriarchy.

Liberal_feminists: We condemn the moral policing of the fringe groups.

Secular_newspaper: Once again, Valentine's Day was celebrated despite threats from regressive elements.

Breaking News — Times of Hindustan
18th December 2013

Maharashtra Assembly passes anti-superstition bill

MAHARASHTRA: The Maharashtra Assembly has created history by passing the much-awaited Anti-Superstition Bill in the Assembly. This new law seeks to drive out superstition, black magic and blind faith perpetrated by self-styled Godmen, tantrics and witchcraft practitioners.

Under the prevention and eradication of human sacrifice and other inhuman, evil and *aghori* practices and black magic law, a violation is any of the following:

1.   Pretending to expel ghosts by tying a person with ropes or chains, whipping a person, making them inhale chilli smoke, hanging a person to the roof

2.   Displaying so-called miracles to defraud and earn money

3.   Instigating or encouraging others to follow inhuman practices that cause grievous harm under the guise of obtaining blessings of a supernatural power

4.   Instigating or encouraging human sacrifice

5.   Creating fear of devil possession or evil consequences if advice of those possessed is not followed

6.   Declaring a person an incarnation of the devil with the intention of making their life miserable

7.   Creating an impression that black magic diminishes the milking capacity of cows or accusing a person of bringing misfortune to others making lives of such people miserable

8.   Assaulting a person or parading them naked in the name of black magic

9.   Preventing a person from taking medical treatment and encouraging them to adopt cures offered by black magic

10.   Claiming to perform surgery by the laying of fingers or claiming to change the sex of a foetus in the womb of a woman

11.   Assuring a woman of motherhood through supernatural powers

12.   Creating an impression that a mentally-challenged person has supernatural powers and using them to rob others

Chapter Twenty
18th December 2013. Time: 11:00

Even the sunshine flooding into the morose room did not have the power to lighten the tension. Hari sat on the bed, his head bowed with Lata beside him, her hand on his slumped shoulders.

This is the closest I've felt to him, she thought as her husband wept.

"Shall I make some turmeric milk for you?" Lata asked. "I can even put in a strand of saffron. It'll soothe you."

"This bill is not anti-superstition as they call it. It is anti-religion. It's anti-Hindu." Hari said. Lata consoled him by increasing the pressure of her hand on his shoulder. "They can't put a stop to our religious traditions by calling them superstitions. They cannot! They'll stop us from going to the temples next. Lord Ganesha festival is always on their radar. They will ban the Ganesh festival by calling it superstition."

Lata nodded, making soothing noises. *I've never ever seen him like this. Almost endearing in a way.*

Hari got up and switched on the TV. All news channels were covering the passing of the bill.

"Our state has taken one step towards progress. Fraud and human rights abuses under the guise of religion can now be firmly dealt with." An intimidating woman was speaking confidently into the microphone.

"Who is this woman?" Hari asked with disgust.

"That was Aparna Soman, volunteer with the Rationalist and Anti-Superstition Society of Maharashtra," the news anchor said, concluding the interview as the celebrations continued.

"What an aggressive woman," Lata said.

"Hindu women are now disparaging our religion. Soon the Muslims will take over while we simply sit and watch."

Lata murmured soothingly.

"When women get out of hand, there is nothing but chaos in society," Hari said with a pained expression. Lata nodded.

Hari took his mobile phone lying on the bed beside him. He searched for Aparna Soman and followed her on all social media platforms. Lata continued to look at the TV.

"I don't belong here," Hari said. "This nation is relentlessly pursuing me and my religion. Wish we could leave, but where would we go?"

And then, a year later, everything changed.

Breaking News — Times of Hindustan
16th May 2014

Hindu nationalists take over India

Hindu nationalists secure victory in India's elections with an unexpectedly wide margin. Amidst warnings from the opposition party that a Hindu nationalist government would be disastrous for India, the victory has been secured on a grand scale not seen since 1984.

Chapter Twenty-One
16ᵗʰ May 2014. Time: 11:00

Lata was at home in her faded, brown nightie, practising the breathing exercises which the world-famous Indian yoga guru prescribed for everyone via television. Kashi was asleep after a long night studying. Vijay was taking an early afternoon siesta. A religious song was playing the background. As she huffed and puffed, her ringtone which was India's national anthem, interrupted her activities. *Never a peaceful moment.* She lowered the volume and answered.

"Lata, prepare something sweet today. I'm coming home early for lunch." Hari had to shout into the phone against the background noise of *dhols*, cheers and jubilations.

"Oh, what's happened?" Lata asked, but Hari had already hung up.

When Hari finally came home, Lata could hardly recognise him. He was covered in saffron dust, but there was something else different about him. A new aura of power. She could see it in the confident, relaxed tones in which he spoke; in his assured gait as if the nation now belonged to him and all the decisions were his to make.

"What are we celebrating?" Lata asked, ladling out the *kheer* which she had hastily prepared.

"Let us sweeten our mouths first." Hari took a spoonful of *kheer* and fed it to Lata.

"*Ishya,*" Lata blushed.

Hari finished the *kheer*, standing.

"At least tell me now," Lata asked, "what happened?"

"You'd know if you'd care to switch on the news channel once in a while. *Arre*, we have a Hindu government in power now. The journey towards our very own Hindu nation has begun. This government will listen to Hindus. We will no longer be just an after-thought."

"But you'll continue to work for the needy, won't you? Your social work will not stop?" Lata asked in a soft voice.

"It will change now! The minorities have been dominating us for so long, making it difficult for Hindus to survive. It's our turn now. The Hindus have arrived! We will show them," Hari said, broadening his shoulders. The politics of Hindutva had begun.

"Baba, where are you?" Hari shouted.

"He is sleeping," Lata said.

"At this hour? No, no, we must wake him up." Hari went to the old man and shook him awake. His father awoke with a start.

"Baba, Baba, we have a Hindu government in power now."

"What?" Vijay put on his glasses wearily, trying to focus.

"The Hindu nationalists have won the elections," Hari shouted. "It's time for celebrations. Have some kheer."

Hari looked at Lata who scampered to the kitchen to prepare a fresh batch.

"Good, good," the old man said smiling toothlessly, "Hindus will rule now. We will get back our past glory. No licking the feet of other religions. Time for Hindus now."

That day, the nation turned saffron, the colour of Hindu nationalists. Saffron flags were raised. Saffron turbans worn. Saffron balloons hung outside the party offices. A nation that loved noise, food, and colour celebrated the victory of the new government with all five of their senses. Drums were beaten; colours thrown in the air. People exchanged jubilant hugs and rich cholesterol-inducing sweets. Loudspeakers blared patriotic songs from Bollywood interspersed with popular dance numbers so that everyone could dance without forgetting their patriotism. Smell of gunpowder clung to nostrils as tons of firecrackers exploded on the streets. Temples bathed their deities and offered fragrant flowers. And a young Muslim student was killed in Pune to prove a point. The pictures of his murder were circulated on social media akin to winning a prized trophy.

The months progressed. Celebrations continued. Hari purchased a small new car. The first thing he did was to put a sticker of a Hindu god on the dashboard. A sticker of the Indian flag followed.

"Being Indian means being Hindu. Understood?" he said to Lata, who'd wanted to purchase a sticker of a kitten for the car. "Show pride in being a Hindu. Take pride in your language. Have you seen how these English-speaking people are now walking around with their tail between the legs? Now, we'll show them," he said, thumping his chest.

On an impulse, he got tins of paint and painted all the walls of his house in saffron.

"Orange walls?" Lata asked, attempting to mask her dismay.

"Saffron. The colour of Hindutwa. Our colour," Hari said while she covered her nose with her *pallu* to get rid of the smell of fresh paint that cloyed in her nostrils.

Soon after, he changed his social media profile picture to that of a Hindu god in a warrior pose. His cover photo was that of the garlanded holy cow.

Two days later, Lata felt a tap on her shoulder as she slept. She woke up with a start to realise it was Hari. Her phone displayed the time to be half past four in the morning. Hari was getting dressed.

"I have some important celebrations to attend today," he said.

"What's happened?" Lata asked. Seeing Hari in a good mood made her day easier.

"Today, we're going to celebrate Nathuram Godse," Hari said with a smile.

"Gandhi's killer?" Lata could not help gasping.

"A true patriot and a true Hindu. Our textbooks have been misleading us all along. He was never given his due. Anyway, you're too naïve to know these things. Trust me when I say, Godse deserves to be celebrated."

Lata simply nodded.

"You don't know how it is now," Hari said. "We will show those who laugh at us. Those who don't take our religion seriously. These English-speaking elites—these children of Macaulay—practically have orgasms at the thought of the West. Our youngsters will study our religious scriptures. They will chant shlokas. Take pride in our culture and religion and worship the holy cow—our mother. We will force it down everyone's throats."

Vijay entered the room just then. "I heard voices, so..."

"Baba, they've asked me to join politics," Hari said.

Lata's head shot up. Hari hadn't told her.

"Politics? Hope you've refused?" Vijay said, hobbling towards Hari and placing a hand on his shoulders.

"It's a new nation, Baba. They require people with my ideology and experience." Hari paused, "They said I'm a rising star for the local right-wing party." He couldn't prevent the joy from creeping into his voice.

"But politics?" Vijay asked gravely. "Is that you want to do? It's a dirty game."

"Baba, I've decided to quit my job and work for the *Dharma Sanstha* full-time. I've thought this through. The renewed funding that the *Sanstha* now receives will be more than enough for us. There's a lot of camaraderie amongst the cadres now. Huge enthusiasm. Would be a shame to waste all that."

"You're willing to let go of a regular income?" Vijay asked. "Is that wise?"

"The party in power will take care of Hindus like us. I want to do something great for the nation. Something great for my faith."

"If that's what you want..." Vijay started to walk out of the room, "who am I to stop you?" *The pischaaz still rules.* The old man muttered to himself.

A flurry of mythological TV programmes now flooded the TV screens. Every night, dinner-plates on their laps, Hari and Lata watched the *Ramayana* TV serial.

"Finally, I belong," Hari said to Lata one night. "This is how I always wanted my nation to be."

He walks and talks like a king! Secure in the knowledge that people will wait for him, listen to him, take orders from him. This new confidence... no, not confidence. This new power he radiates... as if nothing is too big for him. Everything can be managed... everything will be taken care of. He is more like a fixer these day—meddling in things that do not concern him. When I married him, he was in the business of helping the needy. Now, he is on a mission to teach the others a lesson, constantly looking for a point to prove. I'm a proud Hindu but these walls of saffron all around have started to suffocate me.

But Lata kept her doubts to herself.

Aparna Soman's Blog
17th December 2014

Seven months after the new government came to power, the nation has witnessed drastic changes. Intelligence, achievement, and rationality are now ridiculed and equated with elitism. Superstition, mythology and ancient Hindu culture now mingle with science, and seep into areas which, until now, were considered sacrosanct. An insecure nation that hungered to become a major superpower now finds its glory in the ancient past instead. The right-wing propagandists continue to tout ancient India's glory while the hungry masses lap it all up. The funding for science is cut, but pseudoscience flourishes. Ridicule prevails. Indian pseudo-scientists are mocked by the liberals. Godmen, attired in saffron robes and spouting mumbo-jumbo are the new superstars. News media firmly divides into two: the right-wing and the secular. Fake news is rampant. Headlines rule, and no one bothers to read comprehensive, analytical news stories. Hate speech is celebrated. Bigotry is now an aspiration. Stories of harassment of Muslims are shared and celebrated. Bollywood movies are scrutinised. If found to be questioning Hindu religion, screenings are disrupted, resulting in severe losses to the producers and cinema hall owners. Artistic freedom is throttled. Books believed to be offensive to Hindu religion are disallowed. When monetary losses occur, the easiest option is to give in and listen to the goons. Movies steer clear of controversies. Book publishers oblige.

Dinner room conversations have become divisive. Friends forget to eat during meals—so caught up are they in debating the liberal versus the right-wing politics. Friends and relatives are lost to each other forever because of the divisions created.

Chapter Twenty-Two
12ᵗʰ January 2015. Time: 11:00

"*Beta*, a new office? How can you afford it?" Vijay asked in a weak voice as Hari guided his father to the family car.

The Sabnis family glittered in festive wear to celebrate the launch of *Dharma Sanstha*'s new office. The old man, wearing a new bush-shirt he had received as a gift for Diwali, huddled in the back with his granddaughter while Lata, in a turmeric *Paithani* sari with jasmine flowers in her hair, sat in the front with her husband.

"We have all the funds we need, Baba. It's the time for Hindus now. Things have changed," Hari said with a smile as he drove. "Not only a new office in Pune, but offices in several states, plus we also have a swanky new website now."

"That thing you see on the screen?" Vijay asked.

Hari laughed. "Yes, Baba. That thing I see on the screen." He took a sharp right turn and was greeted by a volley of horns. Vijay squirmed in his seat. "Our work is carried out all over India now. But there's more. I plan to buy weapons and organise weapon training for the young."

"What on earth for?"

"We must be militant and self-sufficient to face every threat."

"There's the army for that," the old man said in a tired voice.

"This will be our own local army, Baba."

"There's the police for that. *Beta*, use your skills for good, not for hate."

"Violence used against evil is not violence. Insults to our religion and culture will not be tolerated. It was you who taught me, Baba, remember? About the Muslim takeover if we're not vigilant. And you were right. We are right."

The old man remained silent. They had arrived. A flurry of people surrounded the car as soon as Hari parked. When Lata got out, she was greeted with respectful *namastes*. Her back became a little straighter.

A coconut was handed to Hari. He broke it in front of the office entrance to loud applause. They went in. The *Dharma Sanstha* offices had a huge hall for functions. This was where Hari gathered his colleagues and volunteers. Despite the fans whirring above, aiming to calm emotions, the mood of the room was celebratory in an aggressive way.

"Long live Hindus."

"Jai Sri Ram!"

"Long live our Hindu nation."

Chests were thumped. Slogans raised and drums beat until Hari got up on the podium, adjusted the mic and called for silence.

"Now, listen carefully, all. The time is now ours," Hari spoke to his cadre. "The rationalists are the enemies. Draw up a list of these anti-nationals. These atheists, rationalists and anti-superstition campaigners. We will send a Hindu army to deal with them. We have a strong force behind us and there's no shortage of funds. If any social media post, any actor, author, comedian, movie or book dares mention a single sentence against Hindu religion, file a case of sedition or blasphemy. File multiple cases. File them in multiple states. Hassle the bastards. Let them do the court rounds. Frighten and harass them to silence everywhere including social media."

The room thundered with applause as the drums beat again. Vijay sat cowering in his seat amongst the celebrations. Despite the fans, he was sweating.

Breaking News — Times of Hindustan
3rd March 2015. Time: 11:00

Maharashtra bans beef

MAHARASHTRA: The state of Maharashtra has introduced a draconian beef ban, with up to five years imprisonment for sale or possession of the meat.

Upper caste Hindus consider cows as sacred. The beef ban has only been possible due to the efforts of the Hindu nationalist party which had included a ban on beef in their manifesto.

This is one of the toughest attempts to prevent beef-eating in India, with Maharashtra's law banning the slaughter of cows and the sale of beef. The possession of the meat is now to be considered as contraband. The state imposes a punishment of up to five years in prison for violations.

Chapter Twenty-Three
3rd March 2015. Time: 20:00

Hari fiddled with his phone, quickly composed a tweet and posted it. He sat with Ganesh and Prahlad in his brand-new office. Twilight hour was the time for plans and decisions.

Dharma_Sanstha: The Dharma Sanstha celebrates the ban on beef. We request capital punishment for those who kill, transport or consume cow meat.

His accomplices were silent for a while and then Hari looked up.

"Today is an important day," Hari said "My dream has come true. Not only my dream but my father's too." He raised his voice and thumped his chest. "The holy cow will no longer be slaughtered on our streets."

His lazy audience were jolted into action. They whistled, clapped and hooted. Hari held up his hands for silence and continued in a low voice, "But remember! We have to be vigilant at all times. Our work has increased. I'm setting up cow vigilante groups in the city. It's our job to enforce the cow slaughter ban. Burn down the shops of anyone who sells beef. Sort it out, then and there. I don't need to spell it out, do I?" They laughed. "Remember, it's the law now."

"Very good, Hari *bhau*," Ganesh slapped him on the back, "we will do everything. Don't you worry."

"Secular India is slowly turning into a Hindu India," Hari said as his friends laughed raucously. "Look at Kerala. People still eat beef there and what do they get? Floods which caused so many to lose their lives! Had they given up cow slaughter, this wouldn't have happened."

"Very true, Hari *bhau*," Ganesh said, "only a matter of time

141

before our Hindu Government bans beef in all states."

"The nation will prosper when the holy cow is respected."

"Take weapons and stand outside Muslim homes and butcher stores. The bastards need to know that we mean business. Any hint of beef and whack them right there."

The young men laughed. They sat discussing their success late into the night.

The next morning, Hari's friends spread the word. Volunteers were encouraged to be on a look out. Muslim homes and shops were identified. An opportunity came their way just three days after the beef ban.

While Hari was performing his yoga asanas one afternoon, there was a knock on the door. Lata peeped out of the peep hole and saw the shining dome of Ganesh. She went to the room where Hari was performing his asana.

"Ganesh is outside," she said in a whisper.

Hari nodded. He put on a shirt and opened the door.

Ganesh came in sweating, a hockey stick in his hand. Without bothering to sit, he burst out, "Hari *bhau*, that Javed has killed a cow outside the Munna butcher shop. He is carrying the beef home to celebrate."

"Call the others. You know what needs to be done," said Hari. He buttoned up his shirt and put on his slippers.

"Already done that. They've assembled near the Shivaji statue next to the butcher."

Hari went in and grabbed a hockey stick. "Let's go."

The fat on Ganesh's face wobbled with excitement.

Both the men marched with hockey sticks in their hands, and after a five-minute walk came to the statue erected for a secular king. Twenty rogues holding hockey sticks had surrounded Javed from all sides in the street. Hari was glad to see they had waited for him.

"Show us what's in your bag," one of them said to him.

Javed, surprised at being asked to show the contents of his bag, obeyed.

"Arsehole, don't you know it's illegal to carry beef?"

"This is not beef. It's mutton," said Javed trembling. "Come, let's go to the butcher. He will confirm."

"You think you can fool us?" Ganesh barked. Before Javed could reply, a hockey stick cracked his skull. It connected with a sickening crunch, splitting open bone like an eggshell. The others continued to thrash him. Hari watched, unflinching. For far too long, Hindus had remained silent, but no more. It was time to teach lessons.

"This will teach them," Ganesh said.

As the blood oozed out from Javed's skull, the young men stood and watched. A Muslim was being taught a lesson. He would not be the first one nor the last to die because of his religion. The gathered crowd burst into applause and went their way.

Javed succumbed to his injuries. Later, investigations revealed the meat was indeed mutton. As the news spread, the newspapers and the liberals made half-hearted noise, but the country had changed. An atmosphere of fear settled down over the nation like a fungus. No one had the appetite to get involved with rogues.

Liberals in their pristine gated communities wept. *A saffron hallucinogenic drug seems to have been released into the air of this great nation that once belonged to us.* A spurt of reports highlighted the ludicrous events taking place in the nation, offering dark, comic relief to the privileged. Since religion was now entrenched with nationalism, the outspoken liberals were immediately given the tag of anti-nationals. *Send them to Pakistan. That's where they belong,* was the usual retort of the cow-worshippers. Behind the comedy, the sinister undertones of bigotry, violence and lynching could not be ignored.

As the notoriety and violence of the *Dharma Sanstha* grew,

liberals made a call to ban the organisation. Instead, the political powers felicitated the organisation in a ceremony, where Hari was praised and garlanded.

Vijay noticed an imperceptible change in his son and was perturbed. He tried one more time.

"I'm proud of everything you've achieved so far. However, it is important to know when to stop. Don't take it to the other extreme," he told his son.

"How can you say that, Baba? Wrongdoings must be punished."

"There's the law for that," Vijay said "No need to become a rogue and beat people up."

But Hari did not listen to him. He seemed to be gripped by a kind of mania which, like the *vetal* on King Vikram's shoulders, refused to let go of him. *This is what I was born to do. Born to preserve and protect my religion. This is the highest form of service.*

One morning, Hari woke up before his father. He let the old man sleep for some time but when he didn't wake up even after two hours, Hari went to check on him. Hari put his hand on the old man's chest and when he didn't feel a beat, he knew. The old man had peacefully passed away in his sleep.

He stood looking at his father's corpse and whispered softly to himself. "You gave me my purpose. I'm on this path only because of you. And yet you could not understand my ambition for the last few years." He sighed. "It's okay, Baba. I forgive you."

When Lata heard the news, a single thought came to her mind. *No one has the authority to control Hari now.*

BOOK THREE

Chapter Twenty-Four
4th May 2016. Time: 08:30

The scorching heat of the day had permeated the air-conditioned room. Manish's thoughts jostled like peak-hour commuters on a Mumbai local as he saw Aparna inert on the bed like a mango sucked dry. No one was around. No monitor or tubes attached. He went closer, his hands shaking. Her right eye had developed a strange, involuntary tick. A brown smudge glistened, stoically, on her left cheek and a patch of blood stained the lower part of her sari. He looked at his wife's face but, for some reason, his gaze kept getting pulled towards the macabre patch of blood. His palms and armpits felt clammy. Sweat droplets made an intricate pattern on his forehead. Though his wife's eyes were closed, he denied his facial expressions the luxury of revealing his distress. A throbbing pulse aggravated the depths of his right ear. His chest ached. *What does one do in a situation like this? All my education, and I haven't got a bloody clue.* He tried not to gag at the stink of vomit.

"Aparna…" he murmured. Without opening her eyes, Aparna mumbled something into the sterile air. Gently, he caressed her cheek.

"They threatened me…" Aparna said.

"They?" He took a step back. "I thought you fainted because you went out without having breakfast!"

"Three of them."

Manish could barely hear her, or maybe he didn't want to, as he moved closer and lowered himself into a chair next to the bed. She sounded delirious. He put his hand on her forehead, but her temperature felt normal to him. It was her vulnerability that shocked more than anything else.

"Tell me," he said quietly. "Tell me what happened."

But his wife remained silent.

Who is this quivering, helpless creature? She doesn't look like my wife.

"I can't," she finally whispered.

"Aparna, what happened?"

He tuned in momentarily to the humdrum of the hospital behind him, craving an escape into normality. Adjusting the pillows around Aparna, he let his gaze wander, unable to settle on his miserable wife.

"They wanted to teach me a lesson... for my idea... my tweet," she finally whispered, "... caused them offence." A silence followed. "Guess I'm lucky. Other... rationalists have been killed."

"Aparna, did they...?"

Now, she opened her eyes and looked directly at him. Somehow, he summoned the courage to meet them. Her eyes were dry, barren and scorched like the River Mula in the peak of summer, but his unexpected tears embarrassed him. He muffled a cough and brushed his tears on the back of his sleeve. She closed her eyes, as if wanting only her pain to be the focus of attention.

"It's going to be alright," he said, knowing the words were insufficient. As his hand cradled her head, she moved into his touch, welcoming it with a desperate gratitude, her face contorting. Needing all his strength to simply sit there and watch, he consoled his wife through his touch until she became calmer.

"Don't worry, alright?" he whispered. "You're safe now. We'll ensure you're safe."

All at once, she sat up. "Contact the police. I want to register a complaint. I'm not letting them get away with this."

"Shh, we can do that later," he said tenderly. "Has the doctor given you anything...?"

"I'm going to make a lot of noise about this," she said hoarsely. "You wait and watch. But first, I need to be examined properly."

He wiped the sweat off his brow. "Are you in pain?" he whispered.

"I don't know..." her eyes appealed.

Drenched in sweat, his heart thudded. His own body, his heart, his mind, seemed to be making desperate pleas for help.

"I need a doctor to look at me." Her voice shook.

"Don't know... we may have to go to a government hospital for, you know, the forensic examination."

"...before anything happens." Her voice cracked.

"But Aparna..."

"For heaven's sake...." Her eyes were moist now.

He dug in his trouser pocket and produced a handkerchief. She grimaced on seeing the smudged piece of cloth and refused to take it. She smiled a little. A flash of normality in the subdued surroundings. He flapped the handkerchief as if to get rid of the impurities. She took it.

"Naseem won't let you get away with this dodgy piece of cloth," she said, dabbing her eye.

A terrifying mixture of determination, panic and incomprehension hovered within them. *How could this have happened to her—to them?*

A smiling doctor in a white sari whirred into the room like a bee on a mission, followed by a peon with insultingly cheerful eyes who placed a glass of water on the table in the corner. Used to an invisible existence, the peon left without glancing at them. Manish drank the water. Aparna picked up her glass.

"Please madam," the doctor commanded, "I request you not to drink." Aparna froze. "Not before your forensic examination," the doctor said in a softer voice.

Manish noticed Aparna's furrowed brow as she placed the glass back on the table. "Doctor, my wife was left alone in this room. Your hospital didn't even bother to call. I got a call from the grocery store, for heaven's sake!"

"Oh, didn't the hospital call? I thought they'd taken care

of that. Sorry, but don't worry, our nurses are monitoring the rooms on this floor at all hours. Your wife wasn't really left alone. She was triaged and then placed here." The smile did not leave her face.

"I need to be examined right away," Aparna said in a tight voice.

"Just a moment," the doctor said and looked at Manish, "Please can I have a word with you?"

Manish asked Aparna a question with his eyes. She nodded. He followed the doctor to an adjacent room, and for the next few seconds, watched the doctor's mouth move as she uttered words confirming what he had suspected. Like a blocked sewer, her words clogged his voice. He choked, and then slumped as if punched. The doctor extended a hand to steady him, but he dismissively shook his head. He clamped his hand over his mouth as his stomach heaved. That one word voiced aloud. That one word bandied about by all and sundry without understanding the weight of trauma it carried within. He needed to get used to that word because he would hear it often. It would get thrown at his family from all sides with meticulous precision. His hand remained on his mouth as he waited for the sensation to pass. After a few seconds, he straightened up, and with a darting gaze at the doctor, gave a brief nod to indicate all was well. Not wishing to leave Aparna alone for long, he returned to her room. The doctor followed.

"I will give you both a list of government-approved hospitals authorised to handle such cases," the doctor said. "I assure you; we have the time to take care of complications. It's a good thing you arrived soon after the incident."

"How can you say she's alright? What if she has fractured a bone or is bleeding internally?" Manish said speaking through his teeth as he clasped his hands together.

She looked at him directly. "Please trust us."

Aparna said in a lifeless voice, "The law has changed. An

assault victim cannot be turned away from a hospital. This includes private hospitals. I should know. I was part of the protest that forced the Government."

"I don't know anything about that. We're unaware of the forensic process that needs to be followed for assault cases. Only a government-approved hospital can do that. I'm sorry," the doctor said. "I'll leave you to make a decision. If no forensics are involved, then of course, we will be happy to treat you." With a final, unwavering look at Aparna, she smiled briefly and left the room.

Manish wiped the sweat from his face. "Nothing more to be done here. We will have to go to a different hospital to collect the evidence as per procedures." He took out his mobile phone from his pocket. "Give me a minute," he said to Aparna, and dialled 100.

"Police control room," a gruff voice said.

"Hello, I'd like to know the process for registering a FIR. Will I have to come to the police station?"

"Which jurisdiction has the crime been committed in?"

"What do you mean?"

"Where was the crime committed?"

"I... I'm not too sure..."

"What crime has been committed?"

"Er... difficult to say over the phone... hold on." Turning to Aparna, he asked in a whisper, "Will you be alright? Just popping out into the corridor." After her acknowledgement, he walked into the corridor and continued in a lower voice, "It was a crime against a woman..."

The policeman made a sound which Manish failed to interpret.

"What kind of nation are we becoming when women are getting punished for their views?" Manish could not help saying.

The policeman did not comment. All Manish could hear was a rustling of papers followed by a burp. *"What is the address of the victim?"*

"Senapati Bapat Road."

"That comes under the Deccan police jurisdiction."

"I thought…"

"You may register the crime over the phone, but the details must be provided to the Deccan police." He cleared this throat. *"Name, age and address of the victim?"*

"Survivor… she's a survivor. Aparna Soman. Age forty-five. Address, Prerna Bungalow, Senapati Bapat Road, Pune."

"Speak up Mister. I can't hear you."

Manish repeated the information.

"Date and time of the incident?"

"4ᵗʰ of May. Time: 5:45 am."

"Who is this speaking?"

"My name is Manish Joshi."

"How are you related to the victim?"

"I'm her husband."

"Your FIR has been registered. Please note down this number and quote it in all future correspondence. You will have to give a detailed statement. The victim interview will be arranged."

"Is it possible to send someone to interview her, or does she have to come to the police station?"

"Ring up the Deccan police. They will arrange it all."

Manish noted down the reference number on his phone. He rolled his shoulders, desperate for a release. They loosened as the tension ebbed a little but then, as he looked towards the room Aparna was in, he gripped his hands together until his knuckles turned white.

Chapter Twenty-Five
4th May 2016. Time: 17:00

That evening, when Aparna plodded home with Manish, her home looked exactly as she had left it. The warm, pastel walls of her living room glowed with a jaunty air; the money plant in the corner under the TV was bursting with vigour; the pale yellow curtains swished with a grace she hadn't known they possessed; a hint of saffron in the air; the sound of a spoon swirling in a glass of liquid, and a whiff of the clean lemony fresh smell of her daughter as she bounded out from the kitchen to greet them.

"I've made some lemonade and added strands of saffron," she said eagerly. "You're not going to believe the taste. Ma, you're going to get addicted!"

Aparna was leaning on Manish, his arm around her waist.

"You okay, Ma? Are you going to start your period or something?" Naseem blurted out but then paused.

"Let's sit first..." Aparna said in a thin voice. Manish helped Aparna sit on their worn burgundy sofa, Naseem following. They sat close on either side of Aparna. Manish still had his arm around her. Naseem touched Aparna's cheek and held her hand. Then she gripped her father's hand with force.

Aparna's shoulders hunched over. "We all need to make ourselves strong, okay? Just remember, we're all safe at home right now. That's what matters."

Naseem spotted a faint bruise on her temple. Wrinkles had magically appeared on her mother's face overnight. *When had Ma become so old?*

"Ma, you're scaring me. Tell me. Have you got cancer? Has Baba got cancer?" Naseem's eyes brimmed like the clear, shallow ponds of the monsoon.

How easily she cries, thought Aparna. *We've always tried to keep those tears away but now...*

153

"Naseem..." Aparna started but then stopped. *Is this what they say about clamping down voices? I have no words to explain to my daughter what happened to me.* "Naseem..." she tried again, hoarse. Her effort to string a couple of words together did not yield results. She made a sound of frustration. "Naseem..." she said and then blurted out the word to make her daughter understand. She saw Naseem's eyes die. "I want to be there for you, to help you get through this. I wish I could... I'm sorry," Aparna said, words jostling with each other as they tumbled out. Standing up, she grimaced as a shard of pain shot down her leg. "I think I'll go to my room." Naseem reached out her hand, but she patted it away. "Don't worry about it... I'm fine, just a little tired. I've had a medical check-up. No need to worry."

"Aparna, you go to your room and rest. Don't worry about a thing. We'll be fine," Manish said as he stood up and took her hand.

Aparna turned to look directly at Naseem, attempting a smile which did not reach her exhausted eyes. Naseem stared at her mother, silent tears splashing onto her face, and down onto her lime green kurta where they made a steadily growing wet patch. Manish helped Aparna to her room.

After a few minutes, he came back and went to sit beside his daughter. He put his arm around her shoulder and moved her close. "I don't have the words to tell you."

"How?" she asked. "Who?"

He bit his lip. "We don't know... three of them defending their religion, offended by an idea expressed in her tweet."

He watched his daughter as her determined tears continued to flow. He blamed himself. They'd warned Aparna. She hadn't listened, but he should have persevered. Knowing the rabid atmosphere prevalent in the nation, how could he have given up so easily? His wife's trauma and his daughter's grief... was there anyone else to blame other than him?

"Naseem, please calm down. Everything is alright now. Breathe," said Manish.

Dashing to the kitchen, he got a glass of water for her. Naseem's breathing normalised after a while, but as soon as she took a sip of the water, she rushed to the loo and vomited her lunch out. This started a fresh round of panicked, rasping sobs. He wrung his hands, waiting until his daughter stabilised. After a few minutes, Naseem's sobs subsided, but now she started hiccupping at irregular intervals.

Once again, Aparna appeared from her room.

Naseem looked up and asked her, "Why?"

Aparna walked to her daughter to hold her, hoping her touch would work when her words had failed. "Shh, *pillu*," she whispered. "Stop hurting so much." She rocked her daughter, consoling her. "Give me some space for a few days, will you? Don't get overly worried. With time, it'll be alright."

Naseem nodded. "Yes, Ma, of course. Don't worry. We'll manage," she said in a quivering voice.

Aparna got up with effort, a hint of pain on her face. "It's over for the time being. I'll go lie down... Manish, please will you sleep with me on my bed tonight?"

Manish looked at her and for a second did not say anything. They had stopped sharing beds a long time ago. His snoring and his habit of flaying his arms—a discovery which had caused mirth in the family—disturbed her. An amusing incident came to Manish's mind of Aparna proudly showing their separate sleeping arrangements while giving a tour of their house to Manish's cousin. Manish could clearly see the shock displayed on his cousin's face, but Aparna hadn't even noticed. Now, her request took him by surprise.

"Of course," he said. "Everything is going to be okay. You'll see."

"Traditionalists will say it's my karma. My punishment for not sleeping with you on the marital bed. Don't have an option now." Her laugh was bitter. "They wouldn't hesitate to say this to my face," she mumbled as she walked to her room.

After she left, Naseem clung to Manish. "Will Ma be alright? I can't bear to see her like this."

"She's a strong woman, Naseem. She will soon be the fiery Ma we're used to," he said, though his heart hurt just as much as his daughter's.

"How vulnerable she looked."

"Try not to worry, Naseem. Remember, the worst is over."

"But is it? Will they come for us next? They must have monitored her activities. I feel so scared, Baba."

"Don't worry, *pillu*. We've registered a police complaint. We can get a security guard if that'll make you feel safer."

"Ma was right. Religious intolerance is the root of all the problems here."

"Hush, *pillu*. Let's not even think of those things right now. Are you hungry? Shall I prepare something for you?"

"I'm not hungry. Have you eaten, Baba? Has Ma eaten?"

"Let's not disturb her for the moment," he said. "Look, let's have toast or something. I'll prepare some coffee." He went to the kitchen.

Naseem heard the comforting sounds of spoons clattering, china tinkling and water bubbling. When he came back with two steaming cups of coffee, she felt better. They sat together, sipping.

"You won't tell anyone, will you?" Naseem said, after some time.

"Why is that important?"

"I wouldn't want anyone to know."

"Why? There's nothing to be ashamed of, you know."

"This will be used against me. To shame me, scare me. To ensure I conform. And I'm not even talking about the extremists here. I'm speaking of the common people—the Shirishs and the

Malas, the girls and boys I interact with, my potential employers, my potential suitors, my in-laws... her assault will follow me around."

Manish did not look at her. They sat silently in the dining room sipping their coffee. After a while, they went back to their rooms.

That night, Manish slept with Aparna on her bed. The doctor's prescription helped—she drifted off. He remembered the accusatory looks of the staff earlier in the day at the hospital. Their surreptitious glances with a hint of accusation. Glances that asked, where were you when this happened to your wife? But none of that mattered. Aparna worried him. She was strong but still... Would she be able to cope? What would this incident do to her sense of self? And what effect was this having on Naseem? He would push Aparna towards counselling. That was the right way to go. He watched Aparna's agonised face as she slept, soothed her when she cried, and calmed her whenever her ugly shrieks stabbed the silence of the night.

Chapter Twenty-Six
5th May 2016. Time: 12:00

Aparna Soman's police statement

I left for my morning walk at six in the morning, wearing a white cotton sari with a red border. My blouse was yellow and orange cotton with the traditional *bandhani* print. No jewellery. My walking shoes were white, and my socks were red. I wasn't carrying my mobile phone.

Other than a few early morning joggers, the area was deserted. I saw five joggers at various times before the incident. Taking the main street leading from my house on Senapati Bapat Road, I turned into the third lane on the left. This is my usual route, and the one I've been taking for the past five years or so.

When I entered the lane, around midway, opposite the green bungalow 'Laukik' which has a black gate made with wrought iron, a young man got in my way. He stood leering in front of me, appearing to block my way. He was around five feet and five inches tall. He looked thin and anaemic. Had dark circles under his eyes and a thin moustache. No other identifying marks on his face. Was of wheatish complexion and was wearing a black Iron Maiden t-shirt with faded blue jeans. Must have been around twenty years of age or so.

I moved away but he lightly held my hand. I was annoyed rather than threatened, as he did not appear intimidating in any way. I was surprised by his audacity. He tried to look menacing but failed. Overall, he looked like a malnourished college kid. He uttered my name as a question seeking to confirm whether it was indeed me. I was surprised to hear him say my name. From the periphery of my eye, I realised that two more boys were now silently standing behind me. I wasn't frightened, merely annoyed.

One of them was of stocky build. He was wearing a blue and white striped t-shirt. Fair with a beard. Age around twenty years. Height around five and a half feet. The other one was wearing a white t-shirt with some abstract design, and black faded trousers. Height around six feet. Age around twenty years or so.

I asked them what they wanted. Before I could even finish the sentence, the man standing behind me grabbed me. One of his hands was wound tightly around my waist and the other was on my mouth. I tried to call out. Tried to bite. His palm however was firmly around my mouth, and I could do neither. I struggled. Tried to kick, but he was physically stronger than me. I tried to attract attention by stamping my shoes on the ground, but the soft padding of the shoes did not make an impact. The boy with the Iron Maiden t-shirt ran to sit in the driver seat of a car that was parked next to us. I hadn't even noticed the parked car. They must have parked it earlier and waited for me in the lane. I'm ignorant about cars and therefore unable to tell you the make or the model. I did not look at or note down the registration number. The colour of the car was white.

The man who had me in his grip dragged and pushed me into the car. The third man got into the back with us and made me sit in the middle. The stink of sweat mixed with alcohol and a smell of something sweet pervaded the air. An old gentleman out on his morning walk saw me being dragged into the car. My eyes locked with his even as they were forcing me inside. I was unable to scream. He didn't either. I saw his hand travel to his pocket presumably to get his mobile phone. A domestic worker with a broom in her hand saw us too. She had come out of the adjacent house, the one painted green opposite the bungalow. The men did not seem to care about being seen. I continued to struggle while I was sitting in the car between the two of them, but I realised how pointless it was. They would never let me get away. At that point, I was worried about my life, and... other things. I did not want a brutal death. My only hope was the two people who had witnessed me being dragged into the car. We must have driven for around fifteen minutes. They took me to a construction site which seemed to have been abandoned. I did notice a child's pink dress drying in the corner, but I didn't see anyone else. The three men got out and dragged me out. They told me that they'd had me in their sights for the past year or so. It was for my anti-religious activities, they said. They said they'd been asked to teach me a lesson for conducting activities that were against their culture and religion. A knife was produced from the car. They said I was lucky. Others had been killed. They said they knew everything about my family and there were various things that could be done to them if I didn't stop my anti-religious activities. The incident happened, and then they left. I wandered around until I came to a busy area. I must have fainted. Cannot remember anything after that. They did not mention the name of the cult they belonged to.

Chapter Twenty-Seven
10th May 2016. Time: 22.00

"What in the world are you doing, Aparna?" Manish asked.

Wearing a dull blue khadi *kurta* and a matching *salvar*, Aparna was standing precariously on a stool in the living room, trying to secure an upper window with a handkerchief.

"This window doesn't shut," she said, struggling to fix the errant window.

"I will call Sangram tomorrow. He'll come and fix it. Don't worry," said Manish, "Let me help you down." He extended his arm.

Aparna thought for a second and then accepted it.

"Would you like a cup of coffee? I was just going to make some." But Aparna lumbered to her room without a reply. Manish followed her. She was sitting on her bed staring at the wall opposite.

"Got a call from the police today," he said. Aparna turned to look at him. "A witness has come forward. He says he saw you getting pulled into the car." Aparna turned her face back to the wall. "Only a matter of time before they catch the criminals."

There was a pause.

"How was your appointment with the therapist?" he asked.

"Where did you find her?"

"Online—she had excellent reviews."

"Online? You found her online?"

"Not many people like to mention they're taking therapy, you know. Difficult to find one based on personal recommendations."

"I don't know..."

"Well, you've just had one appointment. Maybe it's too soon to tell."

"It's not going well."

"Why?" he asked gently. "You've made up your mind with just one appointment?"

"She's a Hindutwa supporter."

"*What?*"

"There are photos of Hindu gods in the reception. Before we started our session, while we were chatting informally, she made a remark about the wonderful work the current government is doing."

"Bloody hell! She's turning potential clients away by broadcasting her politics like this."

"She'll get more clients because of her politics."

"This is highly unprofessional of her."

"It is, but so what? Who cares?" Aparna said, "I would like to stop these therapy sessions."

"Do you want me to find another therapist for you?"

"No, thank you. The anxiety medication blunts my emotions wonderfully. For the moment, they will do."

A sense of gloom settled over the household like a coat of unwanted dust. A heavy lethargy came over Aparna. Her night dreams took over. She dreamed of her childhood home as soon as she drifted off. Each of the three rooms; the wooden cupboards; the geranium plants they'd lovingly tended; the colourful designs painted on each flowerpot; the white sink; the place in the kitchen where the dirty dishes were stacked; the bustling sounds of the kitchen when she woke up every morning; salted raw mangoes left to dry on a *batik* blanket in the sun to make pickles; the crunch and the shocking sourness of the first raw mango of the season; the mouth-watering aroma of ghee and sugar used to make an infrequent treat; their mini-temple which had been abandoned after her mother turned atheist; the pale-coloured bucket in the bathroom; the Indian squat toilet with its old-fashioned flush... every excruciating detail appeared in her dreams to torment her. On waking, she desired to view her childhood home, run through the rooms, carefree. But that gloomy home had been demolished to make way for a block of concrete apartments. She envied those with intact childhood homes. Homes they could return to whenever the urge took them. Solid homes they could look at whenever they wished. Hers was gone forever. Aimless, her mind kept drifting.

Both Aparna and Naseem were reluctant to leave their rooms. Lights were switched off, allowing an easier escape into the dark. Plants were neglected. Dishes piled up. Phone calls were ignored. Aparna had taken time off from her activities, feigning sickness. Naseem stopped going to university. Her parents were too busy in their own minds to enquire about her. Rehana was given a holiday because no one had the inclination to cook. The family no longer ate together. Only Manish continued his normal routine. Preparing a quick lunch, mostly an omelette with toast, he would take it to their rooms. Aparna left her food untouched on most days. She slept most of the time. Naseem had lost interest.

Manish left the women alone though he remained keenly aware of Aparna's moods: *Aparna has taken a shower at least four times today. Is this some latent effect of her trauma? I must try and find another therapist for her... The main locks of the house need to be changed... A CCTV would be a good idea. We can afford two security guards. I have a young daughter in the house. We must be careful. I have erred once. Not going to err again.*

Aparna came in from the en-suite as Manish sat on the living room sofa with a newspaper.

"Your behaviour towards me has changed," Aparna said. Her hair looked unruly around her pale face.

"How?"

"You're on high alert when I'm around. Always saying the correct things. Walking on eggshells..." As Manish kept staring at her, she continued, "My neurology is still intact, you know. The good old brain hasn't deteriorated, though the medicines are making me lose my edge a bit. I'm still the same Aparna,

163

and I will not break if you talk too loud, disagree or... anything else."

"Aparna..." Manish said. "I just want to make things as easy for you as possible. That's all I want."

"I thought of hiding it away, you know. Hide it away, and no one would know, but I couldn't keep it to myself. I thought of hiding it from Naseem. Pointless to burden her, I thought. but I couldn't hide it from her either. I just couldn't."

Manish walked over to her and held her. After a few seconds, she separated from him and sat on the sofa. Manish joined her.

"I hate feeling weak," Aparna said as the tears flowed. "I hate this anxiety and... fear. I hate how you treat me as fragile. Hate it!"

Manish turned around to hug her. *Cry it out,* he silently urged her. *It will help.*

"It's alright to feel vulnerable, Aparna," he said, as she started to sob. "Shh, let me... allow me take care of you. No need to be strong all the time." He could feel her relaxing in his arms and for that, he was thankful.

"Can't remember most of it, which is a blessing," she said in a teary voice. She pulled away and wiped her nose with her sleeve. "Atheist blessing, of course."

Manish smiled. "I will ring up the police station today and find out the progress of their investigations. The culprits need to be behind bars."

"Do you know, I feel indifferent to those bloody criminals. Of course, they should be caught and punished, but beyond that, I don't really care. What I do care deeply about is the bloody point they wished to make with this: to prevent me from meddling. They wanted to teach me a lesson. The point is whether they succeeded in silencing my voice. I need to figure that out."

"Aparna, please, let's not think of those things. The time now is to recuperate, not think about political statements or ideologies."

"I expected you to say that. You would love it if I closed shop."

"I don't think this is a fair assessment, especially after what..." Manish stopped.

"Go on. Say it. Especially after bringing this on myself. That's what you wanted to say, wasn't it?"

"Look, let's not discuss this. We can do this later. The priority for me is to look after you and ensure that you heal physically as well as mentally."

"Don't you understand? We shouldn't let them win. I want to discuss these ideas with someone. Their ideology has permeated every field, even professional areas. Ironing out my ideas will leave me with a clear, unambiguous focus of the way forward."

"Aparna, I don't agree. Don't think of your work right now. Please."

"I *am* my work, Manish."

"Think happier thoughts. That's the way to overcome this."

She turned away. "How patronising you sound!"

"Take this opportunity to recuperate. Don't compromise on that. You can get back to work after you've recovered."

"So, what should I do with all these ideas playing tag with my brain? Ignore them and say, 'not now darlings, I'm recuperating'?"

"You can discuss how you feel with your therapist."

"You just don't understand."

They sat on the bed next to each other, defeated.

"There must be something I can do," Aparna said. A string from her kurta had come loose and she pulled at it until it snapped.

Chapter Twenty-Eight
12th May 2016. Time: 10:00

Naseem's laptop was propped up on the adjacent bedside table. She lay sideways on her bed to watch what the reviews called 'a light, wholesome Indian movie from the eighties'. A period when a kiss between a man and a woman was depicted by two roses coming together. She was an avid fan of American movies, but in her current state, the antics of the American characters were too much to take, and it was the bland TV programmes that provided succour and distraction.

Glancing at her phone, she realised she had around fifty missed calls, and thirty of these were from Ronit. His messages to her were unanswered. Naseem did not dwell on them. Her day had acquired a routine that she was getting used to. Sleep was impossible, but she managed to drift off at dawn. She got up at noon and binge-watched shows for the rest of the day and night.

The bell rang and she stiffened. She knew Manish was in the living room, closest to the main door, so she did not bother getting up. She heard the door open, and then voices. Polite voices. Safe voices. She relaxed a little. Hearing footsteps, she hoped they would go away and leave her in peace. The door echoed with a knock.

"Come in, Baba," she said.

"There's someone here to see you, Naseem." Manish opened the door and came into the room, smiling.

"Who is it?" Naseem sat up.

"A good-looking gentleman," said Manish.

Naseem groaned. "Why can't they bloody leave me alone?" she whispered. "Tell him I'm in the bathroom or something and I'll give him a call later."

"Why don't you meet him? See what he wants?" said Manish as Naseem glared at him.

Her oversized, dull grey t-shirt had month-old *dal* stains on the front. Her cotton baggy shorts looked unwashed. Her hair had not been washed or combed in days and hung limp and unruly around her face. She was glad. *I have finally stopped catering to the male gaze.*

"What is that knife doing on your bedside table?" Manish asked, puzzled.

There was a pause.

"I brought it from the kitchen to cut an apple," Naseem said, flopping out of the room in her slippers.

Cutting apples with a butcher's knife? Manish scratched his chin. "But we don't have any apples in the house." he replied,

But Naseem had left the room.

Ronit's face registered joy as soon as Naseem walked in. He stood up. Despite herself, Naseem couldn't help noticing how healthy and handsome he looked in his white t-shirt and ripped blue denims. Shuddering, she flopped down on the sofa, switched on the living room TV, and started to surf channels.

"Where the hell were you? Why aren't you answering my calls?"

Naseem yawned.

"Hello. Are you listening?"

"Yeah," said Naseem, her attention on the TV screen.

"Naseem, I've been loitering outside your house like a dependent puppy abandoned by a cruel owner. Why aren't you answering my calls? I was so worried, babe."

Naseem shivered.

"Stop calling me babe, please." Her voice was tight.

"Hey, is everything okay? Can we go out to get a coffee or something?" He moved close and touched her arm.

Naseem jumped, as if scalded.

"Naseem, what is the matter? Have I offended you in any way? Have I hurt you? Have you heard anything about me from someone? Say something!"

"Look, I need my space right now," she said.

"Need your space? What does that even mean?"

"Let me be, please."

"What happened Naseem?"

"I need some time on my own."

"For how long?"

"I don't know."

"Naseem, this isn't helping. Share your thoughts with me, for fuck's sake. I may be able to help," he begged.

"Are you hard of hearing or something? Or is your brain not powerful enough to understand? I don't wish to talk to you right now."

"What happened Naseem? Don't I deserve to know?"

"I'm not obliged to tell you," she said, staring at the TV. Ronit looked at her for a moment, and then got up and left. She plodded to the door and banged it after him. Listless, she flopped on the sofa, tears starting. When she heard Manish coming into the room, she hastily wiped her eyes and adjusted her expression to neutral.

"Who was the young fellow?" Manish asked, taking in her smudged face and red eyes.

"Just a friend from college," said Naseem.

"Why are you crying, *pillu*? Did you have an argument with him?" Manish asked in a gentle voice.

"Everything is so difficult, Baba. I don't wish to meet anyone."

"How will that do? You have to go out and face the world. Ma is on her way to recovery, and all of us should help her by going out and leading our lives as normally as we possibly can." He went and sat with her. He thought she would place her head on his shoulder, but she didn't.

"I think I'll go and rest," she said, and left the room.

She didn't have the words to tell him how she felt. Her Ma's trauma had introduced her to guilt. For how could she enjoy a man, knowing what Ma had suffered? Wouldn't that be letting her mother down? How could she explain that each time she thought of Ronit, or pleasure, or of sex in general, her Ma's trauma demanded attention, and it would continue to demand attention possibly for the rest of her life.

Chapter Twenty-Nine
12th May 2016. Time: 12:00

Manish's pulse thundered in his ear as he paced around his bedroom. He picked up his phone, intent on making a call, but then threw the instrument on his bed. His pulse made desperate attempts to get attention but failed. Manish picked up his phone again and dialled Shirish. Shirish's recorded voice requested the caller to leave a message.

"Hey Shirish, let's meet for a beer or something. Not in your posh club. Somewhere quicker and closer. Without family." Manish hung up.

Shirish called back minutes later.

"*Glad you called, buddy. Shall we meet today at eight? Excellent idea to meet without the wives. Looking forward to the beer. You pay the bill this time,*" Shirish laughed but Manish remained silent. "*Everything alright?*" Shirish asked, concern creeping into his voice., "*Bhabhi, Naseem doing well?*"

"Er... want to discuss a few things with you."

"*Work or family?*"

"Family."

"*Don't tell me you're looking for a good divorce lawyer,*" Shirish said with a tinge of hope in his voice. Manish didn't reply, and Shirish rushed to make amends. "*Of course, I'm joking yaar.*"

"Let's meet and we'll talk."

"*Sure. Eight?*"

"Six, if it's alright with you. Need to get home early."

"*Okay. Six it is.*"

With that, Manish ended the call. The thundering in his ear no longer terrified him.

That evening, he peeped into Aparna's room. It pained him to see her staring vacantly at the ceiling.

"Aparna, I'm going to pop out for a while. Will be back at around nine. If you need anything, give me a call," he said. Aparna nodded without looking at him. He went to Naseem's room and knocked. A weary voice asked him to come in. He opened the door and found Naseem lying in bed staring at the home shopping channel.

"Why on earth are you watching that, Naseem? Why don't you go for a walk, meet someone...? On second thoughts, maybe not. Probably best to stay at home. Why don't you do some yoga or Zumba?"

"I'm okay," she said, with a tiny smile.

"I'm nipping out. If you need anything, just give me a call."

As soon as he stepped out of the gloom of the house, his mood soared. Traffic was dense but, for once, that didn't bother him. Families were out in droves on the food street. Tiny Chinese stalls, squeezed in between joints selling pure vegetarian food and spicy mutton kebabs; petite ice cream shops and colourful *Mastani* stores to satisfy saccharine cravings. The street offered food to satisfy the palate of the most demanding customers. As a family, they had sampled myriad cuisines there.

The fifteen-minute drive took an hour. He then drove around for another ten minutes trying to find a place to park. Having found a parking place three lanes away, the heat hit him like a hot shower the second he got out of the car. By the time he reached the destination, his face and back were covered in sweat.

The unpretentious bar had neither frills nor glitz. Ordinary lighting and no music. The furniture consisted of cheap, functional chairs and tables with ashtrays placed in the centre. The place had only one purpose: consumption of alcohol. It was full of males of all ages and sizes in various degrees of inebriation. Seated at a table in a corner, Shirish waved to him as soon as Manish stepped in.

Manish sat down. "Sorry, I'm late. Treacherous traffic."

"Glad you could make it, *dost*," Shirish said, shaking Manish's hands over the table. "The usual?" Manish nodded. "Eh *Chotu*, get us two whiskies and some spicy peanuts," ordered Shirish, waving to a waiter.

The waiter nodded. Soon after, the drinks and peanuts were placed in front of them. Manish's shoulders relaxed as he rested back in his chair and sipped his drink.

"Everything alright at home?" Shirish asked after a few minutes.

Manish hesitated. "Yes..."

"That doesn't sound very convincing."

Manish leaned forwards. "Well, the thing is, I'm worried about Aparna."

"What's happened?"

"No, nothing has happened, as such... umm... but her periodical! It worries me. The times are not good. These goons are everywhere, and they abhor rationality."

"I agree. It's dangerous to go on and on about the ill effects of religion. More specifically, about one religion in particular."

"I know you find her annoying, and it's okay. You're not the only one. She does get fixated on things sometimes. People should speak up, express themselves and all that, but in Aparna's case, it's a question of too much, too often. I feel she should give it a break," Manish said, speeding through the words. "I admire her. There's no doubt about that, but I also need to correct her when she's wrong. She will view this as male domination but it's not. It's simply one individual caring for another." Manish blinked back tears.

Shirish relaxed back in his chair. "How's your sex life?"

Manish's head shot up. "Excuse me?"

"Oh c'mon, we are *langoti yaars*—childhood buddies. Surely, I can ask without you getting all offended on me?"

"Sex life is fine."

"Keep this," said Shirish as he produced a contact card from his wallet and handed it over. "She's a call girl. Escort is the more politically correct term nowadays, I believe," he smirked. "Clean, professional and has her own place. No questions asked and satisfaction guaranteed." He leaned back.

Manish scanned the card as Aparna's disapproving face came into his mind. The ethics of it all were displeasing to him as well. He took pride in being a man who respected women. He couldn't believe that any woman would willingly choose this profession. Whichever way you look at it, it seemed exploitative. But he put the card in his pocket.

"I use her myself. Men have needs. Not all women get this."

Manish took a gulp and grimaced as the drink scorched his throat.

"Why don't you ask Aparna *Bhabhi* to take a break from her writing? Lie low for some time?" Shirish suggested.

"She won't listen. The problem is, I'm worried about... our safety. These goons have killed rationalists before. Stupid to instigate these people."

"I agree. *Bhabhi* is too stubborn. She will always do what she wants."

"I hope the bloody Government changes soon. So many activists jailed for the most frivolous of reasons. The country has changed for the worst," said Manish.

"A-ha. That, my friend, is a topic which will take the entire night to discuss," said Shirish with a laugh, "but you said you wanted to discuss something?"

"Er...well, not exactly."

"Is it *Bhabhi*?"

"No, not really."

"See Manish. I've known you since childhood. *Arre*, it's difficult to take on the hassle of these feminist types. Not worth it. Now that you have, show them who is the boss in the house.

173

Very difficult otherwise. Can give you countless examples."

"Shirish, it's nothing like that," Manish coughed. "What are feminist types anyway?"

"Aparna *Bhabhi*, for example."

Manish shook his head.

"They don't allow a man to feel like a man. That's why I've given you that card," Shirish said smirking.

There was a pause.

"Don't agree," Manish mumbled.

"Well?" Shirish asked. "Are you going to tell me?"

"It's nothing specific, Shirish," Manish said as alcohol streamed through his blood. Shirish did not pester him further. The men sat back and relaxed. After a while words became redundant as the men appreciated their drink in peace.

Manish looked at his watch. "Time to go."

"You okay to drive?"

"Of course."

"Well, drive home safely," Shirish slurred.

Manish raised a shaky hand in reply.

His journey home was much shorter. Though he was annoying at times, with a dodgy ideology and a warped understanding of feminism which made disclosures difficult, his childhood friend had managed to calm his fraught nerves. Manish decided to meet Shirish more often.

The house was silent and dark when he walked in. As expected, the women had not moved from their rooms. He changed in his own room and gargled with a strong mouthwash, remembering last week, when Aparna jerked away from the whiff of alcohol on his breath. She startled easily these days, jumping at any sudden or unexpected noise. Unexplained aches and pains without any apparent cause had also besieged her. He prepared a black coffee for himself. Sleep eluded him, anyway.

Chapter Thirty
13ᵗʰ May 2016. Time: 15:00

The doorbell rang. Manish went to open the door and found a policeman standing outside.

"Aparna Soman?" The policeman asked in a gruff tone.

"Yes," Manish replied. "How can I help you?"

"I've come to deliver this summons to her. Ask her to be present at the police station on the 1ˢᵗ of June at 9 am."

"Summons? For what?"

"A police case has been registered against her. All details are in there," he indicated the sealed envelope. "Sign this to confirm delivery."

"Hold on, she's not in a condition to meet anyone right now," Manish protested.

"I don't know anything about that. Please can you sign? I have to leave."

Manish signed the piece of paper that the policeman thrust towards him. The policeman took the signed paper and left. Manish opened the envelope. A case had been registered against Aparna under section 295A of the Indian Penal Code, for deliberate and malicious acts intended to outrage religious feelings by insulting religion or religious beliefs.

Holding his stomach, he laughed. He went to Aparna's room and showed her the summons.

"You wished to normalise blasphemy, didn't you? Well, they found that blasphemous," he said, throwing the summons on the bed next to her. "How many fools were offended this time? Who knows?"

"What is it?" Aparna asked in her tired voice. She was lying, as she usually did, staring into the air.

"A summons asking you to be present at the police station. There are calls for your arrest."

Aparna was too tired to react. She read the piece of paper, folded it, and placed it under her pillow. Then she continued to stare at the ceiling fan.

How can they do this? Manish thought. *What kind of a bizarre joke are we in? There must be something we can do. We must get a lawyer. Can we afford one? We can always sell one of the houses. Does her tweet even break the law? I'm fairly certain that the case has no merit, but does that matter? Harassment is the main intention here. Harassment of dissenters.*

He looked outside and was alarmed to see a media crew waiting outside his gate. He switched on the TV and was aghast to see headlines about Aparna's tweet broadcast on all news channels. The call she made for preventing hate was attracting hate. The news was just breaking, and debates were being held on most news channels:

"Freedom of expression versus religious sentiments. What would you choose?"

"We have never given priority to freedom of speech and expression. We forced exile on world-renowned painter MK Hussain for painting nude Hindu deities. We did not see the art - all we saw was a Muslim painting Hindu gods in the nude. We banned Salman Rushdie's book because we didn't want to offend Muslims. There is no reason to believe we will act differently now."

"Hindu religion has always been ignored because we are peace-loving people. Ask her to say the same about Islam. Would she dare?"

"Why should I listen to insults about my religion? Don't I have any human rights? Don't I have the right to practise my faith peacefully?"

"I've been reading the rubbish that this woman writes. Her writings are filled with anti-Hindu sentiments. Ban her magazine and arrest her."

He switched off the TV. Fearfully, he sneaked a look at Aparna's Twitter account. It had exploded with trolls spewing hate, threatening Aparna and her family. A few of them had posted Naseem's picture detailing the list of things they would do to her if Aparna did not stop authoring hate-filled articles about their religion.

The thundering in his ear started again. He picked up the phone and dialled 100.

"Police control room."

"I want to report an online threat."

"Call up the cyber cell for that."

"No. I'm not going to."

"What exactly is the problem?"

"They're threatening to r——sexually assault my daughter. They're threatening to disfigure her face. Burn her alive. Register my complaint and arrest those criminals."

"Give me your name, please."

"Manish Joshi."

There was a pause. *"Aparna Soman's husband?"*

"Yes. Write down the complaint, please."

"Not to worry sir. We will pass this on to the cyber cell. They will track down those accounts in no time at all."

"If anything... if *anything* happens to my daughter in the meantime, I will personally hold the Pune police responsible."

"Don't worry, Saheb. Trust us."

"Please. Do things quickly. Our lives are at stake."

"You have my assurance, Saheb. Don't worry."

Manish checked the news which informed him that six states had now registered cases against Aparna, and the number was expected to rise even further.

He rang Shirish.

"I was about to call you... just saw on TV. Bloody hell! What the hell is happening?"

"Shirish, I need a good lawyer."

"Of course. Let me speak to a few people and I will get back to you with a name. How is Bhabhi?"

"She's asleep."

"Sleeping? Manish, this is no time to sleep!"

"Shirish, you don't know the pressure we're under."

"Hey! I understand, buddy. Look, my suggestion would be to keep a couple of security guards around the house until this thing dies down, as it surely will."

"But all these cases against Aparna in different states... how do we handle it all?"

"Don't worry. There are ways. Just lie low until things die down."

"I'm worried, Shirish. Things are so bad, I'm scared of letting Naseem out of the house," Manish said, his voice breaking.

"It would be good to stay at home for a couple of days. I don't know whether Bhabhi *will agree though."*

"She isn't herself these days. She hasn't been feeling great for the last few days."

"Well, take care. This will be over soon. I'll do what I can," said Shirish.

"Shirish, is the offence bailable? Will she get bail?" Manish could not keep the desperate tone out of his voice.

"I'm not sure. You let the lawyer handle it all. Let's just hope for the best."

"Thanks, *dost*. I would have liked to have a whiskey together soon, but I don't know whether it's possible now."

"Don't worry and take care." Shirish said goodbye and hung up.

Manish googled section 295A and stared at the words his search had thrown up: *The offence committed under Section 295A is cognisable and a non-bailable and non-compoundable offence. Non-bailable offence means that a person arrested would not have the right to be released on bail soon after arrest. In this case, it is at the discretion of the court to grant or refuse to grant bail.*

Chapter Thirty-One
14th May 2016. Time: 20:00

Aparna sat at her writing desk, holding her head in her hands as she thought. *I have ceased to think of those goons as individual entities who have committed a crime. I think of them as a single homogenous mass. A rotting, reeking mass of fanaticism rendered blind by religion. A rot that goes right to the top echelons of power. How does one fight the offshoots of a government gone rogue? The foot soldiers, the toadies, the delusional, and the supremacists. When an army of criminals is created to threaten, torture, assault, murder and intimidate voices of dissent. When an atmosphere of fear is created to stifle rationality. When the media, the judiciary, and all other institutions that signal the democratic credentials of nations are controlled. When fake news is used to spin a narrative. Where judges are purchased to pass favourable judgements. When even the political leaders that have won elections from rival political parties are purchased using huge sums of money. An impotent population of 1.3 billion hungry for peace, prosperity, and a corruption-free environment, yet unable or unwilling to keep a rogue government in check. A huge mass of people that have traded the very things they hunger for—peace, prosperity, and a corruption-free environment—for one thing only: religious supremacy.*

Lifting her head, she gazed at the wall opposite.

The individual criminals who perpetrated this crime against me will be arrested. My fight is broader—it is against the power that has galvanised its forces to assault a woman to ensure she remains mute.

She brushed off an unexpected tear with her hand impatiently.

There is nothing new in women being blamed. It is the norm. My case is no different. Ultimately, they will all get together and blame me. Why did you express such a radical opinion? They will say. Couldn't you have toned it down a little, coated your view in jaggery, made it more banal; more acceptable, more satisfactory to the goons and society in order to avoid trouble? Couldn't you sit on the fence with your opinions, they will say, instead of being so in your face?

They will all blame me for expressing an unacceptable view. A view unacceptable to the majority. Yes, even those closest to me——my loved ones will find a way to blame me.

She left her tears untouched.

Will I be able to fight their clout without forfeiting myself as a wife and a mother? And isn't this finally about Aparna, the woman? Not Aparna, the mother or Aparna, the wife. Will it all be worth it in the end?

Chapter Thirty-Two
16th May 2016. Time: 13:00

Their dining room circulated an air of melancholy like residual memories after a favourite child's departure. The carefully selected paintings created by renowned artists looked ashamed to be surrounded by such misery. Aparna had requested a family meeting. The three of them, listless, huddled around the dining table.

"I've decided to speak out," said Aparna, in a clear voice.

The old Aparna is back, Manish thought, jubilant. The humdrum sounds of the afternoon outside the dismal room—birds chirping, the cacophony of horns, vendors calling out, children laughing, domestic staff gossiping—managed to bring in some cheer.

"Speak out? How?" Manish asked, leaning towards her.

"I've decided to go public," said Aparna, looking at Manish first, and then Naseem, her gaze steady in her hollowed face. "I will speak to the media," she said in an eager voice.

Naseem shoulders sagged as her vacant eyes looked to the floor.

"About what?" Manish asked, a hint of a frown on his forehead.

"About the extent they went to," said Aparna. "My silence will only encourage these cowards. They will continue to kill, maim, torture and assault. They're banking on my silence, but I will speak. How dare they stop diverse, radical ideas? They mustn't be allowed to get away with this."

"Ma, don't. Haven't you been through enough? Haven't all of us had enough? Let's just put this behind us," said Naseem.

"I can't," said Aparna, miserably.

Manish squeezed Aparna's shoulder. "Aparna, it's not only your decision to make. All of us are in this together."

"With due respect, I'm the one who had to suffer the consequences. Don't I have the exclusive right to decide?"

He sighed. "What do you hope to achieve by doing this?"

"Make a statement. If I don't, then who will?" said Aparna, looking out of the window.

Manish shook his head. "It's not safe. These men are dangerous... the political environment is dangerous."

"That's why I must speak up. When my situation becomes public, they will hesitate to try anything new. The public will support me. I have full faith... full atheist faith."

No one smiled.

"You're giving them a lot of credit. Don't forget, these cults, organisations, offshoots, loonies—whatever you want to call them—have killed before. They don't care."

Naseem held her mother's hand. "Ma, please don't do this."

Aparna's face puckered. "Naseem, don't you understand? We mustn't give in to patriarchy, remember? I want to overcome this. I must do this to feel better. Nothing else works."

"I won't be able to show my face in college."

Aparna pulled back slightly. "Why not? Are you afraid of being called the daughter of a rape survivor?"

"Aparna, that's harsh. And unfair. Your decision affects all of us," Manish said.

"Then, I guess it's time for you two to pay the price of being my husband and daughter. Whoever said it was easy being married to me? Or being born to me?"

"Aparna, our daughter has her life ahead of her. Is it right to hamper her future? It will even affect her marriage prospects."

"A-ha. Spoken like a true Indian male. Why would Naseem wish to marry anyone who would judge *her* for what happened to her mother? Naseem, can't you see? There's no shame in this."

Naseem pursed her lips, shuffling on her seat.

"Aparna, you understand Indian society. You know how their minds work."

"But, what has this got to do with Naseem?" Aparna asked.

"Ma, don't. You're asking for too much. It will even take its toll on *you*."

"Naseem, I've always put you first, but this is something I need to do. I'm lucky not to be killed, they said. It's time to show them, yes, I'm lucky to be not killed."

"Aparna, your interview will not make the slightest difference to anybody other than us."

"I don't agree, Manish——"

"Ma, don't," said Naseem in a small voice.

"We're voiceless right now, but my voice will initiate a dialogue. It will prevent the bullying that goes on in the name of culture and religion. There's so much to do!"

"Aparna, let us think calmly. Think about this for a few days, and then decide."

"My mind is unlikely to change."

Naseem stood up and walked to the window, gazing out. "Why can't you think of me even for a moment?"

"There goes the princess throwing a tantrum. Naseem, I have given you the best part of my life, putting you first always. I'm sorry you're unable to see that. I can't keep thinking of your wishes first all the time. I have to do this."

Naseem turned on her. "Well, you shouldn't have given me the best part of your life, then," she shouted. "Did I ask you to breastfeed me? Did I ask you to dedicate your life to me? It was your bloody decision all along. But I'm asking you, requesting you, begging you... don't carry out this crazy plan of yours. You want to reinforce the very point that has offended them? Can't you even see how this will affect all of us? Are you that blind? Baba will be ridiculed. Don't you care even a little? Put out a public apology for that irresponsible tweet of yours. Apologise and take back your call for normalising blasphemy."

Naseem's hands were shaking.

"You're crazy! You want me to apologise to those goons? Never!"

Naseem's voice cracked. "Well then, there's nothing more to discuss. Normality will end the moment you speak up. For you, me and Baba."

"My mind is made up," Aparna said quietly.

"I feel like killing myself," said Naseem.

"Stop with the melodrama. It's time you grow up."

"Aparna, think this through," Manish said.

"See you on the other side. We'll see what happens. To all of us," Aparna smiled.

Naseem yelled, "It's about you all the fucking time, isn't it? You and your ridiculous ideals. I'm bloody tired of all this. I'm sick of having a dysfunctional mother."

And so, the nurturing goes for a toss in the nature versus nurture debate. This girl, my daughter, whom I lovingly nurtured with my feminist ideas, goes all patriarchal on me. I seem to have failed. Not as a mother, but as a feminist. "I need tea," said Aparna, rising.

BOOK FOUR

Chapter Thirty-Three
6th May 2014. Time: 12:00

Two years after his daughter's birth, Hari hoped for a son, but despite his best efforts (he made Lata narrate thirteen different *shlokas)*, Lata could not conceive. Kashi would remain their only child.

When Kashi was five, she was besotted with a stray dog loitering in the neighbourhood. After feeding him scraps of *bhakri* for two consecutive days, the dog parked himself permanently outside their house waiting for Kashi, and then followed her everywhere after she emerged. He was a scruffy, skinny creature, but Kashi was smitten.

"Don't bring that dirty mongrel inside the house," Lata shouted.

"Aai, he wants to be a part of the family too. I've named him Ganu, short for Ganesha."

"You cannot name him after a god, you little fool," hissed Lata.

"But why? I love him," protested Kashi, hugging the dog.

"You can't. Dogs are dirty. They don't wash their bums. Call him something else. If your father finds out, he will be very angry."

Kashi, held onto Lata's sari, refusing to let go. "He won't. Ganu is such a nice name."

"Ugh! Don't touch me after you've touched that dirty beast. Go and wash your hands at once. You don't know what diseases he is carrying."

That afternoon at lunch, Kashi hollered, "Baba, why can't I have a tail?"

Hari looked up, speechless. Lata, worried about an eruption, muttered inconsequential words which made no sense but softened the sudden silence. Then Hari laughed, and the room became happier.

"Why do you want a tail? Yuck! Dirty little things hanging off bums."

Kashi giggled. "Tails are not dirty, Baba. I so want one. Please can you get one for me?"

The family laughed and thought that was the end of it, but Kashi kept up a constant refrain of wanting a tail. Finally, Hari fashioned one out of a towel for her. She stuck it in her knickers and frolicked with Ganu.

"She will forget about it tomorrow," Hari said, in a low voice.

"Thank God for that," Lata sighed.

Kashi did not forget. The tail, tightly tucked in her knickers, mocked them again the next day.

What's with the child? Is she going to carry the tail for the rest of her life? Lata worried about her daughter. That afternoon, she spotted Kashi lifting Ganu's tail and peering underneath. Lata caught hold of Kashi by her frock and dragged her away from the dog.

"I was just looking at the attachment. His tail is attached differently to mine," said Kashi.

That night, Lata narrated the incident to Hari. "Her behaviour is abnormal. Instead of playing with dolls, she is interested in mongrels and their tails!"

Hari grunted. "Don't worry. I will teach her shlokas. The act of memorisation will help her."

The next morning, after Kashi had her bath and was about to go out to play, Hari stopped her. "Today, I'm going to teach you something new."

"What?"

"A new shloka. If you chant this shloka every time you have a bath, you will feel refreshed and have more energy."

"I don't want to," said Kashi, the tail hanging resolutely behind her. "I already have lots of energy. See." She flexed her arm muscles to show him.

"Kashi. Wait. You will find this interesting." He led her by the hand and made her sit in front of him. As he chanted, a glazed look appeared on her face and then she nodded off despite the morning hour.

Hari got up in disgust. Lata did not have the same fondness for shlokas that Hari did, so Kashi was left alone.

When the time came to choose a school, Lata wanted to send her to the posh, English-medium convent school which had opened in the neighbourhood. Hari wasn't keen, but Lata assured him, "The language does not matter. Beliefs are important. She is your daughter and will not do anything to tarnish your good name."

"Do what you want," Hari said. "English or Marathi, she will be flying off to her husband's home anyway."

Kashi's antics continued. One day, Lata caught her putting rice and dal in the Tulsi *vrindavan* in the courtyard.

"You naughty girl. Why are you wasting food? Don't you know there are lots of hungry children in our country?"

"Not wasting food, Aai, just feeding it to our Tulsi," said Kashi. "We give her water but never any food. She must be hungry."

Lata peered into the pot and saw a mound of rice and dal along with scraps of *bhakri*. Maggots swarmed due to the moist heat. Lata grabbed Kashi's arm, dragged her inside the house and scrubbed her hands clean.

"Should we ask a doctor or someone about her? Her behaviour isn't normal," Lata complained.

Sitting on the sofa in his vest, Hari was reading a newspaper article on the reproduction rate of Muslims and answered without looking up. "Umm? She will grow out of it."

A dancing bear visited the neighbourhood that week. Peering out of her window, Lata was aghast to see Kashi engaged in a deep conversation with the bear man.

"Kashi come back in at once," shouted Lata, going out. *What is the girl up to now? She could easily get kidnapped. People are always on the lookout for fair girls.*

"What were you doing?" she asked when Kashi flopped in.

"I was asking him if he would be willing to leave the bear with us for a few days," said Kashi.

"Are you mad? What is wrong with you, child?"

"I just wanted to observe the differences between bears and dogs, that's all," said Kashi with a look of surprise on her face. "Don't worry Aai, I would have fed him food from my own plate."

When Kashi was ten years old, her schoolteacher summoned her parents.

"Kashi's teacher has asked me to meet her. God knows what the girl has done now," Lata said to Hari. Hari had no words of reassurance to offer, and Lata spent the night worrying.

The next day, dark circles prominent under her eyes, Lata set off for her meeting.

"Good afternoon, Mrs Sabnis. Thank you for coming in," an eager teacher with brown, curly bobbed hair said to her in English.

"Er, I will speak in Hindi…" Lata stammered. "My English not good."

"Of course. No problem," the teacher said, smiling.

"What has my daughter done, madam?"

"A week back, I told my class the story of Madame Marie Curie," the teacher said.

Sweat glistened on Lata's forehead. "Marie Curie… who is she?"

"A famous scientist! The passion with which she pursued her research on radioactivity despite hardships fascinated young Kashi." The teacher smiled again, but Lata could only stare back. "Kashi dug up a copy of a book on Curie's life from the school library and now spends her free time engrossed in the pages."

Lata's eyes widened.

"Your daughter is fascinated with science, Mrs Sabnis! Encourage her curiosity. Get her books on science. If you can, allow her to join extra science clubs. Nurture her interest and watch her flourish."

At last, a smile appeared on Lata's face.

"Really?" she asked softly.

"Yes. You've got an intelligent child who is curious about the world around her. Encourage her curiosity."

That evening, when Hari came home from work, he saw his wife and daughter at the dining table, the fan whirring above their heads. Lata was sifting the rice grains for maggots and Kashi had her head in a big book of scientists. It was half past six. Lights were switched on in the Sabnis household exactly at seven, but for some reason which Hari attributed solely to Kashi, the lights had been switched on earlier that day.

"Why do I constantly see you reading books by British and American authors? Where are the Indian authors?" Hari asked as he took off his shirt and hung it on the rail in the corner.

Kashi looked up and said earnestly, "I read Indian authors too, Baba. Look at the wonderful discoveries these scientists have made. See, there are Indian scientists here too—Aryabhatta, Homi Bhabha, CV Raman and several others. It's so much fun to read about them."

"All the discoveries you're reading about were made in India ages ago. The West simply stole our knowledge and inventions. We had technology long before other countries. It says so in our Vedas," Hari said.

"Where's the proof, Baba?" Kashi asked.

"The proof is in the Vedas. You should read it someday. You will get answers to all your questions," said Hari.

"You mean Newton, Einstein are wrong?"

"They've stolen knowledge from our ancient books," Hari said. "We documented it all long before them."

191

Kashi pouted, crossing her arms across her chest.

Hari growled, "These bloody English schools!"

"Kashi's teacher was praising her a lot today. She says Kashi has developed a passion for science which must be nurtured. We must buy science books for her. Are there any science clubs around that she can join?" said Lata.

The girl couldn't recite a single line of shloka. It's a wonder she is doing well in school, thought Hari and ignored Lata's suggestion.

But Lata wasn't willing to give up so easily. She scrimped, saved and purchased all the required aids for her daughter. When her own funds fell short, she nagged Hari until he gave in.

"I want to become a scientist when I grow up," Kashi announced at lunch one day, and Lata's face glistened with pride.

Afterwards, when Kashi discovered the Internet, it made her feel complete. Finally, she could get valid and verifiable answers to all her queries.

"There is a lot of information out there. Don't just read everything you come across. Ensure it's from a trustworthy source," her teacher explained.

With that advice firmly lodged in her mind, Kashi set forth, towards what she hoped would be a life full of science and rationality.

Chapter Thirty-Four
16th March 2016. Time: 16:00

A few days after her seventeenth birthday, with a pencil secured behind her ear, Kashi was jotting down relevant points from a science video she was watching for her college assignment. It was almost four and she was hungry. With just a few minutes left for the video to end, she wondered whether to hoist herself up to go to the kitchen for some crunchy nibbles which she knew her mother had fried the previous day. The video ended but she continued to watch, her attention arrested by another video which had started playing automatically as soon as the first one ended.

"I grew up in an environment of rationality. We don't have idols of gods or goddesses at home. The women in my family don't restrict themselves in any way due to religion. In my opinion, religion is not always kind to women." A pretty girl was uttering these shocking words in confident tones in the video that had grabbed Kashi's attention.

Kashi watched, riveted.

Who is she? How and why doesn't she believe in gods? Do girls like her exist? Girls, who belong to families who do not worship! Why haven't I met one before?

"I grew up as an atheist humanist, and I will remain one until I die. No problem, however insurmountable, is going to make me turn towards religion," the girl continued.

How audacious she is about religion. What kind of a family allows this?

Atheist humanist! Kashi looked up the meaning of the term. *Why haven't I heard this term before? In my world, nurtured by religion, atheism is offensive, an impossibility. Why haven't I met any atheist in my life? Why didn't my school ever discuss atheism?*

She paused the video and minimised it, to sneak a quick look at the title. It was an interview with the daughters of women achievers from Pune.

Hmm, so she is the daughter of some woman achiever. Let's see what and how much her mother has achieved.

Kashi waited for the video to end to see the name of the girl. *Naseem Joshi.* The name flashed on the screen.

She searched for the name online. Daughter of rationalist and anti-superstition campaigner, Aparna Soman, the search results informed her.

Rationalist? Anti-superstition campaigner? What in the wide world is that?

She hunted for Aparna's social media profile and scanned Aparna's tweets.

Why doesn't her husband or father stop her? How can they allow her to write this way?

Following the links, she fired up the Rationalist and Anti-Superstition Society website.

They counter superstition with facts!

Her hunger forgotten, she scratched her head as she read a list of the most commonly followed superstitions in the nation. In a few minutes, she had ravaged their entire website, hungrily reading all the words.

I am a person of science, and yet I believe every superstition on this list! How could I have been so ignorant? And so stupid.

She looked at the wall opposite, on which hung the Hindu calendar and her mind traversed forbidden places. *What would an atheist life be like? A life with no restrictions! Freedom to mingle even when I'm on my period. Freedom to cut my nails and wash my hair on any day of the week. Freedom to eat all kinds of food. But best of all, the freedom to think without guilt. A place in my mind where ideas are free.*

A tiny possibility opened in her mind. A minor freedom. And a temptation.

But then, I will also lose the security that religion offers. I will start to fear death.

I envy Naseem, but not enough to turn into an atheist myself. I will always be a believer. But can a scientist be a believer? Can science peacefully co-exist with religion? Who should I ask? Someone like Naseem or her mother?

She learned that the society was seeking volunteers. The idea soaked in her head for two days. On the third afternoon, when her mother was folding freshly washed clothes, Kashi showed her a printed copy of the call for volunteers and said, "Aai, look here, this organisation that busts superstitions is keen for more volunteers. I thought of volunteering and busting some superstitions. Volunteering for such an organisation will be so cool!"

"You will not volunteer for any such organisation. There must be some Muslim agenda behind it all. Keep away from it," commanded Lata in a low voice.

"No, Aai. Muslims have got nothing to do with it. The organisation busts miracles performed by Godmen. Volunteers perform miracles, like the Godmen do, in front of believers, but then they explain the scientific theory behind the miracle. Fascinating stuff. I'd love to volunteer my time with the organisation."

"Hindu Godmen?"

"It doesn't say."

"Are you crazy? We're not like those people. We believe in a culture of peace. Our religion shows us the true path and will enlighten us."

Kashi made an exasperated sound. "This isn't to do with religion. It's about superstition—superstitions that harm. In fact, most of the traditions we follow don't stand the test of rationality."

What is wrong with this child? Where does she learn these things? If I give her too much freedom she will get out of our hands. "Keep away from these people, Kashi. They do not believe in God."

"Yes. That's true. Isn't that shocking?"

"It's stupid. That's what it is. My faith protects me from harm. I feel secure with a god looking after me. It prevents me from doing wrong."

"They say religion is just a comfort blanket."

"And what's wrong in having a comfort blanket?" Lata asked, "God knows, I need one."

"You just don't understand, Aai," Kashi said, walking off in a huff.

Afterwards, she left a comment under one of Aparna's tweets. *I'm fascinated with the work you do and would love to get involved.*

Just as she was about to log out, after completing her assignment that evening, Hari marched into the room and whacked Kashi on the back of her head.

The unexpected blow stunned her. With eyes full shock and indignation, she glared at her father and touched the back of her head gingerly. Her father never hit her. Nostrils flared, eyebrows in a frown, she inhaled deeply.

"How dare you correspond with that obnoxious woman?" Hari yelled with eyes full of angry betrayal.

She stared at him and said quietly, "What are you talking about?"

"That bitch. The Aparna Soman woman. I read your tweet," Hari spluttered.

Lata hurried in and made scared, consoling noises.

It took Kashi a few minutes to understand what he was talking about.

"How can you hit me like that?" she said. "The law——"

"Hush, hush Kashi," Lata buzzed in. "Don't say anything."

"What did you say?" Hari advanced towards Kashi, but Lata got in the way. "You are teaching me law now? You? The midget who was born yesterday?"

"I don't know why you're so angry. For one message?" Kashi said in a small voice. Then she saw her mother cowering and wringing her hands. Kashi's jaws and neck muscles tightened as she said in a louder voice, "Most of our traditions are illogical. In fact, they can be harmful to us. Now, this practice of covering the walls and the ground with cow dung—"

Hari pushed Lata out of the way and whacked Kashi again.

Lata rushed to her side and looked up at Hari, "No, no. Please don't."

"She reminds me of those English-speaking bitches from college," Hari shouted.

"If you hit me again, I will call the police," Kashi said.

"Kashi, stop talking, please," Lata whimpered.

"What have you been reading, Kashi?" Hari asked in a tight voice.

"Nothing. Just the website of the Rationalist and Anti-Superstition Society. They have a list of regressive traditions we follow, and a rational reason for why they're harmful. They have all these amazing women working for them. I thought I'll volunteer my time there."

"Over your dead body," Hari snarled. "And what is this photo of the woman doing here?" he shouted, pointing to a photo of Aparna Soman from a newspaper clipping Kashi had stuck to a desk board.

Kashi remained silent.

Hari ripped off the newspaper and threw it out of the window. "Have you seen the incidents of divorces in the West? Now, you bloody want to imitate them?" he bellowed, glaring at Kashi.

"But..."

"Anti-superstition is just another label for anti-religion. A lot of people have problems with our religion. Some, like those missionaries, are eager to convert us to their own religion. Never did I think that my own daughter would fall for the vile

197

tactics of these people. I hold you responsible," he said, pointing his index finger at Lata.

Lata mumbled something inaudible.

"They are anti-superstition, not anti-religion," Kashi said quietly.

"If I see you gallivanting with those fools, you've had it." With that, he strode out of the room and left the house, banging the door after him.

Lata rushed to her daughter, cradling her head in her arms. "Did he hit hard? Does it hurt?" Tears flowed from her eyes. "Don't answer him back, Kashi. Let him vent. Don't debate with him. It's disrespectful. I can't bear him hitting you. Please, Kashi."

Kashi's body slumped as she allowed her own tears to flow.

"What is wrong with him?" she cried. "He cannot threaten me like this."

"Listen to him, Kashi," Lata said. "Just listen to him."

"I can't, Aai. I have a mind, too."

That night, Kashi went to bed with thoughts of rebellion crawling in her head like maggots over rotting food. Her father had forbidden her to interact with Aparna Soman, but it didn't matter. *I can always create another social media ID under a pseudonym.* Behind her late-night thoughts, a singular one rankled: *Why was Baba reading Aparna Soman's tweets?* And then: *How can I protect myself from him?*

Chapter Thirty-Five
17th March 2016. Time: 09:00

Standing outside the office of the Rationalist and Anti-Superstition Society at nine in the morning, in a professional *salvar kameez*, a nervous Kashi rang the bell. A tall woman, dressed in a white cotton sari, with greying hair and Gandhiji glasses, opened the door. She looked like what her father would have called "the activist type".

"I'm here for the interview," Kashi said.

"Of course," the woman said, leading her inside. "Do come in. I'm Kumudini, by the way." She led her into the room which doubled as an office. There was no one else around.

"I'm so glad to meet you, ma'am. I've read everything about you."

Kumudini smiled. "Will you like to have a kokam sherbet?"

"No, thank you." Kashi smiled back and relaxed her shoulders.

"We have a very informal setting," Kumudini explained. "Do sit down." She indicated the mattress. "Let me quickly get your CV." She went to a wall shelf, shuffled some papers and came back with one in her hand. She sat on the opposite mattress, the paper on her lap.

"Why do you want to volunteer with us?" Kumudini queried.

Kashi thought of giving a safe and politically correct answer, but she couldn't. "To be perfectly honest, I come from a religious orthodox family, and I'm a believer. Yet, my passion is science. I discovered the work of your society fairly recently, and believe me, I'm enthralled by your activists. Your thought process, your ideology is so new to me. New, but appealing. I want to stretch my mind and expose it to ideas that will challenge it. I want to discover myself," she said.

Kumudini smiled. "What about your studies? You're studying..." She paused as she looked at Kashi's CV.

"A BSc degree in Genetic Science. In my first year now, hoping to qualify as a research scientist in two years."

"Very good, but do you have the time to volunteer? What about your studies?"

"I can spare one hour every day in the afternoon. My lectures take place in the morning. Other than my lectures and studying time, I'm willing to dedicate my time to the society."

"Several youngsters who join us have this image of travelling to remote villages and bringing to account the Godmen and Godwomen. The work we do requires a lot of filing and paperwork. We haven't moved our information to the computers yet. The work is office-based."

"Yes, that's fine. I want to help in any way I can."

"Well, good. You may start from tomorrow."

"Er... Aparna Soman... is she not here?"

Kumudini laughed. "So, you've heard about our most famous campaigner. Don't worry. You will get to meet her soon."

"I'd really like that," Kashi gushed.

"Well, see you soon. Hope you enjoy working with us."

Kashi waved and left for home. After her father's outburst the other day, she had no plans to disclose her activities to them. Surreptitiously, she started volunteering for the Rationalist and Anti-Superstition Society.

On the third day of her volunteering, she met Aparna Soman. Aparna's entrance was a disruption, impacting everything that came in her way. Within an hour after meeting Kashi, Aparna used a deadly swear-word against some injustice that she narrated. Kashi was shocked. *Nope. I do not like this woman. What kind of a woman swears like this?* But then she analysed this. *It's not about the swearing. She is unafraid of judgement. That's what it is! And it's refreshing.* When Aparna mentioned that her husband cooked more often than her, Kashi was flummoxed. *What kind of a woman makes her husband cook for her? What kind of a man cooks?* When Aparna aggressively vocalised equal rights for women, Kashi hoped some of Aparna's defiance and strength would diffuse into her. *She is outrageous. She is outspoken. She is fierce. I want to be like her.*

After volunteering at the society for a month, Kashi created two neat compartments in her mind. One compartment was for home. Within this compartment, foremost was respect: respect for authority, respect for her parents, respect for religion, respect for traditions. Her primary role in that compartment was to obey and never question. It was ruled by emotions and duty. But then, this other compartment lurked behind the first one. Within this, she allowed her mind to enter forbidden areas. Allowed her thoughts to sweep over the enforced boundaries. She became the Sita who crossed the Laxman Rekha. She dared to dream. To be brazen, audacious and outrageous. This compartment was ruled by aspirations, facts, rationality, and logic. *Which Kashi will emerge stronger? I don't know and I'm in no hurry to discover.*

Her daily visits to the society's office became an addiction. Hari did not have a clue about the detour in his daughter's life, but that was the least of his worries because Kashi was grappling with something much bigger than her infatuation with Aparna. Something that had the potential to disrupt their life.

Chapter Thirty-Six
19th March 2016. Time: 23:00

It was almost eleven. The lights of the Sabnis household were switched off but Kashi couldn't sleep. After her grandfather's death, her parents occupied the bedroom while she slept on her grandfather's small cot in the living room. She got up in the dark and went to the closed door of her parents' bedroom. She listened. Their deep breathing through the closed door assured her they were asleep.

Kashi got her torch and diary out from under her cot mattress . By the light of her torch, she scribbled in her diary:

An unbuttoned blouse here. The smooth curvature of a waist there. Lush, dark tresses and long, slender backs. Eyes that smile. An intelligence that banters. A wave of dopamine that unleashes itself on me unexpectedly. Longings feel like an adversary impossible to defeat. Meeting the eyes of a stranger across a room... sensing that she has similar inclinations. Enticed by body parts on surreptitious display. Totally dry on the entry of macho Bollywood heroes, but an unequivocal proof of my lust when a voluptuous heroine enters, gyrating to the music. Once upon a time, my country created the Kamasutra *which views gay love as an art form to be engaged in and enjoyed, but now my nation proudly proclaims that no lesbians grace her shores. Lesbians are invisible here. I'm unsure. I want proof. Further proof. And I've got a plan.*

Kashi read what she had written. A sudden fear consumed her. She tore off the page into tiny pieces, rushed to the toilet, and flushed them away. Her diary and the torch went back under her mattress as she made desperate attempts to sleep.

An hour later, she sat up. *This won't do. I must put my plan into action.*

Chapter Thirty-Seven
20th March 2016. Time: 11:00

For several months, Kashi had been aware of the wistful looks Suhas gave her in class. During lectures, whenever their eyes met, he threw looks full of shameless longing at her. During the lunch hour in the college canteen, he tried to hover within her gaze. Sometimes when she looked at him, he swept his hand over his hair in typical Bollywood style. For Valentine's Day, he had bowed before her and given her a red rose, consuming her friends with laughter. She had missed a class, one day. The next day, when she arrived on campus, he crooned a Bollywood song about a lover missing his sweetheart. It was obvious. He had the hots for her.

That morning, Kashi went to college earlier than her usual time. Standing tall against the wall of the main porch, she waited. There was still half an hour before the lectures started, so she had plenty of time. She waited for twenty minutes, shifting weight impatiently from one foot to the other. With just five minutes left for the lecture to start, she spotted Suhas trudging in through the main gate, looking as if he had just got out of bed. Kashi straightened her posture which had slumped as the minutes progressed, and gave her hair a pat.

She went up to Suhas whose eyes ignited as he saw her approach him, and asked, "Do you want to kiss me?"

A glint of joy mingled with mischief sprang in Suhas's eyes.

He's not going to back off due to shyness. I'm glad I've chosen him for my little experiment.

"Er... now?" he asked.

"Yes," she said throatily.

"Miss the lectures?" he whispered.

"Yes." She lowered her eyes seductively like a Bollywood goddess.

Suhas leered. Brushing his hand lightly over his lips, he made a spluttery kissing sound with his lips.

What a fool! Kashi thought. *This country should give young men lessons on how to interact with girls. But no backing out. My experiment continues.* "Meet me behind the toilets. No one will be there at this time. It won't take long."

Suhas gave her a salute and sprinted to the location. Kashi saw his thin, eager bum scampering to the toilets. Sighing, she trudged to their place of rendezvous. Leaning against the wall with the help of his right elbow, his right leg crossed over the left with the right toe pointed and resting on the ground, he had struck up a ridiculous pose while he waited for her with a glint of impatient mischief in his eyes. Lust poured from his face. He smacked his lips again.

Kashi arrived and suppressed a laugh as she looked at him. A choking sound escaped her. He looked at her enquiringly, but she gave a nonchalant wave of her head to indicate everything was alright.

She stood in front of him. He held her waist and brought her close. His hug was so tight, her ribs hurt. Kashi tolerated the loud smack on her lips. But when he tried to put his tongue in her mouth and spluttered, Kashi couldn't bear it. Gently, she freed herself and wiped her lips with her sleeve.

"What?" Suhas asked.

"I used you and I'm sorry for that," she said gently, preparing to leave.

He wiped his lips suggestively. "No problem, darling. You can use me as much as you want." He grinned.

Kashi fled.

That night, she smiled to herself. *No more confusion. I feel relieved and excited about my life ahead. But how do I go about it? Why can't I see girls in love with each other? Why can't I see them dating each other? Why can't I see them marrying each other? And what if I wish to do all these things?*

Chapter Thirty-Eight
21ˢᵗ March 2016. Time: 10:00

"Aai! When did you first get attracted to a man?"

Lata was busy preparing *rotis* for lunch. As she hunched before the gas, Kashi stood tall, her back against the fridge.

Lata stood up straight, eyes wide. "Hush Kashi, we never got attracted to anyone. We never vocalised such thoughts. We weren't those kinds of girls," said Lata, relieved Hari was not at home.

"That's really abnormal, Aai. There must have been someone," said Kashi.

"No, there wasn't anyone. I got married before such thoughts erupted in me." The smell of hot *chapattis* wafted in the air. Kashi shifted her weight to her left leg.

"You know, sometimes I find myself thinking of women instead of men."

"Think of the women, then. Who is stopping you, silly?" Lata said with a giggle as she turned over the *chapattis* on the pan. "Our religion, our culture, our traditions, and our family sets certain rules and responsibilities that we women must follow for our own good," said Lata, rolling the dough on the kitchen board.

"So many rules for women! Who made these rules? I'd like to know," Kashi sighed.

"The learned men who wrote all the rules in our religious books."

"Why haven't women written down any rules?"

"Women cannot create rules. Only men can," said Lata as she roasted the chapattis to Hari's preferences, down to the exact level of brownness desired.

"And you're okay with that?"

"Of course. The wise men know best."

Kashi crossed her arms. "What if one were to decide not to follow the rules without breaking any laws? What then?"

"Depending on the severity of the rule you have broken, society will punish you. Throw stones at you. Burn you. Ostracise you. Insult you. There's no getting away from rules."

"What if the family of the woman supports her against rules? What then?"

"Then the entire family will be ostracised. Very few families will dare to go against societal norms, unless they are big and powerful in society... like those shameless Bollywood superstars. It's much easier to make the girl conform instead. Also in her best interests," said Lata. "But why all these questions? You're lucky you belong to a modern family. We've never prevented you from doing anything that you want, have we? Get a good education and cultivate your interests until you get married. Get involved in science - you enjoy that, don't you?"

"Science isn't only about formulas and experiments. It is a temperament. It is rationality and logic," said Kashi.

"You're giving me a headache now," groaned Lata, turning away from her.

"I asked you about women and look where our conversation ended up!" Kashi said in a huff. "Aai, I think I'm a lesbian," she announced and waited for an outburst.

"Of course, you aren't, silly. Where do you get these ideas from?" Lata said with a laugh.

"Aai, I'm serious. I get sexually attracted to girls!" *For the first time in my life, I've mentioned the word containing three letters that cause Indian families to go off like surface-to-air missiles, to the extent of murdering their unmarried daughters for their lost honour in the act of their daughter's imagined copulation. So feared is the three-letter-word, good families do not mention it. Mothers do not inform and educate their daughters about it. The pleasures associated with the word are dismissed, and only the havoc remains.*

206

Lata let her rolling pin drop to the floor with a crash.

Kashi looked insanely happy. *At least I'm taken seriously now.*

Leaving her frying pan on the stove, Lata rushed to Kashi and gave her a slap, leaving a patch of flour on her cheek.

"Don't mention that word in our house ever again. Have you understood?" she whispered to Kashi.

"In our house? Do you want to go outside then, so that I can mention the word?" Her cheek smarted, but she did not soothe it.

"Don't act smart with me, understand? Get a grip on yourself. If your Baba hears of this, he will kill you," said Lata, holding Kashi by the shoulders and shaking her hard.

"At least, try and understand what I am saying..." Kashi started to say.

"Stop it. Don't you understand? Stop talking," Lata commanded, with a tremor in her voice.

"It's foolish of me to expect understanding from someone who drinks the urine of an animal. Urine which flows over the shit still sticking to the animal."

"How dare you?" Lata picked up the fallen rolling pin and advanced, holding it aloft in her hand. Kashi did not move, a challenging stare in her eyes. Lata retreated.

"Go on. Hit me again. Why did you stop?"

"You don't feel scared of me but at least fear your dad."

"It's not in my hands," Kashi said tearfully. "I thought at least you'd understand."

"I fear for you, Kashi," Lata said, close to tears herself.

"Well, what are *you* doing about it? At least I stand my ground in front of Baba." A sob escaped from Kashi. "And I hate it how both of you are always trying to whack me nowadays."

She ran to her parents' bedroom, shut the door and fired up her computer, trying to find succour in the virtual world.

Chapter Thirty-Nine
21st March 2016. Time: 17:00

That evening, Lata went to Kashi and caressed her cheek. Kashi looked up with eyes red as the blood of an honour killing.

"Do you want to come to the temple with me?" Lata asked.

After a moment, Kashi nodded. She put on a sequinned blue dupatta over the *chikankari* white cotton kurta she was wearing. They walked to the temple.

Like a shining, pink mountain peak, the steeple of the temple glittered in the evening sun. Kashi remembered reading somewhere that the steeple of the temple symbolises the mountain where the deity resides. Ever since she was a child, Kashi had loved visiting temples. The serene, welcoming atmosphere and the small rituals had always soothed her. She thought it a bonus if the temple was kept scrupulously clean as this one usually was.

Kashi placed their *chappals* under a stone to hide them from prowling thieves known to favour temples. They walked around the circumference of the temple once—a ritual symbolic of the endless cycle of life and death. They went in and Kashi breathed in the thick fragrance of incense, flowers, milk and yogurt. Sugar mixed in milk or yogurt was often the easiest *prasad* to offer to the deities and somehow the aroma seemed to have permeated the thick temple walls. The priest beckoned to them and gave them a piece of the sweet *pedha* which had been offered to the gods that day. As a child, Kashi had always looked forward to the sweet temple offerings, but as a young adult she was suspicious of their hygiene quotient and therefore consumed only the minutest piece of the offering. She gave the rest of the *pedha* to her mother. They rang the bell to awaken the gods and alert them to their presence. After bowing in reverence to the pieces of carved, coloured stone, they sat in silence and observed the inflow of the worshippers.

After a while Lata said, "Shall we leave now?"

Kashi nodded. They retrieved their *chappals* and walked home feeling calmer.

Dinner that night was muted. Kashi kept her face in a book.

Before going to bed, Lata went to Kashi and said, "Baba will never accept it. He will get you married. To a boy. He will use law, religion, society, and hound you till you get married. Understand this. Forget your fancies. He will never let you win."

Later that night, Lata had a chat with her husband as they lay in their bed together. "Kashi is only seventeen, but it's time we found a husband for her. If we start our search now, we can get her married on her eighteenth birthday."

"Funny you should say that. I was thinking the same a few days back," Hari said as he lay on his back, staring at the ceiling fan, his fingers entwined on his chest.

"I'm a little worried about her. She gets all these new-fangled ideas in her head..." Lata mumbled.

"I know what you mean, but she's her father's daughter. She will never do anything to shame me."

"It's difficult to control modern girls," Lata whispered.

"We can always bend the rules and get her married before she turns eighteen," Hari said. "Anyway, Kashi won't bring me shame. I'm sure. There are ways..."

Fear consumed Lata after Hari's words. *He can kill for honour.*

"At least, ask around and find out if a suitable boy is available. We can finalise her marriage now, and she can get married when she turns eighteen," said Lata. "To think that in another three years or so, we could even be grandparents! These worries will then seem like nothing." She bit her lip, her thoughts veering from pros to cons. "But then... she'd have to be taken out of her university, wouldn't she? Her studies... It would be a shame to put a stop to all that."

"Of what use is education to a girl, you tell me? She has to look after her house and her children, after all. Tell me, had you not been literate, would it have made any difference?"

Lata did not say anything.

"Don't worry. Leave it to me," said Hari, "I will find a solution. I don't foresee any difficulty in finding a husband for her. Her fair complexion will guarantee that."

"Should we ask her first? You know, she isn't like us. She has all these strong views..."

"Don't ask. Just tell her that it's time to start thinking of marriage, so she's prepared," said Hari. He got up and switched off the lights, leaving his wife to navigate residual worries.

The next day, Lata found Kashi sitting at the living room table, reading a magazine article. She stood behind her and swivelled her chair around to face her.

"What?" Kashi shouted.

"Thought I should warn you; Baba has decided to get you married," Lata blurted.

"You've got to be joking. You've decided to marry me off in a single night?" Kashi spluttered. "Marrying off a girl who is younger than eighteen is a crime in this country. I will tell the police."

"You know you won't," Lata said dangerously, "Listen to us, Kashi. Forget your new-fangled ideas. Just listen to us, and everything will be alright."

"What new-fangled ideas are you talking about? The fact that I am a lesbian? What can I do if I get attracted to girls?" Kashi shouted.

"That's a psychological problem. It can be sorted out. There are ways." Lata's eyes gleamed. "You have this image of the revolutionary, rebellious woman in your head and you are dying to become like them."

"That's absurd! Don't you even care about what I want?" Kashi's voice choked with indignation.

"Kashi, the world is a terrifying place for a woman. The sooner we hand you over to your husband, the better." She paused. "You're not safe... even from Baba."

Her words paused the conversation.

Kashi looked at her mother questioningly. "You are as much of a victim as I am," she said, almost to herself.

"Give it time, and you'll get attracted to your husband, and then when the babies arrive you won't have time to think of these funny ideas."

Kashi's moist eyes flashed with anger. "I will tell the police. You cannot marry me off against my wishes."

"Do you want to do this the difficult way? I can easily lock you in your room and refuse to let you out. Here, take this. It'll help calm your anger," said Lata, handing over a tincture to Kashi.

"I'm not going to put that in my mouth."

"It's herbal. Take it. You'll feel better."

"I'm not going to take that unless I know what's in it."

"How stubborn you are! We've been taking this for generations," Lata huffed.

Kashi folded her arms. "Well, I won't."

"Listen to us, and things will be alright in the end. We're your parents. We only wish well for you," said Lata. "There is a Godman here in this city. He claims to cure problems just like yours."

"You've got to be joking. I'll go nowhere near a Godman who will use his tricks to rape me," said Kashi, fuming.

"Have some respect! If you don't care about religion, remember that we do," yelled Lata.

"What do Godmen have to do with your religion anyway? They're frauds, that's all."

"Let us go to a doctor then. You trust science, don't you? It is a psychological problem which will be treated as per science. Happy? In a few months, you will return to normal."

211

"Return to normal? I am normal! There is nothing wrong with me. It is not a psychological problem."

"A girl getting attracted to other girls is not normal. It is not natural. Most importantly, it is not a part of our culture," said Lata.

"That's not true at all. Our culture, as you put it, is not as narrow-minded as you suggest. See this?" She waved the magazine in front of Lata's face. "I've been reading. When Maharaja Dilip died without an heir, Lord Shiva commanded the Maharaja's two widowed queens to make love and create a son. So, that is what they did. The son was named Bhagiratha because he was born from two women, and he went on to bring the holy river Ganga to the earth. So, you see, our myths recognise same-sex unions."

"What nonsense do you talk, child? Stop filling your head with garbage," said Lata, worry cracking her face like a jigsaw.

"I thought you love the myths," Kashi said. "Look at pictures of the temples of Khajuraho if you don't believe me."

"Eeks! How horrible!"

"They're temples, Aai."

"Shee! Baba will find a nice boy for you, and we will finalise your marriage. You will get married as soon as you become eighteen."

"What about my education?"

"You can still do that... if your husband agrees."

"I will only get married to the girl I love," said Kashi.

"Hush. Stop this nonsense. Nobody loves their husband on the first day. Love takes time to grow," Lata pleaded as she stroked her daughter's head.

"What about you? Do you love Baba?"

Lata paused, then said, "I don't understand the love a woman feels for a man, Kashi. I do know the love a mother feels for her child."

Lata's confession stunned Kashi. "Surely, you must have experienced it at some point?"

Lata's thoughts went back to the first night of her marriage which had put her off all men for good. *Where was the space for love to bloom in my life?* she wondered. "I'm happy," she said instead. "And so will you be, with a nice boy that Baba finds. Don't worry. Things will turn out fine eventually."

"Learn disobedience, Aai. You'll be happier," Kashi said.

Chapter Forty
21st March 2016. Time: 23:00

People who are left-handed and who are forced to write with their right hand usually develop a stutter...and you are sexually left-handed. The words from the Lancet medical journal on same-sex attraction served as a constant reminder to her. *I'm not abnormal, just sexually left-handed.*

Common to older houses, the water-tank behind the house was constructed to wash dishes and clothes in the open air. No one visited it in the afternoon. Kashi sat on its ledge and cried.

My parents inhabit an illusion with its own rules and regulations, insulated from logic. How do I get them out of their stupor? To have the freedom to lead your life according to your own rules is a privilege. A privilege that I do not have, and probably never will.

She went in and turned to the Internet, trying to find answers to her predicament. Using an anonymous identity, she read the relevant research, contributing and discussing on various international forums. She interacted with lesbians from countries which recognised their identity—querying, learning and understanding.

Sexuality should not be a barrier to success or happiness, they all implied.

I want to speak to an Indian lesbian as our predicaments are unique, but there are none to speak to.

Under a pseudonym, she started her own social media group for Indian lesbians. *An online group which offers anonymity will be easy for anyone who chooses to join.* Within a few days, fifty girls who identified as lesbians joined. As the numbers increased, Kashi's lesbian social media group became her support. The interaction, exchange and sharing helped her, but as the days passed, she felt morose.

Parents refuse to accept the preferences of their daughters. It's the same story everywhere. Suicides, forced marriages, depression, anxiety, and loneliness are the norm. It's so much easier to just give up and get married to a boy.

She became interested in a girl she met online who called herself fiery_lady. Like her assumed name, fiery_lady's bold and outspoken statements impressed Kashi. They became online friends with the vague understanding they could be potential lovers in the future. They did not share their real names, nor did they share photos. The interaction was limited to an exchange of thoughts and ideas, with banter thrown in.

For the time being, this will work.

Chapter Forty-One
23rd March 2016. Time: 10:00

Lata could be resourceful when needed. She found the address of a doctor who claimed to cure same-sex attraction from the classified advertisements in the daily newspaper. She jotted down the address in her notebook, tore the paper off and then placed it in her bra. The only thing that prevented her from going to a Godman for her predicament was the utter disdain shown by her daughter to the proposition. *With a medically qualified doctor, at least I have a chance of getting my daughter's approval.* On a quiet afternoon, she hailed an auto-rickshaw, read out the address that she had scribbled on her paper, and they were off.

The clinic was located in a crowded sari market in a multi-storey building.

'*Dr Gupte's clinic, MBBS*' declared a board. Stairs stained with betel-leaf juice took her to the clinic located on the first floor. A faint stink of urine teased her nostrils momentarily. She entered the clinic, sweating. Despite the heat, the clinic did not have air-conditioning. The advertisement in the newspaper claimed that the Doctor had cured five hundred gay people in the past year, and he saw patients without prior appointments. There were five people sitting in the waiting room. Lata enrolled at the reception and leafed through a Bollywood magazine while she waited. A man sitting opposite stared at her. She was thankful when her turn came up, after a few minutes.

She went in and found a dark middle-aged man sitting behind a desk.

"What seems to be the problem?" the doctor asked, looking at Lata.

"It's my friend's daughter, Doctor Saheb. I don't know how to explain this... er... well, you see, I think she has abnormal tendencies." She looked at the doctor, who nodded encouragingly. "You see, she has this strange notion that she wants to get married to a woman. She gets attracted to girls, you see..."

"She thinks she's a lesbian," Doctor Gupte completed the sentence for her. "We call this sexual deviance or neurosis."

At the mention of the three-lettered word, Lata did not know where to look. She directed her gaze towards the doctor's writing pad. *Times are desperate. I will have to face the terrible word for my daughter's sake.*

"What can be done, doctor?" she asked, hope shining on her face.

"Neurosis can be treated like any other disease," he said, and she sat back a little.

"I will need to interview the patient for fifteen minutes or so. Usually, same-sex attraction occurs because of sexual abuse when young. Has the girl been abused as a child?"

"Of course not! She hasn't. I'm quite sure of that."

"How would you know? I'll have to interview the girl," said the doctor, tapping his fingers on his desk. "If that doesn't work then we can try hormone therapy. If you want quicker results, I'd recommend electroconvulsive therapy. She will be normal in no time at all."

"Electro...?"

"Electric shocks."

A sharp intake of breath. "Electric shocks?"

"The mention of electric shocks is not pleasant to most people. A lot of bad press associated with this, but it's a workable cure."

"Will it make her normal again?"

"I can't give guarantees. All I can say is that this form of therapy has been used for sexual deviancy with reliable results. I remain hopeful."

"But doctor... shocks... seems a bit extreme, cruel in fact..." mumbled Lata.

"It has the greatest possibility of being successful. We will ask your girl to choose five photographs of lesbians. While she is looking at them, we will start giving her electric shocks. We will then show her photographs of different-sex couples and while she is looking at them, we will reduce the intensity of shocks. We will continue to do this alternatively. Her brain will try to avert the pain that she experienced while looking at the photos of the lesbians, and hopefully will try and avoid it in the future. Her thinking can be altered in this way. Along with this, we will also be providing other forms of psychotherapy, like encouraging her to be more feminine by wearing feminine clothes etc. We've had lots of success in the past where the person not only forgot their gay tendencies but also became straight. I must say though that we don't get too many girls as patients. The parents do not think it's worth the trouble because they can simply marry them off and the problem is solved. Think about it for a few days, and then let me know. You can make the payment at the reception outside. Thank you."

And he turned away to look at the screen on his desk. Lata trudged out, disturbed by the extremity of the cure.

The parents do not think it's worth the trouble because they can simply marry them off. Yes, why go through all this trouble and expense when she could just be married off? Getting her married, even using force if needed, seems to be the easier option. This visit will serve as a deterrent to Kashi—stay on the course or else ...

With a grim smile, Lata got into an auto for the journey back home. The task of finding a husband for Kashi would begin in earnest.

Chapter Forty-Two
23rd March 2016. Time: 23:00

The night was quiet, and the house was dark. It was almost eleven. Kashi got up and checked the door of her parents' bedroom. It was locked. She got her laptop out, sat under her blanket to keep out the glare and switched it on. Without pausing, she wrote on social media:

Trying to correct my sexual orientation is a form of sexual abuse.
By threatening to take me to a clinic to change my sexual orientation
By threatening to marry me off to a male knowing that I am a lesbian
By threatening to give me medicines to cure my sexuality
By treating my sexuality as a psychological problem
By forcing their sexual orientations on me
They are abusing me sexually. This is rape.
Is there a law to prevent this kind of assault on my sexuality? Will the police help me if I register a complaint against my parents? If they take me to a clinic, I will run away or I will kill myself, or I will kill them. If they force me to get married to a man, I will kill the man.
I will do my utmost best to prevent my abuse.

She sighed, read what she had written and deleted it all.

Chapter Forty-Three
26th April 2016. Time: 10:00

With rising anger, Hari read Aparna's article on normalising blasphemy. He caught up a glass paperweight on his desk and smashed it to smithereens on the floor. Lata scampered in with a broom and without a word swept and cleared away the broken glass pieces. After reading about the reward of fifteen *lakhs* for Aparna's nose, he composed a tweet from the *Dharma Sanstha* account, implying approval and posted it. Soon, he was contacted by the media requesting a byte on the developments. Exercising his right to freedom of speech, Hari spent the day giving interviews to TV channels on just how wrong Aparna's article was.

His phone shrilled. Baba Alok Shastri was on the line. Baba Alok Shastri, owner of a multi-million-dollar empire based on spirituality and irrationality, was a spiritual guru with two pending cases accusing him of rape against his name.

"Hari bhau, do something about that woman," Baba Alok Shastri pleaded. *"Look, I'm just a spiritual man, but since you move around in those circles, I have come to ask you for help. The rationalists are after me now, desperate to find something that will put me in jail for a number of years. I can't allow this to happen. Take the thorns away from my path."*

"Babaji, I'm sorry to hear that. You know I think very highly of you. But I worry that taking away one woman will not solve this. The rot is deeper."

"Look, set fire to her office... I don't know."

"Babaji, this woman has gotten inside my nose and blocked it. Have you read her article?"

"Hari bhau, demeaning Hindu culture has become a fashion, unfortunately. I don't care what you do, or how you do it. Just get it done. Money will be in your hands, in cash, soon after."

"Babaji, I'm a simple man. What will I do with your money? You can donate it to *Dharma Sanstha* where it will be put to good use. How much?"

"*Fifty lakhs. It will give me great pleasure to see the money used for propagating our religion and culture.*"

"You are very kind. I will keep you informed."

At home, in their bedroom, Kashi read Aparna's article on normalising blasphemy with conflicting thoughts. *I don't want blasphemy to be normalised, but an opinion, a view or an idea will neither make my belief fragile nor my religion weak.*

Fearfully, she looked at the Twitter account of the *Dharma Sanstha.* Hari's tweet about Aparna consumed her with fear.

Whose side are you on? she asked herself. *Aparna uses words like feminism, patriarchy, misogyny, sexism—words which always had a negative connotation before I met her. But now, I understand these words. I recognise them. I see a patriarch in my father. As a victim, even Aai is propagating patriarchy. What gives my father the right to condone violence against a woman? What gives him the bloody right? How did I not recognise the signs in him before meeting Aparna? Or maybe I did, but never had the strength to acknowledge them.*

As Kashi read various tweets related to Aparna, she started to sweat. It wasn't only the *Dharma Sanstha;* the entire country seemed to be celebrating the call for Aparna's nose.

What is wrong with everyone?

Breaking News – Times of Hindustan
27th April 2016

Rationalist M.D. Kuber shot dead

Nashik: Nashik's most vocal rationalist, M.D. Kuber was shot dead early this morning by two gunmen when out on his morning walk. Mr Kuber took a bullet straight in his heart and died on the spot. The activist was known to target Godmen and superstitious practices state-wide, earning the ire of the religious right-wing. His press conferences were often disrupted by Hindu extremists, but he did not take the threats seriously and refused police protection.

Chapter Forty-Four
27th April 2016. Time: 18:00

"Others have beaten us to it," said Hari. It was the twilight hour. Sounds of children playing *lagori* chimed in from outside. A baby was bawling somewhere. A woman called out to her daughter. The aroma of jasmin incense from a neighbouring home wafted in the air. Sipping water from a coconut shell, Hari was in the living room of his home. Prahlad and Shakti were glugging beer with him. Lata had gone to visit her parents, and Kashi, her friends. Both were not expected any time soon. A newspaper lay open at the page reporting the death of the rationalist.

"Who did this *bhau*? Any idea?" Prahlad asked.

"Not a clue. Some lone organisation somewhere," Hari said, scratching his nose. "His name was on the list, you know."

"Kuber's?" Shakti asked.

"Yes, the rationalist. One by one, they all will fall." Hari paused. "Since childhood, I've wanted to do something that will make me proud, something for my faith, my religion, my country."

The room remained silent for a few seconds.

"Weapons are difficult to procure, Hari *bhau*. Guns are almost impossible nowadays," Prahlad said.

"How did the Nashik group procure them?" Hari asked. "Ask around. Someone will be able to help."

"We don't have those kind of contacts, Hari *bhau*," said Prahlad.

"What about swords?" Hari asked.

"Not easy to kill someone with a sword in a public place," said Prahlad.

Hari nodded.

"Who is it that you have in mind, by the way?" asked Shakti.

"That Soman woman. We can't have women like her changing the set order. God knows we have fought long and hard for this. We're not going to have that taken away because of the noise a woman makes."

"Anything personal?" Shakti asked.

"This battle is ideological. If we don't fight for our religion, who will?" Hari said.

There was a pause.

"Teach her a lesson she will never forget," Hari said, slowly. "And make an example of her."

Outside, the children had gone home. The baby had stopped bawling. The pleasant twilight had given way to the night. In no time at all, darkness had forced her way inside. Shakti got up to switch on the light.

"*Bhau*, that won't be easy. Even the punishment is harsher nowadays, I believe."

"Don't worry about arrests. I can guarantee, no one will get caught," Hari said.

"How?"

"Contacts," Hari said.

Prahlad shifted on his chair. Shakti dug into his nose.

"When women get out of hand, it's our duty to discipline them," said Hari, his face serious. "An errant woman's core is a dark and malicious place. It's our duty to detoxify. Even our gods have used such tactics when needed. Indra disguised himself as Ahalya's husband, Gautama, to have sexual relations with her. When Gautama found out, he cursed them both. She was turned into a stone." Hari cleared his throat "The demon Jalandhar would disguise himself as the husbands of the women he met, and then deceive them into having sexual relations with him. When the husbands found out, they tried to defeat him in a war. They couldn't kill him because of the loyalty and purity of his chaste wife, Vrinda. Finally, Lord Vishnu disguised himself as Jalandhar and deceived Vrinda into having sexual relations with him. Her loyalty and chastity were thus destroyed, and Jalandhar was longer protected by her virtues. It was easy to kill him after that."

"Correct, *bhau*," said Prahlad with a burp. "Our religion does not shy away from teaching women a lesson when needed."

"Exactly," Hari said.

"Her name was topmost on the list we made," Shakti said.

"Her tweets! And those blasphemous articles! If we don't stop her, she will start breaking idols of gods in the streets tomorrow. The Muslims will then join in. There's no other way. The woman must be punished to prevent the assault on our religion and culture. Thankfully, there aren't too many like her."

"That woman has gone completely out of hand," Prahlad looked angry. "You are right. She must be taught a lesson."

"Who should we choose for the task?"

"Somebody who can get it up," said Prahlad.

They laughed.

"He is right. Not everyone is up to it."

"*Bhau*, why don't you go?" Shakti asked Hari.

In a sudden movement, Hari caught Shakti by the scruff of his neck.

"You've said this once. Never say it again. These jobs are for our foot soldiers. Not for me. Understand?"

"Understood, *bhau*," said Shakti, choking. Hari loosened his hold.

"Three men are required. All three need to know how to drive well. They need presence of mind. Try to find three who have done something like this before," instructed Hari.

"I know someone, *bhau*. He's been boasting..." Prahlad leered.

"Remember, this is not going to be easy. This is an aggressive forty-five-year-old woman that we're talking about here."

"Our lad is strong..." They laughed.

"It's not about that, you fool. The woman will not be easy to subdue. Use the element of surprise and then figure it out," Hari said. "The entire nation wants to teach that woman a lesson, and everyone is with us."

"Good to know, *bhau*. I will talk to a few people and let you know soon enough."

"Conduct a recce before the actual event."

"Will do, *bhau*."

With that, the plan was made.

Chapter Forty-Five
27th April 2016. Time: 21:00

It was almost nine. Hari had informed Lata he would be working late. Lata was glad. Things were always pleasant when Hari wasn't at home.

She dampened the cotton-wick in ghee and lit the steel *diya* kept in front of the gods in their small home temple located in the kitchen. With the height and width not more than a foot each, the home temple still managed to house an idol of Shiva, the monkey god Hanuman, a colourful photo frame of the god Dutta and another one of Goddess Laxmi. Lata gave the tiny steel bell a jingle. She bowed in front of the deities, chanted a short prayer under her breath and switched off the kitchen light. Her work there was done. Going to the bedroom, she started getting the blankets out for the night. While her mother was in the bedroom, Kashi sneaked into the dark kitchen and blew out the flame of the *diya* which her mother had just lighted. Pests, particularly rats, greedy for the ghee, were known to escape with lit cotton wicks and setting fire to the entire house. Kashi had read about one such case. Instead of arguing with her parents, she just blew out the flame every night. Her task complete, Kashi went to the bedroom and slid into her parents' bed while Lata plumped the pillows.

"Given a choice between me and Baba, who would you choose?" Kashi's face was solemn. Lata's instinct was to joke about Kashi's question, but her daughter rarely talked to her these days. Having no friends, not even acquaintances, Lata missed the chats with her daughter.

"Children are all that matter to a mother," Lata explained gently. Kashi started to cry.

After withstanding her daughter's rebellious moods single-handedly for the past few weeks, the tears surprised Lata. She sat on the bed next to Kashi. Her daughter placed her head on her lap.

"What happened, Kashi? What's the matter?"

"There will come a time when you have to choose. I know you love me. Not sure whether you love Baba, but Aai, it's time to be independent from his grip," Kashi said.

"What do you mean? I don't understand you, child."

"What if Baba isn't here tomorrow? You should be able to cope on your own," Kashi said, a little desperately.

"Why won't Baba be here? He's not going anywhere." Lata made a face.

"The time may come sooner than you think. So be prepared."

"What are you saying, child?"

"Remember, I love you too. I'm unsure about Baba. When things happen, don't blame me. It was the only way, remember."

"You're scaring me now. What is it that you're planning? Out with it."

"Nothing. I'm planning nothing. Take care, Aai." Kashi stood up and left the room.

She left behind a puzzled mother whose heart ached with her daughter's words. Lata knew she wouldn't sleep, now stuck in a negative cycle. She thought about all the potential tragedies that could befall their home.

BOOK FIVE

Chapter Forty-Six
17th May 2016. Time: 02:00

Naseem's eyes caressed the wall opposite as she sat cross-legged on her bed. It was two at night. *The air around me reeks like the smell of death mingled with ash after a cremation.* She craved oxygen. *Why don't my lungs feel free?* A dog cried somewhere. *They can sense approaching death*——a belief scoffed at by her family, but which terrified her now. The stench of her unwashed body radiated at periodic intervals. Not having showered for three days, she caught the stink of grime on her, and for some reason, she found this uncontrollably funny. Holding her belly, she guffawed. Her face, with a mind of its own, contorted, eyes watered, mouth gaped, and the laughs continued. Laughing manically, she switched on her laptop and started to read.

How should the daughter of a raped woman behave?

She grabbed a fistful of her hair and pulled.

When a middle-aged man sent birthday wishes to me on social media with a photo of his private body part, I felt loud, excruciating shame. The action was his. The shame was mine. When even a virtual message has the power to induce shame, then what about a rape? They will shame Ma for getting raped. They will shame Baba for letting his wife get raped, and they will shame me because my mother got raped. They will shame us all. Shame is big here. It's thrown in copious quantities at women. Did your elderly relative grope you? Hush! Have some shame. Don't tell anyone. What will people say? Did that boy wink at you? It's because of your short skirt. Have some shame. Did that man stalk you? It's because you went out so late. Which respectable girl does that? Have some shame. A middle-aged man sent you a picture of his body part? You must have led him on. Boys will be boys. Men will be men. But women must have shame. You got raped. How shameful! Let's all get together and stigmatise! Talk in low voices when the raped woman's daughter enters the room. Avoid her glances. Keep our sons away from that raped woman's daughter. Don't call the woman's family for weddings or birthdays because they carry that grey cloud with them. Who are you talking about? Oh, that raped woman's daughter? Let's all get together and shame her because her mother had the audacity to get raped.

While changing tabs on her laptop, she came across a photo of the three of them.

Just the three of us, as we once were. Ripe and juicy! No hint of pain. Wide, open smiles. Secure and confident about our world. Who are these people?

A glance outside her window revealed that morning had arrived surreptitiously.

What would be the least painful way to end your life?

Chapter Forty-Seven
19th May 2016. Time: 21:00

The Times of Hindustan News channel took pride in their secular credentials. For this reason, the channel was abhorred and shunned by the right wing. Aparna was to be interviewed by the channel head, Ashok Sinha, a man with impeccable journalistic credentials. Because of his reputation, Aparna's impending interview was promptly labelled as biased by the right wing before it could even be aired.

"Due to the complexity of the topic, we've decided to give this an hour-long slot instead of the usual thirty minutes we normally schedule for prime-time interviews," Ashok said to Aparna during a pre-interview call. *"I'll need to ask tough questions, so be prepared."*

"Please do. I want to get this right," Aparna said.

"Well, good luck and see you soon," Ashok said.

Before leaving home, Aparna sensed the familiar signs of an impending anxiety attack. Her medication tempted her. Reluctant to fill herself up before the interview, she ignored her cravings. She reached the studio well ahead of time and was directed to a waiting room.

Hanging on the walls of the waiting room were pictures of women anchors of the channel in confident poses. She gazed at them for a while and then turned away. Painted in red and black, the room induced claustrophobia. She wished there was a window.

While she sat in agonising isolation, she could see young men and women buzzing outside the room carrying papers and messages, testing and correcting equipment whose names she did not know. From where she sat, she could spot the interview room. It was empty, but people kept going in and out of it on seemingly important errands.

Not wishing to rush through the interview without giving it the deserved importance, her hands fidgeted with a kind of an obsessive compulsion. The dark rings under her tired eyes were reminiscent of a solar eclipse; the once taut skin now hung in soft, loose folds on her face like an ageing *chiku* fruit; her forehead and eyes had shrunk within themselves instead of confronting the world as they once had.

Ashok bounced into the room from somewhere. "Let's go!" He indicated the interview room with a movement of his head. She followed him.

Myriad equipment around her was adjusted and tested. A young girl came on to dab some foundation over her. Aparna refused.

"Just a little," the girl said and dabbed some on her face anyway.

Now seated opposite Ashok, amidst the sudden hush that took over the room, Aparna thought to herself: *An hour or so after the interview, our lives will change irrevocably. A couple of months down the line, we'll know whether this was a good decision.*

"Viewers, this is an exclusive. Aparna Soman, well-known feminist, rationalist and author is joining us today. Aparna Soman, thank you for coming to our channel tonight. You are live on Times of Hindustan News. There's something important that you wish to tell our viewers, Aparna. Over to you now. Ladies and gentlemen, presenting Aparna Soman."

"Thank you, Ashok," Aparna said. With effort, she managed to look like herself as she once was—calm, confident and eager to put forward her view. Only her eyes gave away the trauma she'd suffered.

"On the 4th of May, I was assaulted for my views," Aparna said in a clear voice.

"Please can you elaborate?" Ashok leaned forward.

"Three men accosted me on my morning walk. They pushed me into a car, drove me to an abandoned construction

234

site and..." Aparna took a moment, "they raped me."

Naseem, who was watching at home, felt something stir within her when she heard her mother utter the weighted word.

"Aparna Soman, are you declaring live on TV that you were gang-raped?" With eyes twinkling greedily, Ashok looked as if he would burst with the sensationalism of the disclosure.

Aparna sat straight. Her face scrunched up for a milli-second. "Yes."

"But why?"

"For everything I stand for. My anti-superstition campaigns, my rationality, my atheism, my gender, my view. All of it was offensive to them."

"Did you know any of those men, Aparna?"

"No. They were strangers."

"Ladies and gentlemen, this is an exclusive! Aparna Soman admitting on live television that she was assaulted because of her aggressive campaigns perceived to be anti-religious."

The channel had obtained an exclusive sensational news story, and liberal or not, they planned to spin it to gain as many eyeballs as possible. Aparna looked down.

"Aparna, the law protects the identity of the rape victim. Why did you decide to speak to us today?"

"Because you and people of your profession don't speak up!"

Ashok, the seasoned anchor, merely smiled.

She's enjoying herself, Manish, who was watching the show, thought to himself.

"No one expects," Aparna swallowed, "a... a raped woman to speak." In a voice which shook periodically, she continued, "They want us to hide behind shame, hide behind culture and tradition. Such a woman is a guilty one in their eyes." She paused. "I'm not a lesser woman, not lesser by any degree, simply different." Looking directly at the camera, Aparna said with a faint trace of a smile, "After all, a woman is more than her vagina, isn't she?"

The word 'vagina' was beeped out of prime-time television, but her smile was telecast into all the living rooms that evening.

"An assault that took place in the morning, not far from a public mainstream road. It's shocking, but the scenario doesn't fit in with incidents of sexual assault you normally hear about in our country," said Ashok.

"The men didn't care about being seen. It was irrelevant to them. They seemed supremely confident they would get away with their actions without any consequences."

"Are you hinting at something?"

"Not hinting, but I'm saying this loud and clear. They couldn't have been so brazen without a reason. Their audacity speaks. They have support, the backing of a mass of people with a blindness only religion can induce. This gives them power" Aparna paused. "The power to do as they please without fear of consequence. They are assured in the knowledge of someone powerful watching their backs."

"Who in particular?"

"That's for the investigating agencies to find out. Rationalists are being killed, threatened, assaulted. It's obvious, the criminals fear rationality. They fear atheism."

"Aparna, have you changed your views on religion after this incident?"

"That's a silly question. My views are clear as always. I don't have a problem with those who quietly practise their faith. My problem is with the misuse of faith. The minute your belief tramples on the human rights of others, it's a no from me."

"But why promote atheism so aggressively? This call to normalise blasphemy: like, really?"

"What is the need to promote religion with so much pomp and show? Why this exhibition? Practise your faith quietly. If a person of faith can rave about their religion, I have an equal right to promote atheism," Aparna stated, her anger rising. "Let people choose."

Ashok raised his eyebrows. His eyes glittered. Though he remained seated, he drew himself up in his chair. "But who are you to tell us what to do, Aparna?" He smiled. "I warned you; I will have to ask difficult questions."

Aparna broadened her shoulders and raised her chin. Looking at Ashok directly, she answered, "Well, who are *they* to tell *me* what to do? I speak as a woman who has paid a heavy price for expressing a view."

"But, but, but Aparna... faith must be respected," Ashok said in a softer voice which men regularly adopted around Aparna as if explaining things to a child.

"Why?" Aparna asked in a loud voice. "Why is your faith so fragile? Can't it even tolerate a radical idea? Why feel so threatened?"

"You believe that by speaking up you will change mindsets and divert people away from religion?"

"It's my right to speak. I should be allowed to put forward controversial ideas without getting mauled or killed. That's all I'm saying. I'm not breaking any law by sharing my views," she said, "and if I am, then the law needs to change. You cannot arrest someone for an idea."

"Isn't your atheism extreme as well? You're giving this interview to prove a point. Doesn't that make you a fanatic? As extreme as the religious fanatics who did this to you?"

"With all due respect, I haven't mutilated or killed anyone to promote my views. The difference between them and me is pretty obvious, I think."

"What would you say to other rape victims? Would you encourage them to speak up?"

"Survivors..."

"My apologies... rape survivors."

"It's important for me to speak up. Each woman should have the full freedom to decide what she wants to do without

237

giving a thought to our culture, religion, or society."

"You seem very normal after such a traumatic incident," Ashok said. "What I mean is, you don't look traumatised."

Aparna cursed under her breath, raised her voice and asked, "What does a traumatised woman look like?"

"There is a section that believes you're cooking up this story to avoid arrest. What would you say to them?"

"I've brought my forensic medical report here with me. Anyone who is interested can look and judge for themselves. It provides details of the different ways my body was abused."

Ashok lowered his gaze. "There have been several brutal sexual assaults in our country where girls have ultimately paid with their lives. I'm told there wasn't a single stain of blood on your clothes. What do you have to say to that?"

"What do you want me to say? Should I express my thanks to those criminals for sparing me the brutality?" Aparna wiped off the dampness she felt on her forehead. "I'm sorry, a..." she cleared her throat, "a rape by its very definition is brutal."

"You seem very normal after such a traumatic incident. That's what I'm getting at. You don't look like a woman who was sexually assaulted."

"How does such a woman look? I would like to know." Aparna touched her brow and wiped off her sweat.

Kashi was watching the interview transfixed. *What a woman! What chutzpah! She had them all by their balls. I want to be like her.*

"You have your own blog. You also publish a monthly periodical. Why didn't you write instead of attending an interview on TV?"

"TV has a wider reach. It goes right into the depths of our villages. My blog is only read by six *lakh* readers, but I will write extensively about this," said Aparna.

"It sounds very much as if you are using your assault to promote your views."

"I didn't ask..." Aparna took a sip of water, "to be assaulted."

"What is the point you wish to make through this interview?"

Aparna sat back and relaxed in her seat, but her face displayed her urgency to make her point. "An environment that allows satire and mockery. Making fun of mythological characters has always been a part of Indian tradition. Haven't you seen the *Ramleelas* full of risqué humour? We've always ridiculed blind faith. Stop being so fragile that even a word, a sentence, a view, an article, a cartoon, a film, or a TV programme offends you. Do we need an archaic anti-blasphemy 295A? Scrap it. Let's normalise blasphemy. Let religions evolve with the times."

"Oh, that's impossible. Normalise blasphemy? Have you even thought about how Islam would view this?"

Aparna raised an eyebrow. "I don't know if you're aware, Ashok, but liberal atheists born into Islam have been fighting for this for decades. Imagine the resources, not to mention the time, the justice system would save if we stopped throwing every comedian and cartoonist in jail for expressing unpopular views. It's time for some maturity."

"Do you think the atmosphere right now is conducive enough to do that?"

"It isn't. An atmosphere of intolerance, hate and bigotry prevails in the country. Now, more than ever, we need humour and sanity. Who are these religion guardians to decide what is blasphemous and what is not?"

"What do you really think of our country, Aparna? Accusations of you being an anti-national were levelled. So, I ask you now. Is Aparna Soman an anti-national?"

Aparna thought for a moment. "I speak as a concerned citizen. Initiate a dialogue instead of sticking labels on people you disagree with!"

Like a contented lion after a kill, Ashok gave a satisfied smile. "Thank you, Aparna. You've been incredibly brave.

Finally, is there anything you would like to say to our viewers?"

"I would like to quote a few lines from the beautiful poem written by Bismil Azimabadi:

'Jism bhi kya jism hain jinse na ho khun-e-junun
Kya ladhe tufan se jo kashti-e-sahil mein
Sarfaroshi ki tamanna ab humare dil mein hain
Dekhna hain jor kitna bajue katil main hain
Sarfaroshi ki tamanna ab humare dil mein hain.'"

"What's the use of a body without passionate blood? How can a person conquer a typhoon while sitting in a boat near the shore? The desire for struggle is in our hearts. We shall now assess the strength of the opponent."

With those words, Aparna smiled at the camera and the interview concluded. The cameras switched off. With the adrenaline still surging in her body, Aparna felt euphoric.

"Hey, you alright?" Ashok asked Aparna. "That was a brilliant interview. Our TRPs will go through the roof."

Aparna nodded; her face serious. She asked for a glass of water. Ashok requested a studio boy to give her the water and left. Aparna waited in the visitor's room for Manish. She felt the familiar anxiety creeping in. Her heart knocked loudly, making a plea for freedom. She attempted to breathe deeply, counting the numbers in her head as she had been taught, but the breathing did not help. With a tremulous, clammy hand she reached for her anxiety pill and gulped it down with a sip. The effect, when it presented itself, managed to blunt the edge of fear, making her emotions muted and dull. She embraced the uncomplicated succour.

Her phone rang. Her first cousin, Santosh was on the line. She hadn't heard from him for the past twenty years.

"*Have you lost it?*" Santosh shouted down the phone.

"Wha—?"

"*Can't you keep quiet? First, it was on social media. I didn't say anything. And now you're actually giving interviews on TV? Exhibiting yourself in the most shameful way possible. What will people think? Our family has a certain respect in society. Have some shame——*"

Aparna cut him off. Her phone rang almost immediately. Without thinking, she took the call. Manish's uncle, Sriramji, was on the line.

"*You've taken it too far, beti,*" Sriramji said, without even a hello. "*Do you even give a thought to your husband before doing such shameless things? If you have no shame, at least spare a thought for your family. How many times have I told you to stop writing? This social media nonsense... why do you crave attention so much? All these likes and comments and all that virtual nonsense. When the time comes, it's your extended family that will stand with you. Your husband, his family. Stop——*"

Aparna cut him off.

Her phone rang again. This time, Aparna took a moment to view and process the name of the caller. It was Benazir.

"*Why didn't you tell me?*" Benazir asked.

"Things happened so quickly——"

"*But bravo, girl! I couldn't be prouder,*" Benazir interrupted.

"What's the time in your country? Isn't it late out there?"

"*Not really. Look, it's easy for me to say, but treat this like an accident you've had. Recuperate physically and emotionally, and then put it behind you.*"

"I don't have an option, do I?" said Aparna.

"*Do you want to come and spend some time with me? I'll give you your space, I promise,*" Benazir offered.

"I've got a police case against me. They delivered a summons the other day."

"*The bastards! Have you found a lawyer? Should I find one for you?*"

"No, I'll take care of it eventually."

"*And look, I cannot stress this enough. Find a good therapist. Do not be lazy about this. Find one that you gel with. Change therapists until you find the one that you like but do find one, pronto. How's*"

Naseem?"

"I haven't had much time to think about her, to be honest. She's young… will bounce back."

"*I would recommend therapy for her too. From what I know about her, this TV interview, not to mention your own trauma, must have traumatised her in turn. She is sensitive and loves you to bits. Please ensure she gets help.*"

Aparna made a non-committal sound. There were pressing matters to deal with, and Naseem had a good head on her shoulders.

Chapter Forty-Eight
19th May 2016. Time: 22:00

At home, Naseem watched as her mother smiled on national TV. *This will follow our family around like a bloody stench!* Her phone rang. The screen spelt Ronit's name. Without thinking, she clicked the symbol to accept the call.

"*So, that's why you've been avoiding me,*" Ronit's clear voice resounded from her phone. "*You should have told me.*" Naseem noticed that his voice did not soften with sympathy when he said this. "*Your mother is in another league all together, I must say.*" A quick sarcastic laugh escaped from him. "*Well look, full disclosure. Something's brewing between me and Seema. Thought you should know. I would have liked to meet personally to... er ... officially break up, so to speak but you never gave me a fucking chance. Well, good luck.*"

Naseem went into the kitchen and opened the medicine cabinet. She overturned the plastic bottle containing paracetamol tablets on the kitchen board. The tablets spread out prettily like a girl's skirt. She counted them. Thirty-six. *Will they be enough?* She took a plastic bag from a drawer and swept all the pills into it. Hiding the bag under her grubby t-shirt, she escaped to her room.

Chapter Forty-Nine
19th May 2016. Time: 22:00

Hari watched the interview at home, alone on his laptop with his headphones on. Not wanting the incessant chatter of his wife or daughter to disturb him while he watched, he shooed them out of the bedroom and locked the door. Switching off the room light, he watched silently, but steadily grew restless.

So, the bitch has decided to fight back. He grabbed a glass vase and hurled it at the floor.

"Are you alight?" The annoying voice of his wife outside infuriated him further.

If women stop fearing shame, where will that leave us? But then his mind took a different turn. *This Soman bitch is the only brazen one. If she wants to make a fool of herself then she can go ahead. In fact, her public speech fits very much into our narrative. Others like her will be warned. They will think twice before insulting our faith and our religion. This bitch is too full of herself to see it that way. Let her bark as much as she wants to. She's given us what we want.*

He put in a call to Prahlad. "Get our cadre active. File cases against that woman under section 295A of the Indian Penal Code. I wish to see a minimum of ten cases in different states against her."

Hari did not open the door for the rest of the night. Lata who was stuck with Kashi in the living room wondered what to do.

"Shall I sleep here only?" Lata whispered to Kashi.

"No blankets!" Kashi whispered.

"Doesn't matter," Lata said, "it's a hot night."

Kashi slept on her cot like she usually did while Lata slept on the floor. A bunch of towels were used for a pillow and an old tablecloth for a blanket. The uncomfortable sleeping arrangements raised *oohs* and *aahs* from her throughout the night leading to numerous muted giggles from both the women.

Chapter Fifty
19th May 2016. Time: 22:30

As Manish entered the Times of Hindustan TV studios, he saw a drained Aparna sitting on a tiny stool in a corner of the visitors' room. Their eyes met. He smiled. She simply got up. Their car journey was wordless. When they arrived home, Naseem wasn't up to greet them. Tired, Aparna went to her room and Manish followed her.

"I know you're not happy," Aparna said, sitting on the bed, "but this is something I needed to do."

"What can be bigger than family, Aparna?" Manish asked gently.

"A woman's dignity? Her self-esteem? Her mental health?" Aparna appealed to him with her eyes.

"Let's agree to disagree on this one," Manish sighed, "because we're unable to understand each other."

"Does this change anything between us?" Aparna asked tentatively.

"No," Manish replied after a pause.

"I really appreciate this, Manish," Aparna said. "You know how important you both are to me. I don't have to prove my love, do I?" She paused. "Asking me to let go... apologise to the goons... was a big ask."

"I did not ask you to apologise to them. I would never do that. It was this interview, that's all."

"I couldn't, Manish."

Manish nodded but his face looked troubled. Aparna got up and paced around the room while he sat on the bed and watched her.

"Has social media calmed down now, or are they still after me?" Aparna asked.

"I read some tweets. Most women cannot understand you, I think. Take a look." He handed his phone to her, but she shook her head and got her own from her bag.

Prim_And_Proper: What is the need to go overboard with the anti-religion sentiment in the first place?

Glorious_Hues: Religion is important to us. We will never tolerate insults against our religion.

Indian_woman: I'm a very balanced feminist. I do not approve.

Tit_For_Tat: What exactly is her problem? If you play with snakes, then be prepared for their venom.

Women_of_Ramayana: What is all this bravado going to achieve? Just keep quiet and look after your family.

Sita: She should have kept quiet.

"Not as bad as I thought it'd be," Manish said, reading the tweets.

"Or maybe we're just getting used to it," Aparna said.

"Most of them can't get over your smile. The sympathy you garnered seems to have dissipated after your smile," Manish said. Aparna read further:

Gabbar_Singh: She smiled! Doesn't seem to be under any trauma.

Tony: She looks fine. What's the fuss about?

Yogi_Atma: Does she have no shame?

Devout_Man: She is smiling for God's sake!

Believe_in_equality: These radical feminists are as tough as punch bags. Punch them as much you want, and they will still bounce back.

Alpha_species: I would like to see one of these radical feminists grovel in front of me. Now that would be a sight worth watching. Nothing shakes their egos.

"The National Commission for Women have woken up from their slumber, by the way," Manish said, "and have made a statement saying physical assault will not be tolerated. Human rights organisations have condemned the assault. Let me check what the party in power is saying." He scrolled to locate their tweet.

"They've labelled the interview anti-Hindu," Aparna laughed. "What else can you expect?"

Manish noted her laugh. Her first genuine one since the incident.

Aparna said, "They must be plotting and planning right now; analysing whether their voter base will be turned off by the gumption displayed by a shameless woman. My reputation, and the anchor's of course, will make it easy for the voters to decide whose side they're on. People are not used to audacious radical thoughts, and they can be easily swayed towards culture and tradition."

"Uh-oh, #AntiHindu is trending," Manish said. "They've set forth the bots and Twitter trolls. #ArrestAparna is also trending. Arrest you? What on earth for?"

"They're sharing my views on religion yet again. Diverting the public and creating fear in their minds that their religion is in danger. The public will forget my assault. Nice!"

"Has the ruling party officially condemned the assault on you?" Manish asked.

"Of course, not."

"What's our dear old opposition saying?"

"They're focusing on the lack of law and order. I'm probably too controversial for them to support me outright. Even Muslim voters will turn their backs on them if they're seen to support my call to blaspheme."

"I did read somewhere...I forget where...that they were considering making an offer to you to join their women's wing?"

"Radical feminists and atheists never bring in votes, so that will never happen," Aparna said. "Uff! Twitter has turned ugly again."

Proud_Indian: How dare that brazen woman smile?

Boycott_the_West: Our Indian culture does not allow shameless woman to brazenly give interviews on national television like this. That woman must be taught a lesson.

Pious_Man: She did not learn her lesson even after being raped. Rape her daughter next.

Proud_Hindu: She needs to be thrown in jail. How dare she speak against my religion?

Majestic_India: There is a police summon against her. She just wants to avoid arrest.

Maharaja: This is a conspiracy by Pakistan to cause chaos in our nation.

"Enough of this," Aparna exclaimed, throwing her phone away.

"Hold on," Manish said, handing his phone to her. "I'm reading the praises."

Gluten_Free: I admire this brave woman for speaking up.

Fierce_Feminist: Look at all the mansplaining that's been going around.

Witch_that_cannot_be_burned: Physical assault is traumatic. Period.

Legal_Eagle: This is a criminal offence.

Proud_Feminist: Speaking requires gumption which Aparna has displayed.

Stree: When are the perpetrators going to be punished?

Pumpkin_Latte: Do not hold the woman responsible for her assault.

Only_Organic: India must not tolerate any more physical assaults.

Love_to_Read: A woman cannot be assaulted for expressing a view.

Rebel: Promoting atheism is not against Indian culture.

Common_sense_user: Normalising blasphemy, for our nation, is a radical thought. It will never happen.

Hindu_girl: Religion is important to me, but I respect the fact that my religion may not be important to everyone.

Deepika: Repeat after me—atheism does not mean anti-Hindu.

Radical_Atheist: Normalise blasphemy. Strengthen your faith.

Humanist_Number_One: At least, initiate a dialogue!

Feminism_is_my_Game: Why does your religion fear brave women?

Aparna reached for his phone and threw it onto the bed, where it landed noiselessly.

"So that's that." They looked at each other, sensing that a milestone had been passed.

Manish's phone started ringing. Shirish was on the line. Manish answered to a silence.

"Shirish?"

"Just heard the news, dost," Shirish answered in a low voice. Another silence.

"Yeah..."

"Was this what you wanted to discuss the other day?"

"Kind of... yes."

"You should have told me, dost. Too much for one person to manage." Silence. *"I was astounded at her interview. Why make the incident public? Should have kept quiet. Doesn't reflect very well on you, my friend."*

"Shirish, she always does what she believes is right."

"*Arre, how can this be right? You have a young daughter. You must think of her future. Who will marry her now?*"

"Shirish, the deed has been done. There's no point in speaking about it."

"*People will talk... Hold on, Mala wishes to speak to you.*"

"*Hello Manish. I'm horrified by what I just heard. Listen, we're here for both of you. Anything you wish to discuss, let us know. Of course, I'll ring Aparna too... whenever she's ready to talk. We're here for both of you. That's all.*"

"Thank you, Mala. Really appreciate it."

Aparna raised her eyebrows and Manish said, "Shirish and Mala have sent their support."

"Nice of them," Aparna said.

The doorbell rang. Aparna sat on the bed, suddenly weak.

"Relax." Manish said, "it's alright. I'll go take a look."

"Where's Naseem?"

"In her bed."

He walked to the main door. Looking through the peephole, he saw Rehana's seventeen-year-old son Ijaz standing on the doorstep.

"It's just Ijaz," Manish called out to Aparna. Aparna came to the door.

"They're threatening to beat my mother up," Ijaz said as soon as the door opened. Tears streaked his face.

"Who?" Aparna shouted.

"The Hindutwa guys."

"What?" Aparna said, "Why?"

Simultaneously, Manish said, "Beat her up? Let's go. I'll come with you." Turning to Aparna, he said, "Lock the door, okay?"

She nodded with a frown.

Manish took his glasses, phone, car keys and wallet, and headed out to the car.

Ijaz got in the car with him "When I came home, a crowd had gathered outside our house. Amma had locked herself in. I didn't know what to do, so I came to you for help," he stammered in panic.

Manish drove.

Naseem locked her bedroom door. In the moonlight, from the depths of her cupboard, she whisked out the plastic bag containing the sleeping pills and gazed at them, trying to make up her mind. She shook her head. Opening the window, with a force she did not know she possessed, she swooped out the contents of the bag, hearing soft plonks as they fell and scattered on the paving outside. She seized the skipping rope from under her bed and, within a few seconds, fashioned a noose. Her mind went to a bottle of weed killer tucked cozily in the garden shed. The cabinet under the kitchen sink held a fat bottle of rat poison. She caressed the noose as she gazed at the ceiling fan. Outside the window, the moon seemed to be watching her every move.

Manish parked his car outside the slum area where Rehana lived. They got out and continued on foot to Rehana's house. They spotted the crowd outside her house. Rehana was nowhere to be seen. Manish dialled the police and, pushing past the people gathered outside, he went to the door.

"What is happening?" he asked a man loitering outside the house.

"We don't want Rehana to work for that vile woman," a hefty man panted.

Manish remained silent. It would only be a matter of minutes before they found out who he was. He guessed that he would be viewed more as a figure of pity than anything else. A husband whose wife was disobedient.

The men spotted Ijaz and one of them caught him by the scruff of his neck. "Tell your mother not to work for that

251

woman, otherwise things will turn ugly," the man threatened.

"*Arre*, let him go. He hasn't done anything wrong," said Manish.

"*Saheb*, you can never tell with these Muslims. His mother found the one person who writes against our religion. Couldn't she find anyone else?" the man asked.

Three police officers arrived ten minutes after Manish's call. They waved around their lathis, and the crowd scattered.

"Rehana, are you in there? Please can you open the door? It's me, Manish. Don't be scared. The police are here."

She opened the door and stood in front of them, crying. "Saheb, I just heard the news on TV. Poor Aparna Madam. How is she?"

"She's alright," Manish said. "But what happened here?"

"It's not easy living as a minority, especially in a country where we're hated. A woman always fears that this... this thing will be done to her. And I'm a Muslim woman in a Hindu country. My fear was so much more. But nothing happened to me. They've done it to Aparna Madam, instead. A woman of their own religion."

Manish looked down.

"You know how it is, Saheb. A woman says something that the men don't like, and they go on a rampage and want to beat everyone in sight. Saheb, please try and explain to Aparna Madam. She's an intelligent woman. She will understand."

"Explain what?"

"This constant speaking and writing against religion isn't good. It will bring nothing but trouble. Yes, Aparna Madam has made a mistake, but she has a good heart. They've been too harsh for what is merely a lack of understanding on Aparna Madam's part. Tell Aparna Madam that I will pray for her every day. May Allah give her peace"

"Rehana, if you no longer wish to come to work, we will understand. Your salary will continue until you find somewhere else to work."

"No, Saheb. Why should I change jobs for these stupid men? Aparna Madam has been nothing but kind to me. She needs me now."

"Are you sure? These men looked like maniacs. I was scared of them too," said Manish.

"I've seen them around. They live in this slum. Saheb, nothing that we do will satisfy them. It's pointless, I now realise. They will find some fault or the other with how we conduct our lives. Best to do what you want without bothering about anyone else. I've made up my mind."

A police officer spoke up. "No need to get scared of anyone, Saheb. We will give them lathis on their bums. This *bai* can go and work for anyone she wishes to."

Manish found himself pleasantly surprised. *I must narrate this incident to Aparna.* But thinking of her made him feel morose almost immediately. After assuring Rehana and Ijaz, he left.

Chapter Fifty-One
20th May 2016. Time: 20:00

It got easier after I stepped out of the house on the pretext of getting milk. Of all the absurd reasons... Had one of them stopped me, I would have stayed back, but they didn't. Not that I'm blaming them.

Even the traffic flows smooth tonight. What are the odds of that happening? No snarling car queues to help me change my mind. Only one red light, no pun intended, which lasts for two minutes.

And the desolate two-storeyed building looms into view. Yellow, with shoddy, damp patches caused due to rains over the years. I peer out of my car to take a good look. "Lucky Apartments". Yes, that's the one I want. No one around. That's good. No piercing glances to help me change my mind. Even so, I make a u-turn and park a few yards away in front of a respectable-looking bungalow. Baby clothes hang to dry in one of the windows. Reassuring.

I bend my head and sprint towards Lucky Apartments. The flat is on the ground floor which is a relief. No one sees me. I would have turned back otherwise. I stand in front of the ground floor flat. After a few seconds, I take a breath and press the bell.

The door opens immediately and I enter. I'm expected. The door is closed behind me. A quick professional conversation, and a nod.

The apartment is minimalistic. No paintings, grey curtains. Clean. Nothing much to give away the state of mind of the owner. There's a shoe rack at the entrance. I take off my Kolhapuri chappals. She points to a room. I follow.

Surprising myself, I find it easy to relax and give in.

"Was it good for you?" she says afterwards, sounding as if she genuinely cares.

With her clothes back on, and my pent-up energy spent, she looks... ordinary, like a college student... or like someone's daughter. She is probably Naseem's age. The thought jabs the periphery of my mind, threatening to tarnish the few minutes of physical gratification

I've just experienced. I give her a brief nod.

"If you need my services again, you know where to find me," she says.

"How much?" I ask, a tad hesitant and a little shy. Is there a discreet way of doing this? Guilt threatens to disrupt my peace. She tells me. I give her more than she asks. Why not? She deserves it.

"Er... I'll see myself out," I say to her, feeling foolish. Without waiting for her reply, I let myself out of her flat, and close the door behind me.

I push the dreary flat into a recess of my mind which I never plan on visiting ever again. Let it sit there and rot if it must. At least for a few minutes, I had the assurance of being in control of my life. I need that if I'm to look after everyone.

I get into the car and drive steadily towards our bungalow, back to my wife and daughter.

Chapter Fifty-Two
21st May 2016. Time: 22:00

Manish looked up as Aparna came into the living room. "Coming in just a moment," he said.

Aparna sat next to him on the sofa. "It's okay. Not really sleepy." She stifled a yawn. "What are you watching?"

"A Bollywood movie of the eighties. Did not catch the name. The villain is just lowering the hero's mum via a menacing-looking contraption into his den."

Aparna laughed. "Sounds good. I'll watch with you."

The antics on the screen continued, but Aparna's thoughts strayed. *Post-traumatic stress, anxiety, anger, depression, and panic attacks followed by therapy, anti-depressants, anti-anxiety medication—the cycle continues. I can't command my body nor my mind to heal faster, but things are improving. I can laugh, hum, and sing now. I appreciate those who love, support, comfort, and protect me. I've started to feel more like the me that existed before the traumatic event. Yet, it is always there with me. I don't think it'll ever go away. It shows in me being hyper-aware of the tiniest of sounds. Being unable to sleep without having Manish's solid body in bed with me at night. It makes me dependent but it's alright. Always checking and rechecking the doors, windows, and locks. Brushing my teeth, washing my hands, and taking showers at least a million times in a day. Fearing the stink of alcohol mingled with sweat. Scrutinising the faces of women that I cross in the streets. Have you experienced something like this? Was it a stranger or your own husband? Did you tell anybody? No need for shame. It wasn't your fault. Some of the smug faces stare back. The faces that haven't experienced this. This can never happen to me, the faces seem to say. Some faces are full of innocence and the absence of any kind of trauma. I was like them once. Yes, I do envy those faces sometimes, but then I console myself with the knowledge that things will only get better.*

Manish pointed to the screen and laughed. "And that, is how you defeat the villains. Ready?"

The movie had finished. Manish held out his hand. Aparna took it and rose. She followed him into her bedroom.

Chapter Fifty-Three
22nd May 2016. Time: 2:00

While Aparna slept, Naseem crept into her room, looking for the colossal bag that Aparna usually carried around with her. Finding it tossed on her desk, she opened it and peered in. The brown paper envelope felt cool in her feverish hands. She took it to her room and, with fingers that would not stop trembling, opened it. It was her mother's forensic medical report listing the exact details of how and where her body had been ravaged. Naseem read the full report, looking up the meanings of the medical terms on her phone.

Knowing what has happened to Ma, will I ever enjoy a man's touch as intensely as I did earlier? Will I be able to revel in physical intimacy? With any man? Will Ma's assault come knocking on my mind's door, pestering me for acknowledgement during those intimate moments? Will I be able to keep her away? Will I ever be able to surrender fully to intimacy, get lost in the moment... or will there always be the shadow of Ma's assault over my desire? Desperate to be acknowledged...

Won't I let Ma down if I forget her assault for even a single second? Because I feel this tremendous amount of guilt within me. Guilt, because of what has happened to her. How can I experience ecstasy when she has experienced so much pain? Do I have a right to pleasure when her life has changed irrevocably? Won't it be best to create an environment where the question of physical intimacy does not arise—by avoiding Ronit, by avoiding all men, by repressing lust, and repressing love?

Poor Ma is withered. Does the shame ever go away? Will all the smiles, love and happiness return after we have adjusted? Tears and pain are finite—aren't they?

Her fingers did not tremble as she placed the report back in the envelope. She went to her mother's room and placed the envelope where she had found it, counting the range of anxiety medicines and anti-depressants that had magically appeared on her mother's bedside table. She did not look at her sleeping parents as she left.

She switched off the lights and sat on her bed, rubbing her hands on her arms. Sleep was out of the question. She got up, whipped out her writing pad, tore a sheet and wrote:

Ma, I understand.

Her eyes went to the *chafa* flowers from their garden, floating in a bowl of water on her desk. *Ma must have left them here for me. When did she put them here? Why didn't I notice them earlier?*

As she breathed in the fragrance of the *chafa*, she slumped on the bed.

They shame us because we let them. There is always a way. No point in behaving like a Bollywood tragedy queen.

She took a pair of scissors innocently lying on her desk and cut the noose into tiny pieces. She crumpled up the note she had written and threw the pieces of the noose and her note into her eager dustbin.

It's time to be disobedient. Ma will understand. I'm her daughter after all.

Chapter Fifty-Four
22nd May 2016. Time: 10:00

The rationalists, liberals, free speech advocates, seculars, atheists, feminists, humanists, and the anti-superstitious planned a demonstration for the first of June at 10 am, on the open grounds near the Gandhi statue on Deccan Gymkhana, to protest the assault of Aparna Soman and contest the broader political point of her assault.

Hari heard the news of the impending protest as soon as it started circulating on social media. *This is one protest that won't be going ahead.*

"Disrupt the protest. Create chaos. Riot, if you must, but don't let the protest succeed. Gather all men, and outnumber the protesting bastards," he told Prahlad and Shakti.

"Will you be there Hari *bhau?*" Prahlad asked.

"Handle this on your own," Hari spat. "Go and teach those bitches a lesson."

Shakti nodded. He leered, bared his teeth, and rubbed his hands, as if off on a romantic pursuit.

Prahlad giggled, "Khee, khee, khee. Of course, *bhau*. We'll show them. Can't wait!"

"Do you have enough men?" Hari asked.

"Yes, *bhau*. Our numbers are always growing!"

Kashi logged into her laptop and the news of the planned protest floated in front of her eyes. Immediately, she logged into her LGBTQ group and roused her buddies. *"People, a demonstration has been planned on the first of June at 10 am to protest the assault on Aparna Soman and the stifling of dissent. We must lend our support. Let's make some catchy posters and try and get in front of as many cameras as possible,"* she posted.

The suggestions trickled in.

"We must do something radical that will get everyone's attention," said fiery_lady.

"Do you have anything in mind?" Kashi asked.

"I'll think of something. Give me some time."

Only a few members of the online group lived in Pune. Owing to family pressures, not everyone was comfortable attending the protest under the LGBTQ banner. Only a handful agreed to attend, and this spurred Kashi on. *This is one protest I'm going to be a part of. If no one attends, then I will go on my own. Ready to rebel. Do I have any other option?*

Once, Kashi had shared. Now, she refused to speak to her parents. After completing her assigned chores, she spent her spare time with her books and on the Internet. Hopelessly aware that her father was trying to find a suitable groom for her, her life remained within the virtual world of the LGBTQ community. Plans, friendships, new events and possible loves meandered over her horizon now. *They know me. My parents never will.*

When Vaishali heard the news of Aparna's assault and the planned protest, her first thought was one of relief that her son was no longer involved with the now presumably traumatised family. He had confessed to breaking up with the poor girl. Her next thought was one of indignation. One by one, she called up all her kitties. A plan was made to meet in a café.

On the afternoon of the meeting, the ladies arrived one after another in their cool linen wear sporting trendy sunglasses and expensive eau-de-cologne.

"So, all of you must have heard the dreadful news," started Vaishali.

"What happened?" Mrs Kulkarni breathed heavily.

"You know the news that's trending all over. The news of the rape," Vaishali mouthed the word 'rape' instead of saying it out loud.

"Yes, yes. I heard. Dreadful. To think that a woman of our class can be assaulted so easily in broad daylight is shocking," said Mrs Joshi.

"Exactly," said Vaishali. "See, they have a protest planned on the morning of the first of June. As you all know, I consider Aparna an extreme, over-the-top feminist. My son, by the way, has broken up with her daughter, you will be glad to know. One load off my mind. But this... this is something else. It makes me angry. How easily they assault a woman and get away with it. What are your thoughts about attending the protest?"

"Crowded, chaotic and unsafe," said Mrs Kulkarni.

"The police will be present. It will be safe. This is Pune! Our sleepy town where people shut shop in the afternoons so that they can nap. What can possibly happen?"

"I'm in. I want to protest the assault, and moreover it may be fun!" Mrs Rathi said jubilantly.

"The media will be present as well. Coverage will be at prime time. I'm in as well," said Mrs Kulkarni.

Most of the ladies decided to attend the protest, despite reservations. A plan was made to meet at the venue on the designated hour.

After coming home, Vaishali told Ronit: "My kitties and I have decided to attend the protest for Aparna Soman. Do you want to attend as well?"

"What will I do there, Ma? It's your kitty thing, isn't it?"

"Well, you know the girl, don't you? What happened to her mother is ghastly, although I don't care much for her ideology. Don't you want to take a stand? You can come with your friends."

"When has a protest ever achieved anything, Ma? It is a waste of time. Besides, I have better things to do," he said.

"You know the girl, so..."

"All that is over. I don't think of her anymore."

How quickly the young move on, Vaishali thought to herself. *Well, I'm not complaining.* With that, she started to think of the slogan that would go on her protest placard.

Rehana heard about the protest from another domestic worker called Kirti.

"I heard that they are arranging a protest for your madam," said Kirti to Rehana as they met near the communal tap where they washed their clothes.

"A protest?"

"Haven't you heard? Has Madam not told you? They've arranged a demonstration to protest her assault," said Kiri. "My madam is going as well. That's how I know."

"Kirti, I would like to go. When is it? Will you come with me?"

"Nope. My husband won't allow me, and where will I get the free time?" said Kirti.

"Try. We must do our bit," said Rehana.

"When have they gone out of their way to do anything for us? I'm not interested."

"My madam does have funny ideas, but she means well. Whatever has happened to her is so ghastly that I get nightmares about it. I want to protest," said Rehana.

"Your wish," said Kirti, as the women turned their attention back to the washing of their clothes.

"Ijaz, will you drop me at the protest venue on the day?" Rehana asked her son that night.

"Don't you have work on the day? Why do you wish to go there anyway?" Ijaz said.

"To show my support. Aparna Madam does have funny ideas about religion, I give you that, but she means well. She has suffered enough. We should not let her get arrested. Don't worry, I won't wait long."

"Why do you want to get involved in protests and such, Amma? You are the one who keeps telling me to be careful, and

263

now you want to protest!"

"Ijaz, this is the time that we stand up and support each other. If not now, then when? Listen, just drop me off on the day, alright?"

"Okay," said Ijaz. The decision was made. Rehana would attend the protest.

Chapter Fifty-Five
1st June. Time: 06:00

It was the day of the summons. Aparna was due at the police station at 9 am. Whispers that she would get arrested were strong. That morning, she washed her hair with the Jasmine-scented shampoo Naseem had gifted her several years ago which had remained ignored in her bathroom. *It smells of happiness and nostalgia. Who knows whether I'll get the chance to have a decent shower in jail?*

Looking around her room, she sat on her bed, reminiscing. *This room is full of Naseem's love for me.*

On her seventh birthday, Naseem had purchased a book full of little notes to leave around the house. Most of them had been left in her mother's room.

Always know you are loved, said one, tucked in the corner of the desk lamp.

You deserve a hug was stuck behind the door of Aparna's wardrobe.

I will be there soon to give you a warm cuddle was pinned to her bookcase.

Almost a decade later, the notes were still in her room, and now she was glad she hadn't thrown them away.

Just another thing to smile about.

An assortment of pictures of the three of them—on their travels, at home, with friends, with their achievements and accomplishments— hung haphazardly on the bedroom wall. Everywhere she looked, she spotted gifts that had been thoughtfully selected by Naseem: books with tiny messages of love; paintings completed by her daughter after putting in hours of her precious time; a lamp with a special cosy glow; fairy lights to make the room look friendlier; indoor plants to purify the air; quilts with cerise patchwork rose prints; small artefacts proclaiming *Best Mother Ever* trophy; lip balms with aromas to delight; disarming raggedy dolls. *I marvel at this home I've created—these walls full of memories that give me comfort and support. This room is bloated with love like a pregnant buffalo's belly. It has a physical presence. I can touch it with the tip of my finger, breathe in its richness, sense it on my cheek like a kiss, and feel it on my tongue.* She opened a window to let in some air. *We've always been strong together; just become a little wobbly lately, that's all.*

An inhumanely wintry night in the peak of December came to her mind. They'd walked, a few minutes past midnight. The night was lonely, its colour, rich. On their noses, the cold felt like a reprimand. Their tongues relished the taste. They'd felt it in their bones. Far on the horizon, a fire glinted. They'd walked and chatted. Seeing no one, meeting no one, just the three of them in the cavernous dark. The night, beautiful. Their bond, strong. Their lazy dreams for the future, vivid. *Who needs the idea of a heaven with so much beauty around?* It was at that precise moment that she'd stopped fearing death. *Why fear death amidst such beauty?*

Her thoughts moved back to the present. *Why fear jail for that matter? The Government has arrested so many activists for the past two years that jail would mean cosy conversations and stimulating exchanges of ideas.*

Tying her hair into a bun, she now dressed hurriedly. Draping a white sari around her, she put on her *bindi*. She had to be present at the police station at 9 am sharp. Nipping into the bathroom, she poured water into the tumbler and watered the three plants on her windowsill. Tiny gestures signalling normality, home, and comfort made her sick with trepidation. After putting her anxiety medicines in her bag, she went to the dining room.

Manish, fully dressed, was reading the newspaper. "Have a quick slice of toast before we leave. Shall I fry an egg for you?"

"The thought of an egg makes me want to puke," she said as she placed her bag on the dining chair and went to fill her water bottle.

"Have a toast, Aparna. It may be a long day."

"No. I can't even think of food right now," she said as she placed the full water bottle inside her bag.

"The lawyer will meet us directly at the station." The circles around his eyes had taken on the colour of the henna paste which she sometimes used to colour her hair. His eyes looked sad. Aparna turned away.

"Shall we wake Naseem up to say a quick goodbye?"

"Let her sleep," said Manish. "We'll have a meal together this evening."

"Yes, let's have a nice meal in the evening. We can even open a bottle of wine if we feel like it," said Aparna, "or eat something sugary."

Manish smiled. "Naseem will be pleased." He headed towards the loo. "I'll join you in a minute."

Aparna, needing spare change, opened Manish's wallet he had left carelessly on the dining table. She was rummaging for coins or notes of a lower denomination when her eye fell on the card which advertised the services of an escort girl. Pulling it out, she read the front and the back, and then placed it back into the wallet. She gave up her search for spare change and put the wallet back where she had found it. Her heart palpitations had started again, but she ignored them. Sweat permeated her skin. She breathed in deeply at regular intervals, concentrating on each long breath. Manish came into the room, tightening his belt.

"Let's go," Aparna said without looking at him. She picked up her purse and walked to the main door. Manish took his wallet from the dining table, and the car and house keys from the wall. He sprinted to the balcony where the washed clothes hung and took two clean handkerchiefs. Aparna was already waiting outside the main door. Manish handed one handkerchief to Aparna. They got in the car and Manish drove to the police station. Their journey was wordless.

Chapter Fifty-Six
1st June. Time: 09:00

No one believed that the corpulent city of Pune, the senior citizen's paradise, notorious for lethargy, would suddenly discover her violent streak. Or maybe the fault lay with the women. It was the brazen women who instigated the mad dogs. They shouldn't have ventured out. The nation was not a safe place for them. Didn't they know that?

The day of the protest started off sedate. The city awoke to find the sun shining as it always did, even in the bleakest of winters and the wettest of monsoons. The road vehicles, like competitive interns eager to get ahead, started their ambitious outings from the early hours.

Finding an area to hold protests was difficult in the city. The open-air ground near the Gandhi statue seemed ideal. Not only was it shielded from the brutal traffic, but it allowed passers-by an unobstructed view. The Gandhi statue also added a level of legitimacy to the protest.

By 9 am, the protest venue was empty. Those who used the ground for sport-related activities finished by seven. Now, only the odd stray dog loitered within the premises.

At 9.30 am, a contrasting bunch of secular and right-wing reporters arrived, lending an aura of democracy to the proceedings. Choosing their spots carefully, they set up their equipment. The reporters talked to the camera and informed viewers about the day ahead. Mandatory police officers positioned themselves at one end of the large ground, keeping a lazy eye out for untoward incidents. Sensing an outdoor event with the potential for increased business, the most agile of the street-side vendors had already collected. An eager young boy still in his school years was selling coconut water. A sari-clad woman, her demureness not giving a hint of her enterprising spirit, was

269

selling home-made *idlis* in a stainless-steel container. A shy salesman ensured that his shyness did not prove an impediment to his business by selling samosas so fresh and aromatic that even die-hard dieters were tempted. An innovative tea-stall owner located across the road sent his helper with six glass cups and a kettle of boiling tea. The helper served the customers in the glass cups, ran back to the stall to wash them, and then brought the washed glasses and the freshly brewed tea for the next lot. A few men, with nothing better to do, just stood and watched, waiting for the action to start.

Minutes later, the protesters started to arrive in groups. They held their placards; they chatted; they spoke on their phones; they arranged themselves and debated on the best place to stand. Groups belonging to the same organisations gravitated towards one another. Volunteers and employees of the Rationalist and Anti-Superstition Society thronged together. The reporters ignored them all and continued to speak into the camera keeping an ear out for the action to start. Hari's goons, silent and predatory, infiltrated the grounds in large numbers, waiting for the right moment to strike. As was his style, Hari remained absent. He trusted his men.

Vaishali and her friends arrived together, colour coordinated, looking like a group of dazzling film stars and drawing curious glances from the other protesters. *What are the privileged doing here?* The appropriate dress code had been discussed and debated by them earlier. Owing to the heat of the day and the solemnity of the event, a decision on wearing white cotton salwar kameez had been agreed upon. If a kitty did not have a white one in her wardrobe, then a pastel-coloured one would do as well. Their designer sunglasses contrasted stylishly with their eco-friendly cotton tote bags in which they carried their mineral waters. Their placards matched the samosas in terms of their freshness. They had spent time and effort, and now they looked like young children eager to take part in their first play.

Rehana caught the attention of everyone when she arrived. A problem with the silencer of Ijaz's bike turned annoyed heads at the harsh sound. Rehana was embarrassed to be the scrutiny of all eyes when Ijaz dropped her at the edge of the sports ground.

"How long do you want to wait?" Ijaz asked as Rehana stepped off his bike.

"Fifteen minutes or so?" she replied. "You can wait with me, if you want."

"I'd rather not. I'll come pick you up from this very spot."

Rehana nodded as he rode off on his bike leaving behind split eardrums. She stood away from everyone, and as far away from the cameras as possible. She wasn't carrying any placard nor was she aware of any protest protocols as this was her first protest. Watching the other protesters, she stood there a little shy and hesitant, but determined to show her support for her employer. One of Hari's goons saw Rehana arrive, and her attire informed him of the religion she subscribed to. The sight of her infuriated him. *They are all in it together. The bloody liberals and their beloved Muslims.*

As the cameras focused, the protesters held up their placards which shone with intelligent writing and idealism. The pitch and tone of their voices rose in degrees as confidence and comfort in their role was achieved. It did not take long for the voices to become loud and angry. The pursuit of fairness and justice was uppermost in many minds. The protest had started.

"Speak!"

"Bol!"

"Protect women who dare to dissent."

"Rape will not be tolerated."

"How can a view offend your faith?"

"Arrest the goons."

"Ideas are free."

"Atheism is not anti-national."

The placards competed for distinction. After a few hesitant attempts, the crowd picked up the chant of "Ideas are free" followed by "Rape will not be tolerated" which they repeated periodically. The crowd of protesters seemed to grow as the event proceeded. Cameras chose their angles carefully, focusing on some of the interesting placards and unique specimens of humanity. A liberal news channel spotted Rehana's hijab somewhere in the crowd and, to her embarrassment, focused on her as they wished to highlight the secular nature of the protest.

At one end, close to the cameras, Kashi's LGBTQ group of five protesters was shouting angry slogans with fiery_lady's shouts the loudest. Fiery_lady was a sixteen-year-old girl called Naaz, with curly hair and wild eyes belying the determination she carried within her. These brave protesters were identifying as LGBTQ in public for the very first time. Each of them carried a placard that had the letters LGBTQ carved in large, bold letters. The sense of inclusion was high. The euphoria of protesting was intoxicating.

"About doing something radical…" said Naaz, looking at Kashi with eager eyes.

"Can you guess what I have in mind?" whispered Kashi in Naaz's ear, as the shouts from the other end of the ground rose in tenor.

"What?" Naaz asked, giggling and heady with anticipation.

"Shall we?" Kashi said, her face bright with the *josh* of being alive.

"Let's do it!" Naaz said laughing. The two girls rushed to the cameras which sportingly focused on them, and once confident that they were under the camera's gaze, Kashi gently placed her hand on Naaz's head and guided it to the correct angle. She inclined her head and then in front of the gaze of the cameras kissed Naaz lavishly on the lips. A kiss that went on for several minutes, leaving the reporters and their camera operators aghast at their gumption. The two girls then held up their LGBTQ placards, bold, alive, and jubilant.

The police officers who saw the kiss zoomed in at once and shouted at the girls. "What do you think you're doing?" A policewoman separated the two forcibly while a policeman slammed his lathi on the ground. The girls escaped and got lost in the crowd.

Away from the protest, they sat on the steps of an old building to reclaim their breaths. A few rapid breaths later, Naaz got her phone out and scrolled.

"Kashi!" Naaz shouted, making Kashi, right next to her, jump. "TV channels have picked up our kiss!" She could not suppress her excitement.

"What? Let me take a look!"

Kashi grabbed Naaz's phone, scrolled furiously and then a look of delight appeared on her face. "Conservative, right-wing channels are only showing a still photograph and blurring out our lip-lock." She laughed.

"Would be offensive to their viewers," Naaz said delighted.

"Heavy criticism of the kiss. This anchor is going ballistic in deriding the state of the nation which allows such anti-culture activities." Kashi giggled.

"Secular channels are showing the full video but blurring the kiss."

"No one has the guts!" Naaz said, venom in her voice.

"But look, social media is showing the full video."

"Oh my God, Kashi, it's gone viral."

The two girls held each other and danced.

"Look, how rapidly it's shared," Kashi said, "our faces clearly seen."

"Who will marry you now, Kashi?" Naaz laughed. "You've guaranteed yourself a rejection by any potential male suitor."

"That was the bloody point," Kashi muttered and then laughed.

"You've broadcast your sexual orientation to the entire nation! You've lost your place on the shortlists of Indian men seeking matrimony."

"Mission accomplished!" Kashi said, raising her arm for a high-five.

"Mission accomplished!"

"Well, not quite," Kashi said as her eyes gleamed madly. "I want to go to the nearest police station."

"What on earth for?"

"You'll see."

Meanwhile, the goons who had infiltrated the protest, became hysterical, like rabid dogs on the loose. It started with a few pushes, and some jostling. The police officers looked on, striking their lathis on the ground as a warning. One spoke into his walkie-talkie requesting back up.

It seemed like a skirmish, but in reality, was a well-planned operation with the intention of causing violence, chaos, and harm. Hari's supporters now surged towards the activists from different directions. The police strode in, pushing and waving their lathis, striking at the closest bodies. Pent-up emotion drove the rogues forward. In the chaos, one of Hari's accomplices shoved Rehana. The push, though slight, was enough to trip the lady who fell heavily to the ground, looking up just in time to see the man aim a kick at her head. Her limbs buckled. Rehana's moan was lost in the surge. The crowd consumed everything in its way. A trickle of blood ran down her forehead, but she breathed.

Most protesters were women. As the chaos achieved an unexpected intensity, the starved, repressed, and angry men rushed towards the women from all sides of the ground, pawing, sniffing in their fragrance, mauling, and touching whichever body part was the closest. The rogues fell on the women eager to sample a part of them—the part that the men envied and longed to own and possess—the part that was not merely physical but was present somewhere deep within the core of those women. Untouched. Unattainable. Proud. Years of assumed derision the deluded men had suffered at their hands had to be avenged. A few women tried to fight back but were quickly intimidated. A single, clever touch placed on a protected body part was all that was required for the women to back off. Nothing mattered. The privilege of physical strength belonged to the rowdy males high on testosterone, and that was a winning strategy in the chaos of the day.

The police officers tried to help the women by pushing and beating the offenders with their *lathis*, but the rogue elements outnumbered the police.

The women fled, sickened, humiliated, sad, and defeated, their pride in tatters just like their clothes. The area, which a few hours ago had been teeming with idealism, now looked shamed and insulted at the litter of chappals, dupattas and bags that the women had left behind—along with one bruised, tired body, still breathing. The police called the ambulance and Rehana was taken to the hospital before Ijaz could come to collect her. Hari's men, knowing that the day had been won by them, celebrated the glorification of Indian culture with renewed enthusiasm. Very much like the nation, the demonstration ended up a confused mass of contradictions: some euphoric, but mostly despairing.

At home, Naseem carried out her own plan of disobedience. Aparna had never been protective of her social media passwords. Using her mother's credentials, Naseem logged into her mother's Twitter account. Using Aparna's account, she wrote:

"A heartfelt apology. I, Aparna Soman, apologise sincerely for hurting the religious sentiments of the nation and take back all my provocative statements about religion. I'm even willing to turn to religion in return for the nation's forgiveness, for which I beg."

The sun passed behind a cloud and then reappeared as if winking with mischief.

Kashi, with Naaz in tow, went to a police station. The city police station looked efficient. The reception had three desks but rooms behind hinted at several more. Kashi saw at least twenty male and female police officers working. She went to the nearest desk.

"I want to register a complaint, but I will only speak to a policewoman."

The policeman nodded. He spoke into the phone and directed them to an interior room.

The policewoman reminded Kashi of a Bollywood heroine whose name she couldn't remember.

"I want to make a statement," she told the officer.

"Yes," the officer encouraged. "Go on."

"It was my father who raped Aparna Soman," Kashi blurted out.

Naaz stood still.

The officer did not move a muscle. After a second, she asked, "Who is your father?"

"Hari Sabnis," Kashi said in a confident voice.

"Hari Sabnis of the *Dharma Sanstha*?"

"Yes."

"How do you know this?"

"I heard him planning her assault with his followers."

"This a serious charge. Are you sure?" The officer looked at Kashi. She held a closed fountain pen in her hand with which she scratched her nose.

"Yes."

"You want to make an official statement?" The officer got her notepad out. Pen in hand, she was ready to jot down her complaint.

"Yes."

The officer wrote as Kashi narrated. "I've registered the FIR. You will be interviewed again as the investigations progress."

"What about my safety? I don't feel safe living in my father's house."

"Since this is a rape charge, he will be arrested immediately. The offence is non-bailable. Your identity won't be revealed."

Twenty minutes later, Kashi and Naaz stepped out into the sun.

"What was that about? I didn't know it was your dad who did this to her." Naaz said. The noise of the traffic and the general chatter provided a safe backdrop for difficult conversations.

But Kashi did not reply. She wasn't looking at Naaz. Her gaze was directed straight ahead at a small girl pulling her mother's hand to change the trajectory of their walk. Kashi's lip quivered. Naaz moved closer. Holding hands, they walked the rest of the way.

Aparna Soman reached the police station just as news about her apology was breaking. With their phones tucked away, Manish and Aparna had no idea what was going on. As they entered the police station, they were received with a curtness which Aparna surmised was solely reserved for liberals who meddled. Judging from the energy of the police station, both Manish and Aparna guessed that bail would be rejected.

While Aparna was being questioned, a plain clothes man came and whispered into the ear of the officer in charge. The officer nodded. In a nearby alley, someone scored a sixer in a cricket match. The watching crowd yelled jubilant cheers.

Glossary

Aghori	Ascetics who engage in post-mortem rituals
Baapre	Marathi exclamation to convey surprise
Bhabhi	Brother's wife, usually used as a term of respect to address married women
Brahmacharya	Celibacy
Bhajan	Devotional song
Bhau	Brother
Chakli	Fried snack
Chikankari	Delicate hand embroidery
Durbar	Assembly
Dost	friend
Diya	Lamp
Dhol	Drum
Dupatta	Piece of cloth worn over the shoulders by women
Gayatri mantra	Powerful Sanskrit hymn
Gotra	Segment of a caste. People belonging to the same gotra cannot marry according to ancient Hindu tradition
Ghazal	Poem
Jaggery	Unrefined sugar
Jamun	A purple fruit
Josh	Passion
Lakh	1 lakh = £100,000
Lakshman and Shurpanakha	Story from the mythological epic Ramayana
Lathi	Stick
Laxman rekha	Story from the epic Ramayana. A line is drawn

by Lord Rama's brother, Laxman, around Sita's abode. Sita is urged not to cross the line.

Mangalsutra	Necklace of black beads which married women wear
Namaskar	Indian greeting
Pedha	Indian sweet
Pillu	Cub
Pishaaz	Ghost
Ramleela	Folk drama based on Lord Ram
Salvar	Cotton trousers
Shloka	Poem in the Sanskrit language
SSC	Government education board in India
Shiva linga	An object symbolizing the god Shiva
Topi	Cap
Tulsi	Basil herb
TRP	Television rating point
Vrindawan	Miniature temple-like structure to house the basil herb
Wada paav	Potato based fast-food

Acknowledgements

My deepest thanks to:

My editor and publisher, Isabelle Kenyon for taking a chance on me. This book would not have been possible without your support, encouragement and perceptive editorial comments.

My editor C.J Hartley for her attention to detail.

My husband, Anand and daughter Raavi, my two loves, who had to suffer my frequent bouts of contemplation during my manic period of writing. Thank you for your love, understanding and solid support.

My mother, Anjali Mulay, who introduced me to feminism and sent me out in the world with my head full of ideas. You made my journey so much easier.

Finally:

"Bol ke labh azaad hain tere" is a nazm by Faiz Ahmed Faiz

"Sarfaroshi Ki Tamanna" is by Bismil Azimabadi.

"Hidden from history? A brief modern history of the psychiatric "treatment" of lesbian and bisexual women in England" - The Lancet Psychiatry (2019) by Sarah Carr and Helen Spandler.

The numbers quoted in the Anti-Superstition Society reports are fictitious.

"Where the heart is without fear" is a poem written by Rabindranath Tagore.

About the Author

Sangeeta Mulay was born in Pune in India and now currently works in London as a UX writer. She received an honourable mention in the 2021 NYC midnight micro-fiction challenge. Her book for young adults, 'Savitribai Phule and I' was a notable book of 2020 for The Bombay Review. She has also had a short story highly commended in the Sydney Hammond short story competition. Another of Mulay's short stories will be published in a 2022 Fox and Windmill anthology.

About Fly on the Wall Press

A publisher with a conscience.
Political, Sustainable, Ethical.
Publishing politically-engaged, international fiction, poetry and cross-genre anthologies on pressing issues. Founded in 2018 by founding editor, Isabelle Kenyon.

Some other publications:

The Sound of the Earth Singing to Herself by Ricky Ray
We Are All Somebody
Aftereffects by Jiye Lee
Someone Is Missing Me by Tina Tamsho-Thomas
Odd as F*ck by Anne Walsh Donnelly
Muscle and Mouth by Louise Finnigan
Modern Medicine by Lucy Hurst
These Mothers of Gods by Rachel Bower
Sin Is Due To Open In A Room Above Kitty's by Morag Anderson
Fauna by David Hartley
How To Bring Him Back by Clare HM
Hassan's Zoo and A Village in Winter by Ruth Brandt
No One Has Any Intention of Building A Wall by Ruth Brandt
Snapshots of the Apocalypse by Katy Wimhurst
Demos Rising
Exposition Ladies by Helen Bowie
A Dedication to Drowning by Maeve McKenna
The House with Two Letterboxes by Janet H Swinney
Climacteric by Jo Bratten
Cracked Asphalt by Sree Sen

Social Media:

@fly_press (Twitter) @flyonthewall_poetry (Instagram)
@flyonthewallpress (Facebook) www.flyonthewallpress.co.uk